ROUGH LANDING

I felt our sled bounce when it touched down, throwing us back into the air before we came down to stay, careening across the ground, through underbrush, knocking small trees flat, using friction as much as the reversed thrust of the craft's two engines to help stop us. "Get ready!" I warned my people. "When the hatches pop, get out fast." I don't know if anyone heard me. We were jerked from side to side several times, and when the airsled finally came to a stop and the overhead hatches popped open, we were canted at a thirty-degree angle to the right.

"Up and out!" I shouted over my radio link as I reached up to use the edges of the hatch over my head to pull myself out of the sled. "Head for the rendezvous point."

We were on the surface of an enemy world.

Ace Books by Rick Shelley

THE BUCHANAN CAMPAIGN
THE FIRES OF COVENTRY
RETURN TO CAMEREIN

OFFICER-CADET
LIEUTENANT
CAPTAIN
MAJOR
LIEUTENANT COLONEL
COLONEL

HOLDING THE LINE
DEEP STRIKE

SPEC OPS SQUAD

DEEP STRIKE

RICK SHELLEY

ACE BOOKS, NEW YORK

SPEC OPS SQUAD: DEEP STRIKE

An Ace Book / published by arrangement with the author

PRINTING HISTORY
Ace mass-market edition / July 2002

Visit our website at
www.penguinputnam.com
Check out the ACE Science Fiction & Fantasy newsletter!

ISBN: 0-441-00952-2

ACE®
Ace Books are published by The Berkley Publishing Group,
a division of Penguin Putnam Inc.,
375 Hudson Street, New York, New York 10014.
ACE and the "A" design
are trademarks belonging to Penguin Putnam Inc.

PRINTED IN THE UNITED STATES OF AMERICA

10 9 8 7 6 5 4 3 2 1

If you want to know about the war between the Alliance of Light and the Ilion Federation, I'll tell you—straight and true, to the best of my ability. You won't get all the pious posturing and the high-falutin philosophy and moralizing you've been hearing from the politicians and generals. I've got a different perspective, and I see the war up close and personal—which none of the politicians and damned few of the generals can honestly say. My name is Bart Drak. Friends call me Dragon to my face. Others sometimes use that nickname behind my back. That's okay with me. I'm a buck sergeant leading a Special Operations Squad in Ranger Battalion of the 1st Combined Regiment. *Spec Ops*—we get the dirtiest, most dangerous jobs. If the mission is something no sane individual would attempt, the big shots dump it on us, Spec Ops—the SOS.

CHAPTER 1

I WOKE UP SWEATING AND SHIVERING AT THE SAME time. I'm not sure, but I think I might have screamed just before I woke. That could be what jerked me from sleep. Oh, well, the room was too well insulated for anyone to have heard me if I did, and it wouldn't have been the first time.

The graphic images, the more-than-real intensity of the nightmare, faded quickly once I was awake, but the substance of the nightmare was far slower to recede, and it never completely disappeared the way a pleasant dream or even a moderate nightmare will. This one wasn't even new. I had experienced it many times, with only minor variations, over the past year.

The scene was the divotect world of Dintsen, during my first "visit" there, back when the galaxy was generally at peace—as close to total peace as it ever gets. That had been intended to be merely a training exercise pairing a battalion of rangers from Earth's army with a divotect ranger battalion, part of a series of joint training operations set up by the Alliance of Light to get all of the species in the Alliance used to working with one another. The program hadn't been in effect very long, and there was no great rush about it since we were at peace. Our exercise was only the second or third. Then the tonatin, the dominant species in the Ilion Federation, started a war by invading Dintsen.

We weren't expecting a war, and we were badly out-gunned. It was a slaughter, and it was a miracle that any-one from my battalion escaped. My recurrent nightmare was of the final battle, one that saw most of the men in my platoon killed. When the shuttle landed to take the sur-vivors off—under fire—I was covered in blood and gore. Some of the blood was mine. Most of the stuff came from men killed around me, including my assistant squad leader, Kip Newley, who was blown to pieces by an RPG—rocket-propelled grenade—that exploded as it hit him square in the gut. I was only five feet away, following him to the shuttle. If Kip hadn't been there, I would have been killed by the shrapnel. As it was, I was knocked down, half-covered by what remained of Kip, my helmet knocked off my head. I caught a few bits of shrapnel. One of Kip's ribs went through my shoulder and stuck there, poking out front and back. A surgeon aboard ship had to remove it.

There are times when I think I can still taste what was left of Newley.

SO WE HAD A WAR WE WEREN'T PREPARED FOR—it's not like it was the first time *that* had ever happened. After I recovered from my injuries I was sent to the Ranger School at Fort Campbell to help train new rangers in spe-cial operations tactics. Then the brass came up with the idea for the 1st Combined Regiment. They were going to form a unit that would integrate members of all the species in the Grand Alliance in one outfit, just to prove to every-one—ourselves included—that we could all work together.

There were problems in training—some that had been anticipated, some that hadn't—but we were progressing nicely, if a bit behind schedule when the high command decided that they needed us in action sooner than we had been told. We had to retake one of the divotect worlds that the Ilion Federation had captured before they could exter-minate the divotect inhabitants—the only known sentient

species derived from reptilian rather than mammalian fore-
bears.

The world they sent us to was Dintsen.

For a time, I feared that my second trip to that world was
going to end the way the first one had, in total disaster. It
was a hard fight, in doubt until the very end, but this time
we won, and we beat the IFer forces there. That didn't stop
my nightmares though.

Once the 1st Combined Regiment—what was left of
it—was pulled off Dintsen after we kicked the rumps of
the Ilion Federation occupation army, I managed to draw
three weeks furlough. The regiment was withdrawn all the
way to Earth for reorganization and training of replacements. That was a stroke of luck, as far as the human members of the regiment were concerned. We weren't just sent
back to Dancer, the desolate, unsettled world where we
had done our initial unit training. I went through medical
screening, drew money from my pay account, collected
my furlough papers, and got away from Fort Campbell less
than eight hours after we landed back on Earth.

Two hours after that, I had been in Chicago, in civilian
clothes, starting what I thought might be a twenty-day
drinking binge. *Hoped.* All I wanted to do right then was
forget about the war and the just-ended campaign on
Dintsen, and booze in large quantities is still the best way
to forget.

It didn't work. The first few nights, I couldn't get drunk
fast enough to escape the memories. Each night I got stuck
in the maudlin stage, doing everything but cry in my beer.
Intoxication made the memories more immediate instead
of pushing them out of my mind completely. I didn't give
up on alcohol completely, but I had to forget the idea of
getting plastered and staying that way. There wasn't a hell
of a lot else that seemed to offer any hope of distracting
me, at least not in the first few days. I got a room in the
hotel section of the Wright Tower, the mile-high building
that sits on a man-made island a couple of hundred yards
out in Lake Michigan, connected to the mainland by tun-

nels—road and maglev track. That wasn't a place that normally drew a lot of soldiers . . . which was one of the reasons I chose it.

I didn't have any family on Earth to visit, and probably wouldn't have bothered to look them up if any of them had still lived there. I tried doing the tourist things but didn't have the patience to stay at any of them for long. Zoos and museums bore me. I hit a different restaurant for each meal, tried not to repeat at any bar. I had a computer list of the possibilities, arranged by location, along with directions to help me work my way from one to the next.

It gave me something to do.

I had been in Chicago more than a week before I even started to think about women, other than an occasional admiring glance when I saw an attractive one who was dressed to entice. And it was a couple of evenings after that before I picked up a young lady in one of the bars. We hit a couple more places together before we went back to my hotel. She stayed for an hour and left a little richer. After I closed the door behind her, I found myself thinking how much liquor that money would have bought, debating whether the trade-off had been worthwhile. I didn't come to a decision, then or the three other times I tried the experiment while I was in Chicago.

The nightmares didn't come every night, but my last night in Chicago they were worse than most—more vivid, more . . . *real* than reality ever is. It was about two in the morning when I woke sweating and shivering as badly as if I had some exotic disease that my body's enhanced immune system wasn't programmed to handle. I sat up on the edge of the bed, trying to get the shaking under control, trying to get away from the memories. Not memories of a nightmare, but of the reality that had inspired it. My mouth and throat were dry. I didn't have a bottle in the room—not with anything left in it—so I got up, went to the bathroom, and got a glass of water from the tap. My hands were shaking so badly that I spilled as much of the water as I got in my mouth. Water was a poor substitute, but it did get the sandpaper feeling out of my mouth. Then I stripped off my underwear and took a long shower with the water turned as high as it would go and as hot as I could stand.

I came close to falling asleep, standing under the pulsing beat of the water with my eyes closed, doing my best not to think of anything and coming close enough for practical purposes. After a time, I certainly managed to relax a little. Eventually, I turned the water off, got out, and toweled off. The mirrors in the bathroom were all fogged over; the air was heavy with moisture. The bedroom, when I went back out there, seemed chilly after the sauna-like heat of the shower. It was refreshing.

I crossed the bedroom and leaned on the control that changed the window covering nearly the entire wall from opaque to transparent. I was sixty stories up and in a room facing the open expanse of Lake Michigan, so it didn't matter that I was naked. Nobody was going to see me. I stood there looking out at the sky. I couldn't see much below me, just the darkness and an occasional glint of starlight on the water. It was almost hypnotic. Perfect. After some passage of time—I'm not sure how much—I remembered that this was the last night of my furlough. I had to check out of the hotel in the morning to get back to camp before five o'clock in the afternoon. My vacation was over.

It was time to get back to work. Time to start getting ready for the next campaign, whatever it might prove to be.

EXCEPT FOR TRAINING CADRE AND TRAINEES, MOST of the soldiers normally assigned to Fort Campbell had been moved to other bases in the previous month. I learned that there had been a lot of troop movements all over Earth putting ground units in position near major cities just in case the Ilion Federation got reckless enough to attack one of the most populous planets in the Galaxy. And a number of bases had been opened, or reopened, to offer basic military training to hundreds of thousands of new recruits and draftees—on every continent. While I had been off on furlough, several hundred replacements had arrived for the 1st Combined Regiment, not just humans but some from each of the participating species.

I did get one laugh when I checked in at the orderly room of my company—B Company, Ranger Battalion. Tonio Xeres, my platoon sergeant, told me that Major Josiah Wellman had been transferred to the regimental staff as assistant operations officer. Major Wellman was the SOB who had volunteered me for the 1st Combined Regiment in the first place. We hadn't gotten along at all well in the few months I had served under his command. Wellman was a training-manual officer with no sense of humor and even less imagination. He had cackled quite a bit at getting rid of me so easily.

"Serves him right," I told Tonio after I quit laughing. We had talked about Wellman before. Tonio wasn't just my platoon sergeant. He was probably the best friend I had ever had, more like a brother than the one I had by blood. "Give him a chance to see what it's like, and he shouldn't be able to give me any grief as assistant ops at regiment."

"I thought you'd be pleased," Tonio said, not bothering to hide his grin. "Just try to stay out of his way. Come on, let's head for chow." It was a little past noon. I had left Chicago on an earlier flight than I had originally planned. It wasn't that I was homesick for the army, but . . . at least I would be with people I knew. "I'll fill you in on what's been happening while you were off enjoying yourself."

I didn't bother contradicting him.

I**T WASN'T MUCH OF A SURPRISE WHEN I WALKED** into B Company's mess hall and saw that most of the soldiers eating there had segregated themselves by species. It showed just how tenuous the success of the program of integrating us all down to the squad's level had been so far. Humans here, divotect there; porracci, biraunta, abarand,

and ghuroh in their separate cliques as well. Altogether, there were about eighty men eating, and I didn't see one instance of a member of one species sitting at the same table with members of any other species.

I stopped near the head of the serving line, turned, and looked around the room. Tonio guessed what was running through my head and said, "You're right. We're still not meshing the way we should. Colonel Hansen has talked about it a half-dozen times in staff meetings and sent out as many memos, but. . . ." He shrugged his shoulders and got a tray and silverware.

"I'm surprised he hasn't ordered squads to eat together," I said as I got my tray and silverware and followed Tonio through the line. The whole rationale behind the 1st Combined Regiment was to prove that the different species could function together at the closest level possible—something to give a political boost to the Alliance of Light. In Ranger Battalion, that integration went all the way down to the squad level. In the rest of the regiment, entire platoons, or companies, were of a single species.

"I'm expecting that, almost any day," Tonio said. "It has to come, probably as soon as we get into serious training again."

Our conversation stopped until we had our food and coffee and had made our way to a table—almost halfway between where the other humans were clustered and the next group, which happened to be biraunta. They look something like five-foot-tall spider monkeys, right down to their prehensile tails.

Tonio started with a sip of coffee. "Ranger Battalion is almost back up to full strength."

"I take it that means they haven't decided to forget about their grand experiment?" I gestured around the mess hall.

"No, they haven't. The 1st Combined Regiment continues, and they're talking about forming a second. As far as I know, it's just talk so far. Anyway, that's not our affair." He shrugged.

"We go back into a full training schedule Monday morning," Tonio continued. "They're telling us that the regiment will have at least four months of training before we're deployed again." He shrugged again. "I know. We heard that before. Maybe this time it'll even be the truth. Ranger Battalion has received replacements for those killed in action from all of the species. About half the replacements are fresh out of Ranger School or the equivalent. Not many have any combat experience. There are still about twenty men from the battalion on furlough and maybe the same number still recuperating from wounds. In your squad, the abarand, Jaibie, was released from the hospital yesterday. He's on a three-day pass now, due back Sunday night. The porracci, Kiervauna, is still convalescent. The last status report from the hospital said he'll need at least another two months before he can return to duty."

"Have I got a replacement for Wilkins?" Lance Corporal Fred Wilkins had been assistant leader for my first fire team, the only fatality in my squad during the liberation of Dintsen. He had also been the only other human in the squad—besides me, that is.

Tonio nodded while he finished chewing a mouthful of food. "Lance Corporal Robert McGraw. He said he's served with you before."

I laughed, almost choking on a chunk of beef. "Yeah, Robbie McGraw. Used to talk about his Scottish heritage in a South American accent so thick I could barely understand him half the time. His family had lived in Panama for something like six generations. Had a great-uncle who was governor of the province thirty or forty years ago. A good soldier, at least in peacetime. He seen any action yet?"

"No, but he had just been transferred to the Ranger School here as cadre before we got back from Dintsen. He asked for us and got it, wanted a chance to serve with all of the species. From what I've seen, he should fit in well."

"Puts him one up on Fred Wilkins right off the bat," I said, softly, more to myself than to Tonio. Wilkins had been an extreme bigot. If he hadn't gotten himself killed on Dintsen I would have done my best to get him shipped out of the unit as soon as we got home.

THE ARMY—ANY ARMY—HATES TO SEE SOLDIERS idle, even if there's no real work for them to do. Ranger Battalion wasn't back into a training regimen yet, so those men who were present were put on work details. It was make-work for the most part, doing useless things like raking gravel and bare dirt to make uniform patterns, planting flowers where visitors to the base might see them, KP and guard duty, and so forth. The Friday I reported back, my squad was at the base hospital, sweeping, mopping, and inventorying nonmedical supplies—blankets, pillows, bedpans and what-all. Corporal Ying'vi Souvana, my porracci assistant squad leader, had been in charge of the squad while I was on furlough. When I joined the squad after lunch, Souvana popped to attention and "relinquished" command to me too formally, and without much enthusiasm.

"Just carry on as you have been for now," I told him, keeping it casual. It's an oversimplification, but porracci look something like Terran orangutans, averaging about twice the weight of humans but generally a bit shorter. "I want to go upstairs and see how Kiervauna is doing." Besides that, I wasn't too thrilled with the prospect of standing around supervising the useless chores . . . and I thought it might do Souvana a world of good to get stuck with it for a while longer.

"Lance Corporal Kiervauna is progressing as well as can be expected," Souvana said, almost growled. His face screwed up in a frown, an expression very like the human equivalent. "It requires time to grow a missing leg back. He will not be fit for duty for quite some time yet. He will miss much training."

Souvana and Kiervauna, my two porracci. One of the problems in the squad. Something—I still wasn't sure what—had happened between them on Dintsen, during one of our rare respites from fighting the tonatin. Kiervauna, usually submissive to the dominant Souvana, had assaulted him. We had been forced to pull the two apart. I couldn't convince myself that the hard feelings between them would disappear, despite the threats I had made to both of them about fighting again.

"His wounds were received honorably, Souvana," I reminded him, keeping my voice as gentle as it gets. "He fought well."

"Yes, Sergeant." There was no give in Souvana's voice, no hint of "forgive and forget."

LANCE CORPORAL TRAU'VI KIERVAUNA WAS SIT-ting up in bed recording a letter when I entered the room. He stopped the recording and pushed the stand with the complink terminal off to the side. He even smiled as I approached.

"It is good of you to visit me, Sergeant," he said.

"How are you feeling?"

"I *feel* in perfect health, Sergeant, but I am unfortunately not yet *in* perfect health." He gestured at the tube around where his missing leg should be. It was a form-fitting apparatus like a small medtank, used to speed the growth of his new limb. "It will be quite some time before the limb is usable. My medtech says it will be at least two more weeks before I can even begin therapy to put the muscles in condition."

"Don't worry about that. It takes time. You acquitted yourself well on Dintsen."

He frowned. "When I could recall who the proper enemy was. When I did not forget my place."

"That's behind us, remember?" I said. He was referring to his assault on Souvana. "We might not have fared as well as we did if you hadn't been there."

•   •   •

IN RANGER BATTALION, A SQUAD IS TEN MEN—
ten soldiers—who can operate as a unit or split into two
five-soldier fire teams . . . or function as an integral part of
its platoon or company. Generally we operate at platoon
level or below, drawing the most dangerous assignments in
combat, often behind enemy lines. Special operations.
Spec Ops. We do long-range patrols, target difficult objectives, harass an enemy's "rear" area with guerrilla-type
raids, stage ambushes—anything that's nasty and too dangerous for line troops. I had lost only one man in the liberation of Dintsen, a claim not many spec ops squad leaders
could make. Sure, there had been a number of others who
were wounded, including me, but wounds heal. Even losing a leg, the way Kiervauna had, is only a temporary dis-
ability. Whether or not a person can be an effective soldier
again after a wound like that is a separate question. Any really serious wound might make a person psychologically
unfit for any combat assignment. It depends on the individual, how he reacts to the . . . experience, and you can't
always be sure about their reaction until they get into combat again.

I spent most of that Friday afternoon talking with each
of the members of my squad—except Jaibie, since he was
on a pass. No one objected to being taken away from their
work for ten or fifteen minutes. The talk wasn't just idle
chatter. I wanted an idea of how each of my people was
after coming back from the trauma of combat—and not
just those who had been wounded. Fang, one of our two
ghuroh, had nearly died from his wounds. Nuyi, our divotect, had also been seriously hurt.

I still thought that the entire idea of putting all the
species together at such close quarters had more holes in it
than a chunk of Swiss cheese. The biraunta were terrified
of porracci. Porracci and ghuroh both came from societies
built around a macho physical dominance ranking, and
they seemed to clash instinctively. And just about everyone
despised the divotect—the only sentient species evolved

from reptiles rather than mammals. Abarand and humans. No one seemed anxious to concede that any of the other species could be the equal of his own, let alone possibly *better.*

Still, we *had* managed to work together well enough on Dintsen to win the campaign and destroy the predominantly tonatin garrison that the Ilion Federation had left on the planet. Tonatin were the dominant species in the Ilion Federation, though there were worlds representing just about all of the other sentients in the federation, even humans. Just about all of the others but divotect. The divotect were the least numerous sentient species, and all of their few worlds were part of the Alliance of Light—those that had not been conquered and were still being held by the Ilion Federation.

ROBBIE MCGRAW WAS A WALKING CLICHÉ. HE was tall and gangly, with straw-colored hair that was almost uncontrollable even cut to regulation army length—little more than half an inch. He lounged around with a perpetual grin on his face like some stereotypical farm boy from midwestern North America. When he opened his mouth you almost expected a *golly, gee whiz* drawl. What you got was a mixture of thick Spanish and Scottish accents that made him hard to understand in either English or Spanish if he started talking too fast or got excited. That was the way I remembered him, at least.

He was the last of the people in my squad I came across in the hospital. He had managed to get himself out of the way—where no one would notice he wasn't doing much work.

"Goldbricking again, I see," I said when I finally tracked him down, in a snack room on the hospital's ground floor. He had aged a bit in the few years since I had last seen him—haven't we all?—but he was easy to recognize.

"Good to see you again, too, Dragon," he said over an easy laugh. I raised an eyebrow.

"Sounds as if you've finally learned how to speak English," I said. His accent hadn't disappeared completely, but it wasn't nearly as thick as I recalled.

"Had to," he said, with his usual sheepish grin. "Before they would accept me as cadre at Ranger School I had to go through speech modification—three weeks of learning how to talk all over again. Said I wouldn't be much good if the trainees couldn't understand what the hell I was saying."

"So the army manages to do *some*thing right once in a while," I said. Robbie was the kind of guy you just have to like, whether you want to or not. "I understand you volunteered for this outfit."

"The minute I heard what you'd managed on Dintsen. If I'm gonna be in this-here war, it might as well be in a unit that's showed it's got the balls to do an impossible job. That's why I volunteered for rangers in the first place. Besides, I wanted to know about the other races in the Alliance and this seemed to be the best way."

"You got that much right," I told him. "You getting enough of that yet?"

Another grin, even wider than before, showing more teeth than any one mouth should have. "Sure a tense bunch of fellas," he said. "Been a couple of times I thought I was gonna see all-out fights in the squad bay. One night, I thought Souvana was gonna take on both ghuroh at once. The three of them growled at each other a lot and postured. Souvana had the fur standing straight up on his head and neck. But they all backed away before it got too far. Nuyi got in the middle and yakked up a storm at them. Smaller than any of them and he didn't flinch a bit. Looked like he was ready to stomp anyone who started something."

"Well, once we start training next week, maybe everybody'll be so tired they won't have enough left in them for a fight," I said, not that I had much hope it would be that simple. "Get it out of their systems during the day."

The grin left Robbie's face. "Seriously, how long you

figure we got before we get back out to where the fighting is?"

"Not nearly long enough," I said. "They're promising four months of training, but we can't count on that. We've just got to work as hard as we can, be ready as soon as possible. It's no damned picnic, I'll tell you that. Now, why don't you try to do a little honest work for once? You've had your break, a whole damn week's worth—from what I hear."

CHAPTER 2

THE LIGHTS CAME ON IN THE BARRACKS AT 0515
hours Monday morning—thirty minutes earlier than I had
expected, fifteen before my alarm clock was due to
sound—and the alarm buzzers started their raucous call at
the same time. You'd have to be half dead to sleep through
that and the stream of cussing that erupted within seconds.
As a sergeant, I rated a private room just off the end of the
dormitory room that housed the rest of my squad, and I
could hear some of the cussing through the wall. I got into
my clothes as quickly as I could, then hurried into the
squad bay to make sure there were no slackers there.

"Let's go! Reveille! Reveille!" I shouted as I made my
way from one end of the squad bay to the other. No one
was asleep, but Nuyi and Jaibie weren't up off their bunks.
"Move it!" I yelled again. "Vacation is over. Today we go
back to work." I ignored the protests and the rest, turning
to head back toward my room at the other end. The latrine
is just across the corridor from my room, and I had things
to do in there.

Reveille formation was at 0530 hours. We fell out in
exercise gear. Since it was summer, that meant shorts,
t-shirts, and sneakers for humans. The other species had
their own variations. For porracci, it meant stark naked.

We lined up by squad and platoon. It doesn't take long

for soldiers to get so used to the routine of "falling in" that they can do it while half asleep—and, nearly every day, some do. Squad leaders checked to make sure everyone was present who was supposed to be and passed the news to the platoon sergeants, who passed it to the platoon leaders, who officially reported it to the company commanders: *all present or accounted for.*

I was a little surprised to see Colonel Hansen and all the battalion staff officers and clerks fall out for reveille. It's rare to see the senior officers at reveille—almost unheard of on a Monday morning. Usually, the brass doesn't show up until time for the work formation at 0800 hours, if then, and the headquarters clerks usually manage to escape nearly all formations. I was sure this exception didn't bode well. I was right. After the manning reports were completed—relayed to the colonel—we went through a full hour and twenty minutes of rigorous calisthenics, topped off by a two-mile run.

Since the colonel and his staff did it with us, there were fewer complaints than there would have been otherwise, but a lot of us had been skimping on exercise since coming back from Dintsen. There had been no formal calisthenics there, not in a combat zone. I was sweating and winded in minutes, and there were times when I wondered if I could make it until the colonel took pity—if not on us, then on himself and the desk jockeys. In time, I got to thinking, *I can make it as long as he can.* The colonel was a dozen years older than me and, I was sure, not as physically fit as I was even after a month without regular exercise. But Hansen stayed where he was and kept right with it, by the numbers.

When the torture finally ended, we had an hour to get cleaned up, eat breakfast, and make beds and so forth before work call at 0800.

"Looks like we're back in the army," I told Tonio as I passed him heading back to the barracks. He didn't bother replying. He was still catching his breath.

•　•　•

AFTER THE WORK FORMATION, B COMPANY DREW weapons, marched out to one of the firing ranges, and spent the morning practicing marksmanship. The normal routine is to get everyone on the range at least once a week in garrison. C Company went to hand-to-hand combat training; D Company was split into platoons for exercises in small unit tactics. A Company drew new uniforms. The announcement of that came as a surprise to me. New uniforms: for the first time, all of the species in the 1st Combined Regiment would have uniform uniforms . . . allowing for the anatomical differences among us. When the unit was formed, the members of each species had come wearing the uniforms of their own armies—different styles, different camouflage patterns, and so forth. Now we would all look as nearly alike as possible. Biraunta uniforms had to have arrangements for their prehensile tails to stick out. Divotect units were tailored to cover the remnants of tails they still had. And so forth.

C Company drew its new uniforms before lunch. B and D companies drew the new issue Monday afternoon. As soon as the men in each company had their new clothing they were told to return to barracks and change. We had just enough time to get insignia switched and to make whatever minor alterations were necessary to get the uniforms looking right.

AFTER MY PEOPLE GOT INTO THE NEW UNIFORMS we went to the pits for hand-to-hand combat training. The pits are engineered to minimize the possibility of serious injury. Holes are scooped out. A thick layer of coarse sand—the sort that doesn't completely compact when it gets wet—is spread across the bottom, nearly a foot deep. On top of that, a layer of sawdust and wood shavings is spread. The whole mess is compacted just enough to allow reliable footing, but this "flooring" has enough resilience to help avoid too many broken bones in training.

On Dancer, when the 1st Combined Regiment was doing its initial unit training, hand-to-hand had been put off as long as possible . . . and then a little longer, because of the way biraunta were terrified by the much larger porracci. The porracci resembled prehistoric predators from the biraunta's homeworld. But we needed that training. Soldiers of each species had to learn how to fight soldiers of all the other species. The only species we couldn't train against was tonatin. There were none in the Grand Alliance—the grandiose name given to the combined armies of the Alliance of Light. For want of any better solution, our porracci served as "stand-ins" for the tonatin. They were as close as we could come, but not nearly a perfect match. Tonatin look somewhat like Neanderthals from Earth's past, but larger, smarter, and very aggressive.

There were new biraunta in our company, if not in my squad, and there were a few tense moments during our first hand-to-hand training session, but it wasn't nearly as bad as it had been on Dancer. What *was* as bad was the intensity of the sparring between porracci and ghuroh. Both of them came from societies where individual physical prowess set the pecking order. The difference, which I had been slow to recognize, was that dominance–submission among porracci was solely a matter of individual fighting ability, while among ghuroh it was more a cooperative thing, making the "hunting pack" as strong as possible. It was less combative among ghuroh. But porracci and ghuroh were fairly evenly matched, and both were anxious to demonstrate their own superiority over the other.

The basic anatomical differences among the various peoples of the army meant that there were some pairings that offered little hope in unarmed combat. Biraunta could not hope to defeat either porracci or ghuroh one-on-one and were hard-pressed to hold their own against humans, abarand, or divotect. Few humans could stand, alone, against a porracci or ghuroh, and so forth. So, apart from the one-on-one matches, we did some experimenting with combinations, looking for workable routines, and hoping that we would be able to stay out of the least-favorable situations when the real thing came along.

IYI AND OYO, THE TWO BIRAUNTA IN MY SQUAD, were brothers, identical twins—in a race that offered little physical difference among adult males at best. The only visible distinction between Iyi and Oyo was a slight variation in the coloring of the fur that rimmed their faces. They were almost exactly five feet tall and each weighed about seventy-five pounds. I could have lifted one of them over my head and thrown him without much difficulty. But in combat that would not have been so easily done. They were almost my equal in hand-to-hand combat, their smaller size offset by longer arms, the ability to grip with feet as well as hands, greater speed and agility, and their prehensile tails. I wasn't careful enough in my first match with Oyo that day. He managed to throw me almost with ease.

Pound for pound, humans don't match up well against most of the other species. It works out about even between humans and divotect because we're about the same size and have fairly equal strength, on average, though the divotect probably do have a little the better of it. We have a slight advantage over biraunta because they're only half our size—but that advantage is *very* slight. The only species in the alliance that humans have a definite advantage over is the abarand. They derive from flying mammals and retain rudimentary wings that are no longer sufficient for real flying, but their bone structure is delicate and their musculature not as finely honed for fighting.

UNIFORMS WEREN'T THE ONLY NEW ITEM WE RE-ceived that first week of training. Wednesday, we all received new electronics packages for our helmets. For the first time I would have the same level of communications with all my people that I had with other human members of the company. We could share full telemetry instead of just voice—map overlays, video relay, and physical vital signs. Thursday, we received new rifles for the ghuroh, porracci, abarand, and divotect—slug throwers that used the same ammunition as the primary human rifle. The weapons were still somewhat different, tailored for the anatomical differences among the species, but being able to use the same ammunition would make resupply in combat easier by orders of magnitude. Only the biraunta were going to continue using their original weapons—short-term, at least. Biraunta were so much lighter than the rest of us that there was still hesitation about giving them heavier weapons and ammunition.

"Maybe it'll all help," I told Tonio when we met for lunch in the mess hall Thursday, just after the company had drawn its new weapons. "We're all wearing the same basic uniform now. We'll be firing the same ammunition, mostly. Maybe it'll rub off and we'll start acting more like we're part of the same . . . team." I shook my head a little, mostly to myself. I had almost said *family* instead of *team,* and we were a long way from being that close.

"That's what the colonel hopes," Tonio said. He looked around to make certain that no one was close enough to overhear. Then he whispered, "Lieutenant Fusik even suggested that we might have to find a way to start a few fights—squad against squad—to get our people to bond more closely."

I couldn't hold back a chuckle. "You mean set someone up and wait to see if the rest of his squad comes to his aid?"

Tonio shrugged. His grin looked more than a little self-conscious. "Something like that. The lieutenant isn't sure enough it would work though. He's worried that things might get a lot worse if we staged something like that and it backfired."

"Or if somebody figured out that it was phony," I suggested. "Could get sticky as hell. Damn, I wish you hadn't mentioned that. I got enough crap to worry about without wasting time trying to figure a way to make something like that work." I shook my head and picked up my fork again, but before I could get a mouthful of mashed potatoes to my mouth I set the fork down. "There must be a way, Tonio. But . . ." I felt my face screwing up as if I had just tasted something particularly nasty. "Hell, I'm not sure we're far enough along. It would work better if it happened while we were off-duty—even better, off base, on pass together in town. And *that* hasn't started happening yet."

COMPANY B SPENT THAT AFTERNOON ON THE FIR-ing range, giving those of us with new weapons a chance to sight them in and get used to the new ammunition. The rest of us took our turns on the firing line as well, just not as often. Practice might not always make perfect, but lack of practice can get you dead. Those men with new weapons went first to zero in their sights and familiarize themselves with the action and recoil. Then they went through full rotations from every firing position, single and automatic fire, using close to two hundred rounds of ammunition apiece. The humans and biraunta did a lighter routine—about eighty rounds.

"An inferior weapon," Souvana said after he had finished his last turn at the firing range. "The caliber is too light to be as effective as porracci weapons. We would be better off staying with our traditional rifles."

"You're making me feel like a psychic, Souvana," I told him, working hard not to grin. "I could have predicted your reaction almost to the word, and that has nothing to do with the relative merits of the weapons. You would have said the same thing regardless. You're being too narrow, and too predictable. Porracci engineers *did* design your new weapon. The only real difference between the old rifles and the new is the caliber."

"As I said," Souvana said after a growl, "the caliber is the problem. It is too small for a proper infantry weapon."

"A smaller caliber but a higher muzzle velocity. A hit

from one of these bullets actually has more energy than a hit from the heavier-caliber bullets your old rifles used. They do more damage and have a slightly greater effective range. Of course, if you can't *see* well enough to hit a target at longer range. . . ." I watched his eyes narrow at what I was certain he would take as an insult, but I didn't give him time to start bitching. "The tool works, if the man using it knows what he is doing. If he doesn't, he should be doing something more within his abilities, like digging ditches . . . or cooking for his women."

Yes, I was baiting Souvana, but I had learned a lot about porracci. You have to find ways to challenge them, channel their aggression, get them angry . . . but not *too* angry. I was pushing the limits, since no self-respecting porracci male would be caught dead cooking for females. Even in their army, it is only the lowest-ranking porracci soldiers who get stuck in the kitchen. It is considered a more humiliating punishment than locking them in the stockade.

"I am too good a soldier to rise to your insults, Sergeant," Souvana said after what was obviously a struggle. "And porracci can do better than anyone else, even with inferior tools. But *some* of the races in our alliance do not have that advantage."

"Each of us has something to offer, Souvana," I said, gentling my voice, almost whispering as I moved closer to him, nearly nose to nose. "Each of us has something we are better at than any of the others. That is why it's so vital to operate as a team, taking the best each species has to offer. That's why this unit was formed. And, *that* is how we will defeat the Ilion Federation."

If Souvana had been human, his jaw might have dropped about then. His eyes got wide and his head tilted back, just a little, which was more or less the porracci equivalent of a human's jaw dropping open because an idea has caught him by surprise. *That's it,* I thought. *Work at it a little. See what I've been leading to.* I was feeling pretty proud of myself right then. Just maybe I was finally going to break through one of the remaining barricades in the squad—at least with one of the species.

I watched his eyes and waited. After a moment, he blinked and cleared his throat. "I must see to my fire team," he said. "We need to clean our rifles and make sure we can disassemble and reassemble them quickly." Then he spun on his heel and walked away. I shook my head slowly while I watched him leave.

You just can't face it yet, I thought. *Nobody can. Damn. I thought we were getting somewhere.* I headed toward the safety tower behind the center of the firing line. That was where Tonio and the other squad leaders were gathering, along with the rest of the sergeants in the company.

WE WERE ACTUALLY DISCUSSING THE BUSINESS AT hand, how the men were doing with their new weapons, when the company's lead sergeant, Greeley Halsey, stepped into the middle of the group of noncoms. "I've got news, gentlemen," he started, then he looked around to make certain he had everyone's attention. "We just received a directive from General Ransom." Brigadier General Wallace Ransom was the regimental commander. "Effective tomorrow morning, there will be new seating arrangements in the mess halls. During breakfast and lunch, on duty days, seating will be by squad. That means no more having everyone break apart by species. For now, at least, this will not extend to the evening meal after the company has been dismissed for the day or for the rare off-duty day. Questions?"

Lead Sergeant Halsey looked around the group again. There were no questions. The directive was clear. I glanced at Tonio. This was something we had both seen coming. I was moderately surprised that the directive did not cover *all* meals in the mess hall. Tonio gave me a barely notice-able shrug, as if he might have been surprised by the same thing.

"Oh, by the way," Halsey said, stopping after he had

taken a single step. "There is one other piece of news from regiment this afternoon. Our company commander is now *Captain* George Fusik." Halsey grinned. "That's not just recognition of what he did on Dintsen, it's recognition of what the whole company did. And a measure of what they'll expect of us next time out. Let's make sure we don't disappoint the brass."

FRIDAY MORNING WE INITIATED THE NEW SEATING plan. The tables in the mess hall were each large enough to seat twelve men, an entire squad in a human infantry unit. With the mixed squads in Ranger Battalion, the tables seated the ten soldiers of one of our squads . . . I hate to use the word *comfortably* . . . but adequately. There had been some discussion among the squad leaders in my platoon about how we should work this and we decided to stay with fire teams within each squad. I sat with my fire team on one side of our table, and Souvana sat with his fire team on the other. Team leader on the right end, assistant team leader on the left. The way my squad was arranged, that split the two humans. Kiervauna, the assistant fire team leader on the other side, was still in the hospital, of course, but when we were back at full strength, the plan would also split the porracci.

We went through the serving line together and got our seats. "We're a squad, a team," I reminded everyone. "When it gets down to it, it's *us* against *them*—whoever *they* are. We saw that on Dintsen. We might find ourselves in even more desperate situations in the future." I hesitated because I had just remembered something I had seen in an old adventure vid. A line of dialogue, rather. I was afraid I might choke on the cliché, but I forced myself to say it: "'All for one and one for all.'"

I could *feel* Souvana staring at me before I glanced his way and confirmed it, but he didn't say anything. But closer, just across the table from me, I saw Claw nodding—and almost smiling. Ghuroh are pack hunters by ancestry. I guess that "all for one" idea is something they understand, something they're raised with if it's not a hard-wired instinct with them. *Maybe we can get through this after all,* I thought—not the first time I had tried to sell myself on that notion. At least no one was too upset by the seating arrangements to eat.

IN THEORY, OUR TRAINING SCHEDULE CALLED FOR a five and a half-day work week with Saturday afternoon and Sunday off. That first week, Colonel Hansen showed us that he knew how to get the most out of us in the allotted time. Friday evening our company was sent on a night exercise in squad tactics, giving everyone a chance to work on the spec ops skills that are supposed to be our bread and butter. We didn't get back to barracks until just before breakfast time Saturday morning. Even then we weren't given a chance to sleep. After we ate and showered, we cleaned weapons and other gear, then stood inspection. By the time Captain Fusik released us for the weekend, it was nearly noon.

Not everyone went to the mess hall for lunch, and no one headed to the company orderly room to pick up passes to go into town. Most were content to use their "free" Saturday afternoon to catch up on sleep. Including me. You have to take it when you can get it.

CHAPTER 3

WE WEREN'T IN A COMBAT ZONE, SO MY REAC-
tions weren't particularly quick. When you expect trouble,
you never get all the way into sleep—you never fade so far
from consciousness that you can't respond instantly to a
threat . . . at least not more than once; if you do, you're
dead. It's different in garrison; you expect to be safe in
your own bed. I woke up to what sounded like somebody
trying to dismantle the building with a sledgehammer. For
a few seconds, I remained on my bed, groggy, just lifting
my head a little while I blinked myself fully awake. When
I finally realized that there was trouble out in the squad
bay, I got up immediately and headed for the door.

What I found was no great surprise. Souvana and Fang
were fighting. They were rolling around on the floor and
had already knocked over a couple of bunks and one metal
locker. It must have been the locker crashing to the floor
that had wakened me. The rest of the squad was more or
less trying to stay out of the way of the two combatants, no
one willing to dare getting between Souvana and Fang to
try to break it up.

"Knock it off!" I shouted. "Souvana! Fang! Stop fighting—*now!*" I screamed the last word as loud as I could,
enough to hurt my throat. I might as well have saved my
breath and the wear and tear on my larynx. Neither of them

paid any attention. I couldn't see any evidence that either one even heard me.

"The rest of you, what are you standing around with your thumbs up your butts for? Claw, Robbie, the two of you pull Fang off. Nuyi, help me with Souvana."

I didn't relish the prospect of getting in the middle of that mess any more than any of the others had, but we had to break up the fight before anyone outside the squad came to investigate the noise—and that probably wouldn't be long. The whole company lived in one building, and the fight had to have wakened a lot of the others.

It wasn't easy to get at Souvana and Fang, but with four of us trying to get our hands on them we did at least complicate their fight until we could start separating them. When Souvana still didn't desist, I clipped the side of his neck with the edge of my hand—*hard.* There is a nerve in porracci necks that can be compressed against a bundle of muscles there. It's supposed to be painful. It was enough to make Souvana loosen his grip a little, and Claw got a hand under Fang's chin and pulled back, so we were finally able to get the two men apart. Then we got between them.

"Back off, Souvana!" I ordered, shouting even though my mouth was no more than an inch from his eyes, which were clearly red with anger. "Now, damn it! Back off and cool down." He was still pushing, still trying to get at Fang, and it was all that Nuyi and I could do to hold him back. I didn't dare take even a second to look over my shoulder to see how Claw and Robbie were doing with Fang, though I could hear both of them shouting at him. I had a nasty itch along my spine. Being between two crazed fighters—either of whom could have done serious damage to me alone —was not a very comfortable position.

Souvana continued to struggle so I kneed him in the groin—a maneuver nearly as effective against porracci males as it is against humans. He grunted and doubled over so quickly that it almost knocked Nuyi and me to the floor. But it did take some of the steam out of him. We didn't give him a chance to recover. I shoved back and up, while

Nuyi stuck a leg behind Souvana and the porracci fell backwards, hitting the floor hard, knocking the breath out of him. I got on top of him, one leg across his throat, holding him there while I caught *my* breath. I was puffing from the exertion.

"Cool down, damn you!" I said. "Enough! If you can't control yourself, I'll call the MPs and have you locked up until you can. You hear me?" Souvana couldn't very well talk with my shin pressing against his throat and jaw, so when he finally stopped struggling I took my weight off his neck—without getting so far out of position that I couldn't put pressure on him again quickly. "You hear me?" I asked again.

Souvana had to clear his throat, a couple of times, before he was able to speak. "I hear you, Sergeant," he said. Squeaked. I hoped I hadn't done serious damage to his throat, but mostly because that would have meant taking the incident out of the squad, putting it on the record.

I got up and turned to see how the others were doing with Fang. Claw and McGraw were both sitting on him, and they had his arms twisted under his back, pinning him doubly. Fang had also quit struggling, so I gestured for the others to get off of him.

"That goes for you, too, Fang," I said, moving until I was about equally distant from him and Souvana. "Get a grip on yourself." I sucked in a breath. "Now, get up, both of you." They were slow to rise, but neither had been hurt so badly that he couldn't get to his feet.

Souvana was several inches shorter than me but twice my weight. Fang was a foot taller than me but only outweighed me by forty pounds. They were both stronger than me by more of a margin than I wanted to think about. Ghuroh look rather canine, something like mastiffs but almost totally hairless. I looked from one to the other. They were both breathing heavily. Souvana was still massaging his throat. Apparently that hurt more than where I had kneed him below. *Something to remember,* I thought.

Fang's light tan skin was flushed. There were two long scratches dripping blood on his left cheek.

"Claw, get your first aid kit and tend to those cuts," I said, gesturing at Fang's face. I was stalling. I had to take *some* action against the fighters, but I wasn't sure what. This was too flagrant to let it slide the way I had the scrap between Souvana and Kiervauna on Dintsen. But I didn't want to go the official route, put them up before Captain Fusik for company punishment . . . or the chance that they might refuse that and demand a court-martial. Either way, it would make my job of developing a seamless team more difficult, and that was proving hard enough as it was.

Claw wasted no time and since Fang's scratches weren't serious, it only took a minute to get them bandaged. Not enough time for me to figure out what to do, but I couldn't let it go without letting them know that there was going to be a price.

"Until further notice, you two are confined to barracks. Except for the requirements of duty and training, and for meals in the mess hall, you are both restricted to this room and the latrine. You'll draw every shit-detail I can think of until somebody else screws up badly enough to take your places. If you don't like it, we can take it to the captain, and you better know he'll be rougher than I am. I won't have this in my squad. That goes for the rest of you as well. We . . . do . . . not . . . fight . . . each . . . other." I spaced those words out carefully, moving my gaze around and making each of the men meet my eyes. "I don't care who started this, or why. Souvana, this isn't the first time for you, but it had damned sure better be the last. If it happens again, I'll take it to the captain and you can count on losing your corporal's stripes. Now, Souvana, Fang, get busy and get this place cleaned up." I didn't wait for questions or comments. I spun on my heel and went back to my room.

• • •

I DIDN'T STAY IN MY ROOM VERY LONG. I HAD TO get away from the squad and cool off before I started hollering at Souvana and Fang again. I put on my boots and a fresh uniform shirt, then went into the latrine just long enough to make sure I looked presentable. My face was still flushed, but other than that. . . .

Before I left, I glanced into the squad bay. Souvana and Fang had the worst of the mess straightened out. They were staying as far apart as they could, and the rest of the squad was watching them, not saying anything. Then I left the compartment, out into the hall and downstairs. It was just a little after eight o'clock, Saturday evening. I wanted a drink. Or three.

The NCO club—the private preserve of the regiment's noncoms—was a quarter-mile from our barracks. It was a fairly substantial establishment, spread over three floors of a building it shared with one of the base theaters and a PX—post exchange, sort of a military general store. Within the club there were two separate barrooms, a dancehall, and what was called a coffee shop where you could get a quick meal as well as coffee, tea, or anything else liquid and legal. The coffee shop was kept open around the clock.

I headed for the first bar and ordered a beer before I looked to see if anyone was in there I might want to chat with. Maybe I was hoping that Tonio would be there. I could talk to him about what had happened, and still keep it unofficial. If that kind of thing was happening in my squad, the odds were heavy that it was happening in other squads as well. But I didn't see Tonio. There were only a half-dozen men in the room, and there wasn't anyone I really knew well—certainly no one I wanted to strike up an idle conversation with just then.

The bartender brought my beer and I put a thumbprint on the tab before I took a long pull, drinking from the bottle and ignoring the glass the bartender had set by it. The beer was cold and delicious, but as I started taking my second drink my stomach rumbled and I recalled that I hadn't eaten since lunch. I had slept through supper—not something I do very often.

"Better put some food in before I do too much drinking," I mumbled. A sergeant can't afford to get too drunk on base. As long as he's in uniform, he has to conduct himself with . . . some decorum. I had learned that the hard way, getting busted from sergeant to corporal. It had taken me two years to get that third stripe back.

The barman had already moved away, and there was music playing loud enough that no one was going to hear me talking to myself. Club rules said we weren't permitted to take drinks from one venue to another, so I had to finish the bottle of beer I had before I went upstairs to the coffee shop. It didn't take long, and the waiter upstairs was able to get me a new bottle in short order, so I could start on that while I gave him my food order—a big platter of jambalaya, one of the specialties of the shop; they always had it simmering on the stove. "Bring me a bottle of pepper sauce with it, and some extra onions," I told him. "I like it hot."

I HAD MADE A GOOD START ON MY JAMBALAYA— rice, a couple of kinds of meat, tomato, onion, and spices—and was into my third beer of the evening when Tonio came into the coffee shop and sat at the counter next to me.

"I thought I might find you somewhere in the club," he said when I glanced over at him.

"Slept through supper. Had to put some calories in the tum," I said after taking a sip of beer. I had worked myself through the gulping stage and was down to sipping the beer to cool the burn of the jambalaya on my tongue. The waiter came over. Tonio told him he would have what I was having, jambalaya and beer.

"I understand you had a bit of a ruckus in your squad bay earlier," he said with studied casualness, after the waiter went to fill his order.

"A bit," I conceded. Not much could happen in Tonio's platoon without him hearing about it— sooner rather than later. I waited until Tonio had his beer and food before I continued. "Souvana and Fang, trying to determine who's got the biggest balls, I guess. Nobody hurt bad enough to need a medtech. I'm taking care of it."

"I figured you would. That's why I told the others not to interfere. Keisi wanted to call in the MPs." Sergeant Hiorayma Keisi, a divotect, ran one of the squads in third platoon.

"Am I the only one having this kind of crap in his squad?"

"Unfortunately, no. There've been at least a half-dozen fights this week, just in B Company, and some of the other companies have been having trouble as well."

"Ghuroh and porracci squaring off?"

Tonio shrugged. "Not entirely. A little bit of everyone trying to prove they're better than everyone else. There's only been one fight where anyone got hurt badly enough to need medical attention. A divotect corporal in C Company got banged up pretty badly by one of the porracci in his fire team. Needed two hours in a medtank."

"The porracci being court-martialed?"

"Or worse. He was transferred to one of the porracci line companies for punishment." In the regiment's line infantry battalions each company consisted of soldiers of a single species, except for specialists and liaison people.

"What's the punishment for assaulting a superior in the porracci army?"

"Don't ask," Tonio said. "I don't even want to think about it. Somebody's likely to have that poor bastard's hide for a rug." I wasn't sure, but I didn't think he was exaggerating.

"It wasn't this bad on Dancer, or on Dintsen," I said after making a little more progress on my meal. "The ghuroh weren't with us long enough on Dancer for much, and Dintsen . . . well, we had enough to keep us occupied there, most of the time."

"We'll get past it," Tonio said, getting ready to finally start on his food. "We have to."

I LEANED ON SOUVANA AND FANG HEAVILY ALL through the next two weeks. That wasn't simply punishment—or sadism on my part. The punishment angle *was* important; they had to learn to play by the rules and make nice. But there was another aspect to it. Since I was hard on both of them, I hoped to help build some common ground between them—you know, *them* against *me*. And once the other members of the squad started thinking that maybe I was being too rough on Souvana and Fang, they might all start thinking of themselves as more of a team.

Tonio knew what I was doing. Once I had figured it out for myself, I talked with him about it. I was doing the same sort of thing that drill instructors do with recruits in basic training, and not as extreme as some of the examples I had seen. "Just be careful you don't push it *too* far," Tonio warned. "Don't let it get to the point where one of your men figures that all he has to do is rip your head off your shoulders to end his troubles. Something like that might destroy the battalion."

"It wouldn't do me a damn bit of good either," I reminded him. "Hell, this is the way we turn civilians into soldiers in the first place, give them a drill instructor to hate to focus their minds and get them doing what we want."

"And sometimes that backfires too. You remember Klaus Dietz?" Tonio asked.

I nodded. Klaus Dietz had been a drill instructor, pushing a new batch of recruits through basic training every three months. Klaus was dedicated to his job, perhaps too dedicated. He was rough, but his platoons were always the best each training cycle. Finally, one recruit snapped—decided that he had taken more than he should, or could—and Klaus didn't pick up the signs soon enough. The recruit was in one of the grenade pits with Klaus. The re-

cruit pulled the pin on a hand grenade, then let the safety
hook flip loose while he held the grenade—and while he
held Klaus in a bear hug. When the grenade exploded,
Klaus died almost instantly. The recruit might have survived his injuries to face a court-martial, but the company
commander decided to save the army the trouble and re-
fused medical treatment for him until it was too late.

AFTER TWO WEEKS, I STARTED TO EASE OFF ON
Souvana and Fang—just a little. It was probably several
days before either of them realized that they weren't catching quite as much crap as before. There were fewer make-
work details piled on top of the training routine, which was
hectic enough. I maintained the restrictions, forcing them
to remain in quarters during their free time while the rest
of the squad enjoyed the freedom of the base while they
were off-duty and passes to go into town on the weekends
—when they weren't too tired for that.

Town. There was Clarksville southeast of the base, but
for the most part, *town* meant the built-up strip loosely
known as Gavin City just across the street on the Ten-
nessee side of Fort Campbell, ten miles of taverns, diners,
clubs, and a variety of other businesses designed to take
care of soldiers . . . and separate them from their money.
The local residents got used to having aliens around fairly
quickly. Their money spent as well as ours. It had taken
most of the local business establishments less than two
weeks to start offering merchandise designed to appeal to
each species—so far as possible; after all, there were no
alien hookers on Earth. There were a few . . . incidents, but
those were handled quickly and quietly by the MPs and
civilian police. After six hundred years of coexisting, the
army and the locals were used to living together, and
sweeping the occasional discord under the rug. *Serious*
trouble was rare, even after several alien species had been
added to the mix.

• • •

ON THE FRIDAY AFTERNOON THREE WEEKS AFTER
the fight, I sent the rest of the squad on to supper and held
Souvana and Fang with me in the squad bay. "We'll call it
even," I told them. "You're released from the restrictions.
But you'd better both be clear about one thing. If anything
like this ever happens again in this squad, it will go a lot
harder on whoever is involved. You're either part of the
team or you're out of it. Another incident and I have the
troublemakers transferred back to units composed entirely
of their own kind—with a statement of the reasons for it.
Souvana, you're assistant squad leader. Make certain that
everyone in the squad knows what I said. We either act like
we're a team or we'll find people who can be. Do you both
understand?"

Souvana simply nodded his acknowledgment—with
less obvious resentment than he normally greeted me with.
Fang said, "Yes, Sergeant," in a subdued voice.

I looked from one to the other and back, then nodded
myself. "I hope you do. Now, let's go eat."

B COMPANY, RANGER BATTALION, SPENT ITS
sixth week of training in Brazil, on maneuvers as the "ag-
gressor force" against a South American regiment that had
been augmented with a battalion of porracci. We were
shuttled south Sunday night, spent four and a half days in
the jungle along the Amazon River practicing what we had
learned and finding a few weak spots along the way. Then
we were shuttled back to Fort Campbell Friday afternoon.
It was nearly supper time before we reached the barracks,
and we all wanted to get into the showers and then into
clean clothes as quickly as we could—to get to the mess
hall and eat "real" food for the first time since Sunday. Battle rations aren't designed for flavor, just to provide the
necessary nutritional requirements.

But we had a surprise waiting in the barracks, and that
threw us all off schedule for a few minutes. Kiervauna was

sitting on his bunk, his injured leg in a prosthetic cast that would protect the still-growing replacement limb while letting him walk almost normally. Except for Robbie and Souvana, we all gathered around Kiervauna to ask how he was doing and so forth. Robbie didn't really know Kiervauna, except for a couple of visits in the hospital, and Souvana wouldn't have allowed himself to show any emotional interest even had he and Kiervauna not been . . . rather estranged since their fight on Dintsen.

"The hospital hasn't released you for duty yet, has it?" I asked once we got through the initial babble of everyone trying to talk at once.

"No, Sergeant," Kiervauna said. "I must return by *Taps*, but apart from my scheduled therapy sessions I have the freedom of the base. The doctors seem satisfied with the progress of my new leg." He thumped the cast for emphasis. "It will be another ten days before this comes off, and perhaps a week after that I will be returned to full duty status."

Kiervauna waited for the rest of us to get clean and changed, and went to the mess hall with us. He had heard about the new seating arrangements, and though the colonel's order still did not apply to the evening meal, I had kept it going within the squad on my own, as had some of the other platoon sergeants and squad leaders. It was getting to be a habit for most of us. The segregated groups at supper and during the weekend were getting smaller each week. Of course, Saturday afternoon and Sunday, there were always quite a few men who didn't bother eating in the mess hall—going into town or to one of the clubs or PX cafeterias on base for their meals.

IT WAS THE NEXT WEDNESDAY, OUR SEVENTH week of training, before I had my first face-to-face encounter with Major Josiah Wellman, the officer who had dumped me into the 1st Combined Regiment in the first place. He was observing a training exercise in spec ops tactics and I had to carry a message to him from Captain Fusik. When I got to him, I snapped to attention as sharply as if I were a recruit and saluted.

Wellman returned the salute slowly, glaring at me the whole time. I gave him the message—we were operating under electronic silence so Captain Fusik could not simply radio the major—and Wellman nodded, also slowly. I waited for him to dismiss me, to tell me to get back to my unit, but he seemed to be in no hurry. He looked me up and down, then did some more glaring—one of his two talents, as I recalled.

"I knew you were in this battalion," he said after what seemed like nearly a minute of silence. "You've managed to keep yourself out of trouble so far." The way he said that, he managed to load the sentence with surprise, and disdain, a certainty that the situation would not last for long. I bit back a reply he would certainly have considered insubordinate. I never go *looking* for trouble with officers; it finds me easily enough. Wellman would pounce on any opening I gave him.

"I try, sir," I said finally, since he seemed to be waiting for me to say something. "We stay busy."

"See that you do," he said. Then he gave me a reply for Captain Fusik and told me to get it delivered—"properly and promptly." I thought the comments I would have liked to have said, saluted, and got away from him as quickly as possible.

EVEN WITH SATURDAY AFTERNOONS AND SUNDAYS off, we managed to put in weeks averaging more than sixty-six working hours. At least one day a week, and usually two, we had night exercises of one sort or another, and some of those lasted *all* night, with no rest before or after. Just about everything we did during daylight hours we also practiced at night. In combat, we preferred to operate at night, when the darkness would give us some small advantage. With modern night-vision systems, that advantage isn't great, but you can't see quite as far, or quite as well at night as you can during the day. It can mean the difference between living and dying.

Since we were on Earth and not on an isolated, otherwise uninhabited world like Dancer, we did hear war news as it filtered in from battlefields on a dozen worlds scattered over a volume of space more than three hundred light-years in diameter. So far, all of the ground fighting was confined to various colony worlds established by several species. None of them, to date, were human worlds, though there had been a failed attempt by the Ilion Federation to invade New Providence, one of the last worlds humans had settled before we encountered sentient aliens. New Providence lived up to its name. At the time the Ilion fleet appeared out of hyperspace to attack, several warships of the Alliance of Light happened to be in orbit, on a routine stopover, so the Ilion invasion never reached the ground. One of the two enemy troop ships was destroyed, with perhaps a thousand soldiers.

That was the good news. The bad news was that our attempt to liberate a second divotect world that had been conquered by the Ilion Federation had failed. Two regiments—one porracci and one ghuroh, augmented by a single battalion of biraunta—were cut to pieces on the ground. Seventy percent of the landing force was killed or captured.

For several days after that I expected orders sending the 1st Combined Regiment out to make a second try to liberate that world—despite the fact that we hadn't had half the training time we had been promised. Our time on Dancer had been cut short as well. But no orders came. We continued our normal training routine.

CHAPTER 4

IT WAS AT THE END OF THE NINTH WEEK OF OUR training cycle that Kiervauna returned to duty, his new leg functioning at something approaching 100 percent. He still had a slight limp, sort of a hitch in the normal rolling gait of the porracci, but Kiervauna reported that his physical therapist had assured him that the limp would disappear after a few weeks of normal activity, augmented by a daily routine of special exercises.

Kiervauna reported to the company orderly room just before noon on Saturday—in time for lunch in the mess hall and a free weekend. It was while we were in the mess hall that I had my brilliant idea.

"We need to do something to celebrate Kiervauna's return to duty," I announced, "the fact that the squad is once more complete." I glanced around to make certain I had everyone's attention. "It's Saturday afternoon and no one in the squad has any duty all weekend. I think we should go into town together to have a few drinks to mark the occasion." Short pause while I looked directly at Souvana. "*All* of us. The first round will be on me, since I'm the squad leader, and the second will be on Corporal Souvana, since he's Kiervauna's fire team leader." I kept my eyes on Souvana, silently daring him to object while the rest of the men were voicing their obvious approval of my proposal.

Souvana's eyes narrowed, but he simply took in a breath then nodded, very curtly.

We went back to the barracks so everyone could change out of "work" uniforms—camouflage-pattern fatigues—into "informal dress" uniforms. Those still varied according to species, in assorted tans, browns, and greens. So far, it was only our combat gear that had been made as uniform as possible.

Grain alcohol—in one form or another, with different sources and flavoring agents—is an indulgence all of the known sentient races share. Brewed, distilled, or fermented, we had all discovered booze at early points in our respective histories and maintained the association on our way to the stars. The 1st Combined Regiment had been stationed at Fort Campbell long enough that a fair number of the taverns near base had started bringing in liquor in the preferred versions of all the species who were part of the 1st Combined Regiment.

I kept my eyes and ears open, alert to the way my men reacted to this not-quite-forced conviviality. My idea was to get the squad drinking and hope that the alcohol mellowed those who were antagonistic toward each other. I knew there was a chance this impromptu experiment would blow up in my face, that a couple of the men might get too much booze and decide to duke it out in front of civilians, or trash a bar, but I hoped for better. I hoped that the way I had jumped all over Souvana and Fang for their fight had not yet been forgotten and would restrain any impulses to commit mayhem.

We walked in a fairly loose group to the nearest gate, about half a mile from our barracks. There was some idle chatter among the men—not as much as there would have been had they all been human, but enough to be moderately reassuring. They weren't arguing or fighting. The closest anyone came to that was the inevitable bragging about who was going to drink whom under the table. I didn't join in the chat, but I found myself wondering the same thing. If the only consideration had been body weight, the porracci would have been the hands-down winners since they outweighed everyone else by a considerable margin. But the speed of metabolic reactions differs from species to species. Biraunta "burn" calories faster than any of the larger species. Abarand are almost as . . . prolific. Both of them require more food per unit of body weight than the rest. Divotect metabolism is markedly slower than any of the others; they get drunk quickly and stay drunk longer. And so forth.

Get everyone drunk together so they'll have hangovers to share later? It was just an idle thought, but it brought an amused smile to my face. The problem was that if everyone got roaring drunk the chances were greater that a fight would break out before they reached the point of passing out from the booze.

THE NEAREST BAR WAS A PLACE CALLED GEN'RAL Jimmy's, only fifty yards from the gate, across the highway from the base, with a pedestrian tunnel under the road to cut down on the chances of drunk soldiers getting flattened by vehicles. Gen'ral Jimmy's had only had that name for five years. The decor was supposed to represent a slice of history of Fort Campbell, harking back centuries to a time when many soldiers were trained to jump out of aircraft with only huge sheets of cloth—parachutes—to slow their fall. Seeing the old photographs and the reproduction of a parachute that was draped along one wall was almost enough to make me appreciate our airsleds.

Since it wasn't two in the afternoon yet, the bar wasn't busy. There were a couple of drinkers at the bar and another pair at a table in a corner with a dozen empty bottles between them. We pulled two tables together near the rear of the barroom and got our orders in. I decided to stick with beer . . . and to drink in as much moderation as possible, just in case there was trouble. It wasn't until after the waitress had left that I noticed that everyone had pretty much taken the same positions they had been taking in the mess hall—my fire team on one side of the table, Souvana's fire team on the other side. I had trouble suppressing a grin.

When the waitress returned with our drinks, several of the men hooted with pleasure as I thumbprinted the tab. Once everyone had their drinks, I stood, raised my beer, said, "To the best damned squad in the 1st Combined Regiment," and poured a good measure of beer down my throat. Who said you can't find camaraderie in a bottle? Right at that moment, my squad was as unified as any I had ever served with.

OKAY, MY RESOLUTION TO DRINK MODERATELY didn't work as well as it might have. I'm a little hazy on some of what happened that afternoon. Somehow, we got back across the road and home to the company area in time for evening chow at the mess hall. That was an economy measure, if I recall the discussion. Eating in the mess hall, rather than paying for a meal somewhere else, would save that much money for additional drinking.

Kiervauna and Robbie nearly had to carry Nuyi, who had been hovering near the edge of unconsciousness for more than an hour. They put him to bed in the barracks before the rest of us went to eat. I kept seeing Claw at my side. I think maybe he had to steady me a couple of times. We must have pushed decorum as far as we could in the mess hall, but there weren't that many people eating there on a Saturday evening—and no officers came to look in—so we got away with it.

Except for Nuyi, who hadn't gone to the mess hall, and Oyo and Iyi, who went straight back to the barracks after supper, the rest of us walked, or staggered, to the Enlisted Men's Club once we had finished eating. Noncoms have lots of places to drink on base, EM clubs as well as NCO clubs. I remember going to the club with the bulk of my squad . . . but I don't remember leaving it. My next clear memory is of waking up before dawn Sunday morning—

still in the clothes I had been wearing the day before, right down to my dress shoes—with a raging headache. I think I started groaning before I woke up.

The first thing I did, once it was possible to do anything but lay on my bunk and moan, was to reach for an analgesic patch and slap it on my forehead, right between my eyebrows where my agony seemed to be focused. Then I lay back and closed my eyes again, waiting for the hot thumping to ease off.

Thankfully, those patches don't take long to start working. It must have been less than five minutes before the agony moderated enough that simple thoughts didn't bring new waves of pain and nausea. Once I could hear beyond the pounding in my own head, I noticed that the barracks was silent. Sometime later, I opened my eyes and turned my head to look at the clock on my nightstand. The glow of the numerals wasn't *too* painful. It was a little past six in the morning.

I fought my way up to a sitting position and waited for a brief wave of nausea to pass before I started the difficult process of trying to remember what had happened. There were only isolated fragments willing to be recalled. What was important was that there were no memories of police or fights, or anything else that might have found its way back to haunt me in unpleasantly official form. I *thought* I would remember something like that, no matter how drunk I had been. I certainly wasn't in the guardhouse—always a reassuring bit of knowledge.

Twenty minutes in the latrine, most of it under a steaming-hot shower, had me finally feeling halfway human. I got my shaving kit and finished the morning necessities, then went back to my room and dressed. There had been no sign of life in the squad bay, but I had only glanced in and hadn't switched on the lights. Once I had myself squared away, I walked down the aisle between the rows of bunks in the squad bay just to make certain everyone was present. The sour smell of alcohol breath was heavy in the room, but every bed was occupied. There were a few soft groans, and a few not-so-soft snores. It looked as if everyone had survived my brilliant idea.

I walked the length of the squad bay again. The patch on my head had done its job well enough that I felt hungry. "If anyone is going to want breakfast this morning, you'd better start pulling yourselves together," I said, not *too* loudly. There were a few responding groans, but no one said anything intelligible.

AFTER I CAME BACK FROM THE MESS HALL, I went to the company dayroom to use one of the complink terminals to check my pay account—to find out how much I had spent the day before. Apparently I had popped for several more rounds of drinks after the first, at Gen'ral Jimmy's and the EM Club. It could have been worse. I still hadn't worked my way through all of the pay I hadn't been able to spend during our months on Dancer and our shorter stay on Dintsen, and there had been a few paydays since.

Then I checked the company bulletin board, just to see what was going on. I thought about going to the orderly room to ask whoever had the Charge of Quarters duty if there had been any . . . problems reported, but finally decided not to tempt fate. "Trouble will find us soon enough if we did screw up," I mumbled.

I was just getting up from the complink terminal when Robbie McGraw came into the dayroom. "I don't think there's a pain patch left in the squad, Sarge," he said. "Boy, are there some hurting heads this morning."

"Anyone besides me go for breakfast?" I asked.

"Not that I know of." He sat on the big leather sofa along one wall of the room, leaned back, and closed his eyes. He was still wearing a patch on his forehead, and his face was almost pale beneath the tan of spending so much of every day outside. "I haven't been up that long."

"I think yesterday did us all a lot of good," I said. "Maybe we're finally coming together as a squad."

Robbie made a noise that might have been a soft

laugh . . . or a groan. "That wasn't what you were thinking about before we left Jimmy's yesterday."

"What the hell are you talking about?"

"The way you were coming on to Chrissie, the waitress. For a minute there, I thought the two of you were going to get under the table together and go to it right there."

I started to shake my head when some hint of recall flashed a peek around one of the dim corners in my head—something I really couldn't pull out into the light. "Oh, God, what did I do?" I asked.

"Well, you kept your pants zipped up, if that's what you mean. You gonna keep your date with her this afternoon?"

I wasn't even sure I remembered what Chrissie looked like. Her image in my head was fuzzy. All that stood out was that she had a lot of dark reddish-brown hair. "What date?" I asked.

"When she gets off work this afternoon."

"What time?"

"How the hell should I know? You're lucky I remember that much. I guess I was a little pissed off that you asked her out before I could."

THE FIRST THING I DID WAS CALL GEN'RAL Jimmy's and ask to speak to Chrissie. She did remember me. "I just wanted to make sure you still want to go out with me this afternoon," I said, moving easily into a polite fabrication, "after all, I wasn't in the best of shape yesterday." When she said she did still want to go out, I wasn't sure if I should be happy or not, but there were a lot more men than women around, and there was no way to tell when I'd get another chance . . . at whatever. "What time do you get off?" I asked next.

Four o'clock. She had to get back to work right then, so I told her I'd see her at four. That left me time to sit and wonder what the hell I was getting into before it was time to have lunch and start worrying about what I was going to wear and where I might take Chrissie.

• • •

No, I DID NOT MAKE ANY BASELESS ASSUMPTIONS about what was likely to happen. I didn't go to Gen'ral Jimmy's expecting to have sex before the evening was out. If Chrissie had been a whore, she wouldn't have been waiting tables in a bar. The prostitutes were better organized; their guild frowns on moonlighting; and the local laws don't require subterfuge. I also did not assume that I *wouldn't* be having sex. I didn't know anything about Chrissie except the fact that she worked at that tavern. I didn't know how old she was, what she was like, what she liked. Hell, I didn't even know her last name.

I don't know if anyone in the squad other than Robbie knew that I had made a date with the waitress, but I assumed that at least some of them must have been aware. In any case, no one said anything about it or asked why I was getting spruced up. Most of the men were extremely subdued, quiet, slow to recover from our outing of the day before. Everyone was recovered enough to eat Sunday dinner, always a special occasion in garrison; the cooks pull out all the stops, and it's usually the best chow of the week. After dinner, people wandered in and out of the squad bay, doing whatever they had to do on their day of rest. Wrote letters, read, went to a show, whatever.

I left the barracks just after three o'clock, a lot earlier than I needed to, anxious to get away from the others before somebody noticed that I was nervous and started asking questions. Yes, I was nervous. I could hardly believe that myself. Anyway, I got out of the barracks and did some walking, away from where I was most likely to run into people who knew me. I was wearing a watch so I'd know what time it was, and I kept glancing at it—about every thirty seconds, it seemed.

I TIMED MY ENTRANCE AT GEN'RAL JIMMY'S AL- most to the second. I didn't want to be late . . . but I also didn't want to be early. Chrissie was taking one last tray of drinks out to a table. She gave me a quick smile as she went past and said she'd be ready "in just a minute." I mumbled something back and took an empty stool at the bar, watching Chrissie. The bartender didn't ask if I wanted something, so he must have known why I was there.

Chrissie had to be at least eighteen—minimum legal age for working in a tavern—but I doubted that she was much older than that, which meant that she had to be ten years younger than me. I had recalled the abundant auburn hair correctly; there was so much of that it hardly seemed possible. Chrissie was nearly my height and had brown eyes, and she was attractive. I didn't know how long her shift had been that day, but she was still moving spryly enough. She finished delivering drinks, ducked into the back room for thirty seconds, and came out minus the apron. She waved goodbye to the bartender and came over to me.

"All ready, Bart," she said, proving that she remembered my name. I got up from the stool.

"What would you like to do?" I asked as we headed for the door. "If we made any specific plans yesterday, I'll have to apologize for not remembering. I had a little too much to drink." It was the third time I had apologized for that, but I'm not all that used to dealing with civilians. Sometimes I have the feeling they think we're all barbarians.

She laughed, low and throaty, not a giggle. "Nothing specific," she said. "Are you a gamer? I know the army doesn't let soldiers get hardwire implants, but a lot of the guys who come in use temps."

I turned my head to look at her and caught a slight glint of metal under the hair just behind her right ear—a jack for a direct electronic connector to let her plug directly into a game console. "No, I've never been much for games. I'd be a complete novice at anything. No challenge at all."

"That's okay. No need for us to start competing."

"We could start with dinner," I suggested. "That'll give us time to figure out what else we want to do."

• • •

HER LAST NAME WAS ORLMUND. SHE WAS TWENTY-
one, studying alien languages on-line, and didn't date anyone below the rank of sergeant. We ended up spending
three hours sharing a simvid—some ridiculous romantic
adventure with men in ruffled tights carrying swords and
women in fancy gowns screaming to be rescued from
some extremity or another. I *tried* to get into the spirit of
the sim, but I think Chrissie was disappointed with my effort. Still, she didn't complain. Afterward, we just walked
for half an hour or so, ending up at her apartment.

I didn't go in. We stood at the door for several minutes
and talked. We exchanged link codes and I told her I'd call
when I could. She gave me her work schedule—her days
off. Then I walked back to base, stopping at two bars along
the way—one beer in each. I wasn't sure that I would call
her . . . and I doubt that she had any confidence that I
would. I had the feeling that Chrissie was looking for more
than a casual relationship.

And I wasn't.

CHAPTER 5

THE FOLLOWING WEDNESDAY WE LEARNED THAT four officers from Ranger Battalion and a dozen others from the rest of the regiment were being transferred out, immediately. The rumors we had heard about the formation of a 2nd Combined Regiment were confirmed. The officers from our regiment were to provide some experienced leadership for the new unit. Friday, we learned that a few sergeants were also being transferred to the 2nd Combined Regiment. The only man transferred from B Company was Junior Lieutenant Eso Vel Hohi, the biraunta who was third platoon's leader. Tonio told me that we were scheduled to get a new biraunta JL, but that he wouldn't arrive for another week. All of the officers and sergeants transferred out were supposed to be replaced.

After two and a half months, we were in pretty good shape. Much of the battalion had been together since Dancer and I had been through the combat on Dintsen; all of the wounded were back with their units. With plenty of veterans it had been easier to bring along the replacements for those who had been killed or wounded too badly to come back. All in all, Ranger Battalion was sharper than it had been when we hit Dintsen to liberate that divotect world. That didn't mean we could just sit on our butts. You hone your skills constantly, looking for that little extra sharpness, knowing that it might mean fewer casualties, might even mean the difference between winning and losing.

We had reached the point where we were doing at least one practice insertion each week—simulating combat landings either by shuttle or airsled. We practiced complicated battle scenarios, spec ops missions and deep penetrations with other army units providing the enemy for us to act against. One of those maneuvers was held in the desert of southern California. Another was on the Panamanian Isthmus. Each lasted three or four days.

General Ransom and Colonel Hansen kept us busy. We started doing night exercises two or three times a week, and those included just about every Friday night, which meant that we wasted a lot of "free" Saturday afternoons catching up on sleep. I called Chrissie a couple of times over the two weeks following our first date, and we had dinner together on the second Sunday, but nothing more. She was very understanding. She knew about the training schedule. It was affecting business at Gen'ral Jimmy's. There were a lot of soldiers too tired to cross the street for a beer when they could get one cheaper at a club on base.

The next Sunday I took a bus into Clarksville and visited a professional to get laid. I didn't have to worry about complications, commitment, or polite maneuvering; just a couple of drinks, a few words on what I liked, and we adjourned to a private room. Half an hour later I was feeling much better.

THERE WAS ONE OTHER BENEFIT TO THE INCREASED training schedule. With everybody working day after day until all they wanted to do was sleep when they got off duty, there were a lot fewer fights. I had no trouble at all in my squad, and the spats were becoming minimal throughout the unit. They didn't disappear completely. You're always going to have squabbles in an army unit, disagreements that can get out of hand. What was important was that they no longer seemed to result from bigotry among the species, and the men in the various squads took to stopping them before any superiors had to get involved.

We got through the hottest months of summer and into the slight relief of early autumn, with temperatures rarely hitting ninety. The 1st Combined Regiment was close to achieving the four months of training we had been promised. The general finally relented a little on the schedule, occasionally giving us all of Saturday off, supposedly to make up for the earlier intrusions on our weekends. Even during the week our schedule was a little softer. We concentrated on fine points of techniques as well as continuing the routine of physical conditioning, the firing range, and the hand-to-hand combat pits.

"Just means we're that much closer to being sent out again," I told Tonio. We were eating supper in the NCO club. It was Friday afternoon, the end of week sixteen of training. One more week and we would have our four months in, all that had been promised to us.

"Probably," Tonio said. "This time, I think we're ready for whatever they want us for, even if it's something as insane as liberating another world like Dintsen with too few men. We've had time to jell, time to get most of the problems worked out. We're sure as hell not going to win the war sitting on Earth. Time for us to earn our pay again."

"You heard any hot rumors about where they might send us?"

He snorted. "Hundreds of rumors, none worth the energy to repeat. Rumors sending us to just about every settled world in the galaxy, and to a few that aren't. Anyplace that gets talked about a lot is probably unlikely. Hell, they're not going to broadcast plans when any news might get to the wrong ears."

"I know, but . . . it would be nice to have some idea."

"You've been in the army long enough to know better. Maybe General Ransom and his top staff officers know what's coming, but the odds of the rest of us being told anything before we absolutely have to know are too small to worry about. They'll give us a few hours', maybe a whole day's, notice that we're going to ship out, but we won't be told where we're going until we're aboard ship and moving out-system, too late for it to get to the enemy before we get there."

And we could be shipping out almost any day now, I thought.

THAT STARTED TO NAG AT MY MIND. I WASN'T looking forward to combat—I had been there and knew how horrible it can be—but I was as ready for it as I was ever likely to get. It's the whole reason for all the training, the fundamental reason for the uniform, the job. Every soldier has to deal with the possibility that the next mission might be the one he doesn't come back from. Those of us who had been on Dintsen had all seen comrades die. Many of us had been wounded. You can't forget those things. You just have to find a way to deal with them. You recognize the fear that starts to build as soon as you realize you're going to be going into combat again, and you do whatever it takes to make sure the fear doesn't mash your brains to jelly. Maybe it's easier for some of the other species. Porracci and ghuroh seem more involved with the business of fighting, less concerned with what happens to them personally. But, then, maybe that's just the way it looks to me. There's still a lot about the others that I'm not certain I completely understand.

I did call Chrissie Friday evening, and we made a date for Sunday. She wasn't working that day, so we could spend the afternoon together. I would pick her up at her apartment at one o'clock and we'd decide what we were going to do then. After I linked off, I sat and wondered just why the hell I had called her. I couldn't find an answer.

"YOU THINK YOU MIGHT BE LEAVING SOON," Chrissie said just after we said our hellos—punctuated by a very short kiss, an expected type of thing without passion. She wasn't asking a question, just making a simple statement.

"Sooner rather than later." I shrugged as I stepped through the doorway and she shut the door. "We're not going to win this war strutting around Fort Campbell."

Chrissie's apartment was small and utilitarian, only three rooms—if you include the bathroom as a separate room—bedroom in the back and combination living room and kitchen. Her complink terminal sat on the kitchen table, the screen aimed into the living room area. There was a direct link for her gamer jack in the living room next to the love seat. There were two straight chairs at the table and a single upholstered chair that matched the love seat, simple drapes on the windows, not much else. I've been in hotel rooms that looked more . . . homey. Hell, my room in the barracks wasn't much more spartan.

"We don't have to go out if you don't want to," Chrissie said, moving me toward the love seat. "We could maybe watch something on the link, or listen to music and talk. Whatever. I've got a few beers in the refrigerator."

"Whatever you want to do."

She moved closer to me, until our bodies were touching at several locations. "Let's stay in, get to know each other better," she whispered. She initiated the kiss, and it was more than the ritual little peck we had shared at the door. She didn't have to draw me pictures. Chrissie was ready for our relationship to move to a new level.

What the hell, I thought, moving into the spirit of the moment. We were both adults with full control of our faculties. *We're going to be shipping out soon. No telling where they send us after the next campaign. Might be a world with no human women on it.* There hadn't been females of any sentient race on Dancer, and Dintsen only had divotect women—and their anatomies are too different from humans to make *fraternization* (the formal military term for sex and other frowned-upon activities) possible even if a horny soldier wanted to try.

• • •

CHRISSIE WAS CERTAINLY NO BLUSHING VIRGIN. I hadn't expected that, but she demonstrated a few tricks that made me think she had received expert coaching somewhere. That afternoon I think I had the best sex I had ever had without paying for it. By the time we finished I was limp in more ways than one. We lay together in her bed, tangled together. We had spent most of the past several hours there. I was feeling warm and comfortable . . . and spent, and I remember thinking, *I could get used to this.* I was having difficulty staying awake, but I did a lot of blinking and tried to suppress any yawns. A man has to have standards.

"Much nicer than going out," Chrissie whispered, her lips moving right against my ear, tickling.

"Very nice," I agreed.

"Is this how you got the nickname Dragon?" Chrissie asked, tracing the tattoo on the back of my left hand.

I chuckled. "No, the other way around. I got the tattoo because of the nickname."

"How did you get it?"

"Right after I finished boot camp, I was out on the town with a bunch of buddies and I tried a really stupid trick I had read about, an old sideshow bit that involved spraying a mouthful of a flammable liquid past a flame, like breathing fire. Someone called me a dragon and the name stuck." I shrugged. "That and my hair. It was redder then, not washed out the way it is now."

We stretched the afternoon out a little more, but the waves were gone, and we eventually got out of bed and got dressed. *I* got dressed. Chrissie just pulled on a dressing gown.

"I hope you don't ship out *too* soon," Chrissie said as she showed me to the door. Then, before she opened it, she sort of melted against me in a way that made me think we were both still naked. "I like being with you."

"You're . . . special," I whispered, moving some of her hair so I could kiss the side of her neck in a way she really liked. She raised up on her tiptoes, pressing harder against me. For an instant, I thought maybe it wouldn't be necessary for me to leave quite yet, but it was just another tingle, not the real thing. "I don't think I've ever known a girl quite like you."

She chuckled, then gave me a hard kiss on the mouth. "Call me," she said, reaching around me to open the door.

I KEPT TELLING MYSELF THAT IT WAS TIME TO END it with Chrissie—before we got too involved for me to break it off at all. She wanted something I wasn't sure I could give her. I woke in the middle of the night, sweating and shaking at some dream I couldn't recall—except that it had involved Chrissie and me in some sort of supposedly permanent relationship. *Forget her,* I told myself. *She'll find someone else soon enough. She must have men waiting in line for a chance.*

But forgetting her wasn't that easy. She kept intruding on my thoughts, even after I promised myself that I wouldn't call her, wouldn't see her. It got to the point where I was having trouble keeping my mind on my work, and that can be dangerous even in training. If you lose concentration, you're inviting an accident, and the tools of my trade are deadly.

I held to my resolution not to call her until Thursday. Then I called, just to talk for a couple of minutes. I didn't know if we were going to have the weekend off—or even if we would still be on Earth that weekend—but we made tentative plans for Saturday. She was working the early shift, getting off at four in the afternoon, and had all of Sunday off. Chrissie suggested that we spend all that time together. I told her I'd let her know as soon as I found out what my schedule was.

At that minute, I think I would have almost welcomed news that the regiment was going to ship out on Friday, even if it was to go into combat. *When we left, it would be easier,* I thought. Have time without her so close, then just don't pick it up again when we come back. There was always a chance the regiment would be stationed somewhere else the next time and I wouldn't even have to risk a face-to-face breakup.

I COULDN'T REMEMBER THE LAST TIME I HAD AC-
tually slept with a woman—slept, not just dozed for a few minutes, but spent the entire night in bed with her. It had been a lot of years; since I was eighteen or nineteen. Since then, it had always been briefer. One of us would get dressed and leave afterward. I wasn't certain I would be able to sleep in bed with Chrissie, not without a sleep patch. I had two in my pocket when I left base Saturday afternoon.

On the walk to Gen'ral Jimmy's I kept telling myself that I should turn around and head back to base—hide in my room if I had to—but my feet kept moving. I had a small bag with a change of clothes in it, and I felt self-conscious about that when I went into the tavern, right at four o'clock. I don't know if anyone noticed the bag. At least I didn't have to wait for Chrissie. She was ready to go and met me before I had taken two steps inside, before my eyes had time to adjust to the lower light level. By the time the door closed behind us, we had our arms around each other. We couldn't have been any closer if we had been in a three-legged race.

"We don't even have to go out to eat," Chrissie said. "I went shopping and got everything we'll need. I want to cook dinner for us." That sentence would have sent danger signals through me but I was too preoccupied with the way her body was rubbing against mine, and the way I was already getting aroused. We talked, but I don't have any idea what else either of us said until we were inside her apartment and had gone through a kiss that threatened to suck my insides out.

By the time that had ended we had both started stripping. We got naked, but Chrissie danced away from me before I could start the next logical sequence. "I've got to get supper started first," she said, laughing. "Get us a couple of beers." I wasn't all that steady on my feet, but I got to the refrigerator and got the beers out and open. Chrissie paused to take a sip, but she had already started dinner preparations. I moved back a couple of steps—the better to watch her—and drank my beer too quickly, trying to force patience to the least patient part of my body.

There was something incredibly erotic about watching a naked woman fix food. In five minutes Chrissie had everything cooking that needed to cook and had the table set. "Come here," she said, gesturing with one finger in a come-hither gesture.

I went to her and she wrapped herself around me. We kissed, and then we made love, standing in the kitchen, with Chrissie leaning back against the counter. We finished just before the timer on the stove went off.

I DID SLEEP THAT NIGHT, A COUPLE OF HOURS each time, separated by more sex. Sunday morning, we slept late. It was past ten o'clock before we got out of bed, showered, and dressed. *If I get through today without her mentioning marriage, it'll be a miracle,* I thought when I had a few seconds free for such idle thoughts. I wasn't sure how I would handle that conversation if it started, but an image of me grabbing my clothes and running for my life darted through my head. I wasn't naive enough to think that good sex was enough of a basis for marriage . . . even if I had been inclined toward that sort of thing anyhow.

But the subject did not come up. We ate lunch, then went for a walk in the park—all quite trite and innocent. We spent most of the afternoon out like that, holding hands and walking, talking about nothing much in particular, then went back to her apartment for an hour or so.

"If you leave before we get a chance to see each other again, don't forget me," Chrissie said as I got ready to leave her apartment. She touched my cheek in what seemed to be a very possessive gesture.

"I don't think I'm ever going to forget you," I said—a confession that tripped my tongue a couple of times before I got it all out. We kissed again and I left.

THE NEXT MORNING, WHEN TONIO GAVE ME THE news that the regiment was going to ship out that night, I almost got down on my knees and thanked him. I needed time away from Chrissie before I got in too far to back out.

CHAPTER 6

THE FLEET THAT WOULD CARRY US HAD BEEN gathering over the weekend. The logistics of the move had been planned long before we were told what was coming. Ammunition, food, and other supplies had been loaded aboard transports. Crews from the fighting ships had been given a last chance at liberty, either on Earth or at Over-Galapagos in geostationary orbit. During the day, Monday, our heavy equipment, mostly the remote-controlled artillery and tanks, were shuttled up to their ships. The men of the regiment's Heavy Weapons (HW) Battalion—officers, operators, mechanics, and so forth—were the first to shuttle up to the fleet, before ten o'clock Monday night, 2200 hours in military parlance, as it was time to start thinking in military time again. We were on our way to combat.

We weren't told that before we left Fort Campbell, not officially. All we knew for certain was that the 1st Combined Regiment—some five thousand soldiers—was being deployed with all its equipment and supplies. But there was a war on and we knew what was coming, if not where.

I did take two minutes to call Chrissie. All I could tell her was, "We're shipping out. I don't know where. I don't know for how long." She told me to come back safely. That was all there was. Neither of us mentioned the word *love,* which was a relief. To me, at least.

An interstellar journey is not a protracted affair; a matter of a few hours, not days or weeks. When we got where we were going, we would almost certainly land just about immediately, and if my guesses were right that would be right into combat. We were assault troops, not garrison soldiers—an offensive weapon. We had Monday morning to get our gear inspected and packed. Lunch in the mess hall. Ranger Battalion was told to return to barracks and get what sleep we could, ready to fall in for transport at 2300 hours that night. We would follow the HW men. The regiment's line battalions would follow us.

"Figure that means that the fleet will be heading out-system by 0400 hours tomorrow," Tonio said. He had the platoon's squad leaders in the barracks dayroom. Tonio had just come from a briefing at battalion headquarters. "I can't tell you where we're going—nobody told me—but this is definitely not a training exercise. Make sure your men all get their sleep in today, even if they need patches to do it, because tomorrow is likely to be . . . busier than any we've seen since Dintsen. That goes double for us. Get your men bedded down, then get there yourselves. If anyone doesn't have a sleep patch, there are plenty in the orderly room. Use them if you have to."

I had to. I suspect most of the others did as well. At that point, we had been up for seven hours or less after a full night's sleep. Our bodies weren't ready to go back to sleep without medical assistance. Sometimes, it's when you need sleep the most that it's the hardest to find.

We were wakened at 1800 hours, the day flipped around for us with breakfast waiting in the mess hall after a rare evening reveille formation. I doubted that the timing was arbitrary. There had to be some point, most likely an attempt to get our body rhythms attuned to wherever we were going, to the cycle of day and night on whatever world we were being sent to.

After we returned from our meal, we stacked our duffel bags in front of the barracks to be loaded on trucks and shuttled up to our transport. Then we went to the armory to draw weapons; put our battle helmets through electronic diagnostics routines, replacing any part that did not test out perfect; and waited. I inspected my men. Junior Lieutenant Krau'vi Taivana, our company's porracci executive officer and nominal platoon leader of first platoon, came through the barracks to inspect each squad. A little later, Captain Fusik did a walk-through, not really inspecting, just looking us over, exchanging a few words here and there, and letting us see that he was calm and confident—making a show.

The order to fall out for transport came over the loudspeakers at 2255 hours. It was time to go.

WE ASSEMBLED IN FRONT OF THE BARRACKS, TO be bused to the port and loaded in shuttles. Ranger Battalion's shuttles took off almost in formation, one every twelve seconds until the entire unit was on its way up to our transport.

Once the shuttles took off, conversation was minimized. Military shuttles are cramped, uncomfortable, and noisy, even with the sound insulation of our battle helmets, external audio pickups turned off. The ride to our transport, which was parked two hundred miles up and two thousand miles west of Fort Campbell, took less than forty minutes, but it felt longer. We docked, waited for the hangar to be pressurized and the shuttle secured, then moved through to the compartment where we would spend the trip—strapped into rows of spartan seats. The trips don't last long enough for the navy to waste the volume bunks would need. The ship had beds for a quarter of the battalion. If we ended up spending more than a few hours aboard ship we would rotate turns at the bunks, each man getting a six-hour shift before he had to get up to make room for the next man.

We knew we had a wait of at least three or four hours before the fleet started moving away from Earth—the length of time it would take to get the entire regiment moved to the ships. The troop transports, supply ships, and combat vessels of our escort would all leave at once then, moving out toward the first hyperspace jump in formation. Depending on how far away our destination was, and how far off the most common space lanes were, there would be between three and five or six jumps, each taking only a minute or two of perceived time, and separated by however many minutes it took the computers to make certain of our position and calculate the next jump.

Just after midnight, the officers and senior noncoms—platoon sergeants and company lead sergeants—were called to a briefing. I watched Tonio and the other platoon sergeants from B Company follow our officers out of the compartment. *When they come back, we'll know where we're going and what we have to do,* I thought, and then I repeated the thought aloud for the men in the squad—not that they hadn't already realized that themselves.

It was almost an hour before they returned. Captain Fusik stood at the front of the compartment with our platoon leaders and platoon sergeants flanking him. Since we all had our battle helmets on, the captain used his all-hands circuit to talk to us.

"This is not a training exercise," Fusik started. Big surprise *that* revelation was. "The general staff has decided that it is time to take this war to the enemy rather than immediately continue liberating worlds the Ilion Federation has conquered. Specifically, we are going to invade Olviat, a long-established tonatin colony world and a full member of the Ilion Federation." The tonatin, who look similar to the Neanderthals of Earth's prehistory, except for their larger size and their claw-like four-digit hands, were the dominant species in the Ilion Federation—certainly the most important in their military establishment, both in numbers and influence.

"The invasion of Olviat is a major commitment by the Alliance of Light, our first attempt to gain the initiative in this war," Fusik continued after giving us fifteen seconds to digest the first item. "In addition to the 1st Combined

Regiment, which will once more have the 3rd Firestorm Battalion of the porracci army attached, the invasion force will include the ghuroh 17th Regiment and a regimental team consisting of two biraunta battalions, a divotect battalion, and an abarand scout company. The ground force will number nearly nineteen thousand including ancillary units, supported by three ships carrying aerospace fighters and half a dozen other combatant vessels. This will be the largest operation of the war, so far.

"The civilian population of Olviat is estimated to be slightly over two million, almost exclusively tonatin, but the Ilion Federation is believed to have a military presence of no more than two regiments, along with ground-based aerospace fighters and planetary defense artillery, perhaps twelve or thirteen thousand men altogether, almost exclusively tonatin. We believe that the Ilion Federation considers Olviat safely away from any danger of invasion—good enough reason to hit it. Once we show that we are willing and able to carry the war that the Ilion Federation started to their member worlds, they will have to put more thought to defense of those worlds, which will limit the resources they can put toward invading Alliance worlds. We hope that it will cause them to, ah, reevaluate their policies and help bring this war to a satisfactory conclusion.

"We expect a hostile and possibly actively belligerent civilian population. The military garrison will defend Olviat to the limit of its ability. The Ilion Federation will almost certainly attempt to reinforce that garrison as quickly as possible once they learn of our invasion. We have to conquer and garrison Olviat before those reinforcements come."

"Garrison it, sir?" someone from fourth platoon asked. "We're going to *stay* there?"

"I don't *know* that the 1st Combined Regiment will stay," Fusik said. "I assume the Alliance intends to hold Olviat as long as that seems . . . profitable and practical, as long as it ties up Ilion assets or serves to move their government toward peace. Now, for our role." The captain paused.

"Naturally, Ranger Battalion will go in first, broken down into our usual special operations teams, from single squad to platoon strength. We will secure landing zones for the main invasion force, get behind enemy defenses—particularly around the capital city—to tie down their available military strength, confuse them concerning our overall objectives and areas of operation, and wreak what havoc we can on their military assets and on the infrastructure that supports them. Platoon leaders and platoon sergeants will brief you on details of your individual assignments. All available data on Olviat has been downloaded to the electronic maps of officers and noncoms.

"Good luck, and good hunting." Captain Fusik left the compartment with Lead Sergeant Halsey. The lieutenants and platoon sergeants started moving toward their men.

ALL FOUR SQUADS OF FIRST PLATOON WOULD BE landing together, on airsleds, and operating as a single team during the initial phase of the invasion. Our primary target was the electrical power distribution complex for the capital of Olviat. The city, also named Olviat, had half a million residents, a quarter of the world's population. The power complex was on the northeastern edge of the city, less than two miles from a military base, even closer to several civilian residential districts. There were other spec ops teams being landed closer to that base, their goal being to distract the enemy garrison long enough for us to do our job and get to safer areas away from the city, or off on whatever follow-up mission we were given. One bonus for us was the fact that there was a fairly significant river between the army base and the power station and city. Some of our teams would target the bridges across that river.

We went over the maps together, along with the minimal data we had on the flora and fauna. During the time we were studying the information and the battle plans, the rest of the regiment reached the other troop transports and the fleet started moving away from Earth, toward its first jump point. We had time to get in a quick meal before that first jump. Then we waited.

THE ENTIRE INVASION FORCE RENDEZVOUSED ONE hyperspace jump out from Olviat. Stacked away in the troop compartments, we had no way to see what was happening around us. The ships that had started out from other worlds, those bringing the other units and more fighting ships, all arrived. All in all, we were in normal space for nearly two hours waiting for everyone to get to the rendezvous.

We didn't have the leisure to get antsy at the delay, though. We worked the whole time, going over maps and data, checking out the landing zones, LZs, planning what we would do when we hit the ground, the course we would take to our objective, how we would handle it when we got there. Of course, the advance planning had to be tentative. Everything really depended on what the enemy hit us with once we were on the ground, on whether we lost anyone *in the box*—still aboard the shuttles or airsleds—and whether the airsleds actually brought us down where we were supposed to land. *Make your plans, but be ready to improvise like crazy once you get there. Expect to make changes. It's not often that a plan goes the way it was laid out originally.* There's a lot of truth in that old saw, "If it can go wrong, it will." We try to anticipate that.

Eventually, Captain Fusik passed the word that the last elements of the invasion fleet had arrived at the rendezvous. A minute later, there was an announcement over the loudspeakers that our final hyperspace jump would come in thirty seconds. As soon as that was over, we would move to the shuttles and get into the airsleds. We would come out of this jump ninety minutes out from our launch point, which is why we weren't loaded aboard our shuttles *before* the jump, the way we otherwise would have been.

"That's farther out than we'd like," Fusik commented on a link with all his noncoms, "but our intelligence shows that it's as close as we can come without risking running into their orbital planetary defenses. We need to give our fighting ships a chance to knock those satellites out before we get in range." The fighting ships would emerge from hyperspace a couple of minutes ahead of the rest of us, and closer, vectoring toward the known positions of those defenses.

Give 'em hell, navy, I thought.

WE MADE THE HYPERSPACE JUMP. THEN WE WERE ordered to the shuttles. After our arrival aboard ship, the shuttles had been reconfigured. The web seats we had rode up from Earth had been folded out of the way and the airsleds had been attached—stuck up through the decks of the shuttles—clamped, and sealed. An airsled is basically a length of sewer pipe, five feet, seven inches in diameter and twenty-four feet long, with two small engines and enough lifting surface to give it slightly better glide characteristics than a rock. It holds a single fire team—cramped, claustrophobic and more thoroughly uncomfortable than you can possibly imagine unless you've ridden one. You sit crouched over, about the way you would on a bobsled. The only reasonable excuse for airsleds is that they present a smaller target to the enemy than a shuttle and give you a slightly greater chance of surviving an insertion. The shuttle takes you part of the way in, then launches the sleds while it burns to get out of range of enemy missiles.

We loaded our weapons before we got into the airsleds, but I ordered everyone to make certain that the safeties were on, and Souvana and I did an eyeball inspection to make sure that the order was obeyed. An airsled ride is rough, and if a weapon went off accidentally it could chop up everyone in the tube.

I was the last man from my squad in. That wasn't just because I hate airsleds, though I do, passionately. As squad leader, it's my job to make sure that all my men are in first. Souvana was the last of his fire team in their airsled. As soon as that was sealed, I took my place with my team in the squad's other sled. The shuttle crew chief checked the seals, on all of the sleds in the shuttle—all of first platoon.

Wait. My helmet was linked to the shuttle crew's communications, so I had some idea what was going on, and heard the conversation the pilot had with the launchmaster. The wait wasn't going to be long, but ten minutes in an airsled can seem like an eternity, and we had the ride in after that. At least while we were sitting still inside the ship no one was likely to start puking—and it's almost certain that at least one member of any fire team will upchuck during an airsled insertion.

Launch. The shuttles were lifted out of their hangars by cranes, then shoved away from the ship's hull. The shuttle pilots could not ignite their rockets until we were far enough off to avoid damaging the ship. The shuttles rendezvoused and started their acceleration toward the surface, aerospace fighters moving ahead of us to provide some cover during the insertion—to give the enemy more targets to worry about and give us a better chance of getting to the ground safely.

At the start, we were diving toward the ground, accelerating at full power, adding to the pull of Olviat's gravity on us. *Down* was behind us in the sleds, not out in front where the ground was. It felt as if we were lying on our backs, stacked one on another. Once we hit the upper levels of the atmosphere the shuttle started to shake, buffeted by even the thinnest layers of air, and the buffeting got worse as we got closer to the ground and the shuttles came out of their nose-first dives to get level by the time we reached our drop points.

The shuttle would take us fairly low, to somewhere between five hundred and two thousand feet altitude. Then the airsleds would be dropped on their glide path, giving the passengers an independent ride of no more than a minute or two.

The passengers in an airsled have no control over their craft. It is programmed to make its landing. The shuttle crew can adjust its course, but that's difficult, at best. Inside, we can't even see where we're going—no windows, no video monitors. It's like riding a bullet . . . on the inside. If the sled hits something solid at full speed, the result is about the same. The sleds are supposed to come in to a relatively soft landing, scooting along the ground until friction and reversed jet thrust can stop them. It doesn't always work that way.

I felt our sled bounce when it touched down, throwing us back into the air before we came down to stay, careening across the ground, through underbrush, knocking small trees flat, using friction as much as the reversed thrust of the craft's two engines to help stop us. "Get ready!" I warned my people. "When the hatches pop, get out fast." I don't know if anyone heard me. The ride was about as rough as it gets. We were jerked from side to side several times, and when the airsled finally came to a stop and the overhead hatches popped open, we were canted at a thirty-degree angle to the right.

"Up and out!" I shouted over my radio link as I reached up to use the edges of the hatch over my head to pull myself out of the sled. "Head for the rendezvous point."

We were on the surface of an enemy world.

CHAPTER 7

OLVIAT'S SUN WAS SLIGHTLY HOTTER THAN
Earth's, and a bit farther from the planet. The tonatin had
colonized the world several hundred years earlier, bringing
in plants and animals from other worlds, cultivating them
for their own use and to help control the forms that had
arisen on the world before they arrived. Around the planetary capital, we expected to find imported varieties almost
exclusively.

The day on Olviat was a bit over twenty-seven hours.
We landed two hours after local sunset in the capital, giving us most of the night to operate in the conditions we
prefer—darkness. We moved away from the airsleds as
quickly as feet could carry us. The sleds glowed brightly in
infrared after the heat of their flight and landing, as did the
trails where they had skidded along the ground. Those
trails were clear arrows for anyone searching for us, so we
had to move away quickly.

First platoon's rendezvous was a hundred yards north of
our airsled tracks—a row of hot scratches in the ground,
nearly a half mile long—just about four hundred yards
from where my team's sled had come to a halt. By the time
I had covered half that distance—at a fast jog—I knew that
all of first platoon's sleds had come in safely, on target, and
that we had no one injured too badly to continue. That isn't

always the case. I've seen soldiers killed or injured by rough sled landings.

As each squad reached the rendezvous its members moved into a makeshift perimeter, guns pointing out. My squad was the last in. Lieutenant Taivana had already dispatched the two biraunta from third squad as scouts in the direction of the power distribution complex we were to attack. The platoon went to electronic silence, to avoid giving the enemy an easy way to track our progress and estimate our numbers. Operating together, not using radios was no impediment. Hand signals worked well in line of sight, and when better communications were necessary, we could go face-to-face, lift helmet faceplates, and whisper.

Second squad went on point. The lieutenant put my squad slightly behind and on the left. Third squad was to our right, and fourth brought up the rear. Lieutenant Taivana and Tonio were in the middle of the diamond formation. We started moving as soon as my people reached the rendezvous.

It was winter locally, but we were in a borderline temperate–subtropical zone. Supposedly, temperatures rarely got as low as freezing, and we could expect daytime highs in the low to mid-seventies. Comfortable temperatures, for the most part, since our uniforms were thermal insulators—more to help camouflage us from enemy eyes than to keep us comfortable.

The sensors in my helmet told me that the temperature where we landed was thirty-nine degrees, but I hardly noticed the chill on my hands, the only part of my body not covered. There was a moderate breeze, maybe ten miles per hour, from the northwest. The sky was heavily overcast. We could see the glow of lights from the city. The locals had not gone to blackout conditions yet. Turning out the lights wouldn't hide any targets, though it might make civilians feel safer to hide in the dark.

We had three miles of flat to gently rolling terrain to cover to get to the power distribution center, since we did not take a direct heading toward it—too easy for an enemy to anticipate and counter. Much of the ground was lightly forested, landscaped, with spaced formal gardens. The trees tended to be well-spaced in clear rows, evidence that the arrangement wasn't natural. There were occasional paved or graveled walks. Before we had covered half the distance to our target, we started to hear the sounds of fighting to either side of our route, but we hadn't seen anyone at all, military or civilian. No one relaxed. We knew that the enemy had soldiers not too far away. It was just a matter of how quickly they had been mobilized and how long it would take to deploy them.

The platoon was still a mile from the power center when we finally came under fire.

THREE OR FOUR RIFLES OPENED UP FROM THE left, on my squad's side of the formation. Iyi and Oyo, my biraunta, were farther out than the rest of the squad, covering the flank. There weren't enough trees for them to be high, brachiating, where they operate at their best, so they were on the ground. Still, the biraunta are the stealthiest scouts we've got, and the smallest, so I didn't immediately conclude that Iyi and Oyo had been spotted.

"Dragon, take your squad and see what we've got over there," Tonio said on a radio link. While we were under fire, it wasn't necessary to maintain complete electronic silence. "We'll keep moving. If it's just a small patrol, take care of them. If there are too many for you, give me a call and we'll come around from their left."

I acknowledged the order, then switched to my squad frequency. "Souvana, take your fire team and curve around on the left. I'll take the rest of my team and curve in on the right and we'll pincer them between us. Iyi, are you listening?"

"Yes, Sergeant," Iyi said. "We have the enemy in sight. We count six soldiers. Three of them are in what appears to be an artificial mound of rocks, 120 yards due north of your position. The others are on the west side of that formation, under a low-branched tree of considerable size."

"How far are you from them?"

"A hundred yards from the nearest, those in the rocks. They do not seem to be aware of our presence. They have not taken us under fire. They are shooting in your direction."

"Then stop transmitting. Don't reply. Wait for my signal, then open fire on them."

Souvana had already started moving his team. I signaled to Robbie, and he and Nuyi moved closer, then followed me along the track I had picked for us—Robbie on my left, Nuyi on my right. We stayed low, ducking from one tree to the next. The enemy gunfire was sporadic and not too smartly aimed; most of it went well over our heads. It was as if the enemy wasn't sure where we were, even though they were so close. Maybe they were nervous and hadn't actually had firm targets before they started shooting.

It wasn't difficult to move from cover to cover, though few of the tree trunks were thick enough to be complete protection. Souvana's team moved more quickly than my group did, and they had started thirty seconds earlier. It took them less than two minutes to get into position to take the enemy patrol under fire. As soon as they did, I told Iyi and Oyo to open up from their positions on the other side. Then I got up with Nuyi and Robbie and we charged forward another twenty yards before going to ground again, ready to contribute our part of the action.

We didn't have to. The firefight was over. All six of the enemy soldiers were down—dead or too badly wounded to continue. Souvana's team got to them first, to get the weapons and helmets of the two who were still alive. I switched radio channels to report.

"Tonio, Drak. Six-man patrol. All down. Two of them are wounded. I don't know how badly."

Before Tonio could respond, Souvana came on the channel and said, "The last two are also dead. Their wounds were too severe to give them a chance. I made certain they did not suffer."

You slit their throats, you mean, I thought, forcing down a surge of anger. "You shouldn't have done that without orders, Souvana," I said, keeping my voice low, under control. "We don't kill wounded men who are no threat to us."

"Worry about that later," Tonio said. "Dragon, get your squad back on our flank. If there's one patrol, there are likely to be others. We have to get on with our job. The rest of the invasion force is waiting to come in."

"On the way." The destruction of the power complex was supposed to be the signal for the shuttles carrying the rest of the invasion force to start in, on the calculation that we might knock out enough of their command and control structure to make defense more difficult for the tonatin.

I took twenty seconds to give my people instructions, then we were on the way again. I wasn't certain why I felt so angry about what Souvana had done. Souvana had rubbed me the wrong way since he first joined the squad, back on Dancer. Assuming his diagnosis was correct, that they were wounded too badly to survive until proper medical help could reach them, perhaps he *had* done the humane thing, but I doubted that he had done it for humane reasons, and I would have wagered money that he had done something direct like slit their throats rather than administer painkillers to make certain they did not suffer.

I made a note of the location. If the opportunity came up later, I would check—for my own satisfaction, if nothing else. There was little chance that any disciplinary action would be taken over an incident of that nature. It's hard to generate sympathy for armed hostile combatants.

TWENTY MINUTES LATER WE HAD OUR TARGET IN sight—the main power distribution center for the capital. There were no lights on in or around it. There was a chance that there were enemy soldiers between us and the two buildings that housed the transformers and relays we were supposed to knock out. Some enemy soldiers had managed to cross the river before our teams could blow the two bridges. We had no way of knowing how many enemy soldiers had been south of the river when we landed; the patrol we had run into and the other sounds of fighting we had heard were evidence enough that there had been *some*. With ninety minutes' warning of our coming, they might have moved most of the garrison closer to the city, even right inside.

Assume the worst. I scanned as much of the perimeter of the complex as I could, using the maximum magnification through my helmet's faceplate. The grounds of the power center were clear of trees and bushes. There was some fencing around the edge, but it was not complete and appeared more decorative than functional. Our night-vision systems are as advanced as any, but there is still *some* deterioration from what we could see in full daylight, both in range and in clarity. I couldn't see any obvious targets—hot spots or movement—but if the enemy's thermal camouflaging was as efficient as ours, they might still be there.

In any case, the decision what to do next wasn't up to me. Taivana and Tonio would issue the orders. We had come equipped for this operation. One man in each fire team had a rocket launcher with three rockets. Each of the other men in each team carried two rockets in addition to their normal combat loads. Normally we had one man with a rocket launcher in each squad, rather than two. Generally, those rockets were intended for antiaircraft or antitank use, but they were versatile. They should serve to open large holes in the buildings and destroy the machinery inside. Some of the warheads were incendiary.

We were three hundred yards from the two main buildings, well within effective range of the launchers—they could bring down an aircraft at more than a mile—and my squad had a clear line of sight to both buildings. Some of the other squads weren't so well situated. We were waiting for them to get in position.

Five minutes. "Get your men ready with the launchers,"

Tonio said, a barely audible whisper over the radio. "On my order." I gestured—Kiervauna and Nuyi, the men with the launchers, were watching me for signals. They put the weapons to their shoulders and sighted. Each had extra rockets at his side and someone to load them in the proper order for him: armor-penetrating first, then incendiary. The rest of the squad was ready for whatever response the enemy might have—if any.

"Ready . . . fire." As soon as I heard Tonio's order, I brought my right arm down. Four squads, eight rocket launchers—within five seconds of the order, the first eight missiles were on their way. Six seconds later, a second volley was in the air, not as uniform as the first. The third rounds were being loaded before the first hit.

I would not have wanted to be any closer to the two buildings than I was. Three hundred yards was a little close for comfort. Explosion after explosion erupted. First there were the rockets. Then we started to hear secondary explosions from inside one of the buildings. The taller of the two structures—sixty feet high—came apart at the seams, debris hurling nearly as far out as where we were. A fireball climbed into the sky, briefly overloading my night-vision system, making the night almost as bright as a sunny noon.

Altogether, Kiervauna and Nuyi each fired four rockets into the complex, switching their aim a little for each round. I assumed that the other squads contributed as much to the destruction. Both main buildings were reduced to flaming rubble. Several smaller structures—office space, maintenance facilities, and so forth—were also targeted, hit, and either destroyed or seriously damaged before Lieutenant Taivana came on the all-hands channel to tell us to pull out, to move to the rendezvous point that had been designated earlier.

"You heard the lieutenant," I said on my squad channel. "Let's get the hell out of here before the locals drop the ceiling in on us." No one would repair that center in a hurry. The entire facility would have to be rebuilt from scratch.

I got up and started moving, my fire team forming around me, with Oyo and Iyi in front. Souvana moved his team around to follow us. We were going to skirt the edge of the power complex, as close as we could safely with the fires and secondary explosions that were continuing, so I could get a good view of the damage—a view that would be recorded by the video camera in my helmet so that the higher-ups could review it later for an official damage assessment. We had not come under fire since arriving near the complex, so it looked as if there were no enemy troops between us and the still burning buildings.

The lights had finally gone out in the capital.

CHAPTER 8

I **DIALED UP A CHANNEL THAT WOULD LET ME LIS-**
ten to updates from our CIC, combat information center,
on the flagship—a constant broadcast, repeating when
there was nothing new, a soft voice displaying no emotion.
There was no worry that the enemy would intercept and
learn anything that might aid them. The signals are scrambled with an encryption algorithm so complex that it's impossible to decrypt. And our battle helmets are tuned to the
men who wear them, so even a captured helmet's electronics will not help an enemy eavesdropper.

The rest of the invasion force was on its way down, ac-
companied by most of our aerospace fighters. The fighters
would provide close air support for the landings. Our ships
were in no imminent peril from the Ilion Federation's defenses on Olviat. The orbital defenses had been knocked
out, and the ships could defend themselves against missiles
launched from the surface—if Olviat was equipped with
such a system. So far, the only sizable rocket that had been
launched from the surface had been aimed to keep it as
far from the invading fleet as possible—probably an unmanned messenger rocket carrying news of the invasion.
We had been unable to intercept and destroy it.

Losses in Ranger Battalion had been minimal during our
landings. Only one airsled had been lost during insertion,

and that was accidental rather than a result of enemy action. Many spec ops teams were engaged with the enemy on the ground, or had already been engaged, but it had all been small unit activity. So far, the tonatin military force had been unable to mount organized resistance on any significant scale, but we hadn't done much damage to them either.

After our strike on the power distribution center, first platoon rendezvoused on the move, heading toward the primary road leading into the city. Our instructions were to set up an ambush to deal with anyone coming out to survey the damage or attempt to repair what we had done.

"Fat chance that a few repairmen are going to be able to do anything, sir," I told JL Taivana when we stopped for a minute while the scouts searched for a place for us to establish our ambush. "We'll just be spinning our wheels. We could do more good looking for enemy soldiers."

Taivana's first answer—a soft, almost inaudible rumble in his throat—alerted me to the fact that he wasn't happy with my comments. "We obey our orders, Sergeant," he said. "If a target of opportunity arises while we are waiting, that is something else, but we will perform our assigned mission."

"Yes, sir, I know," I said, attempting to cover myself. "I was not suggesting that we disobey orders, sir, merely pointing out an observation for you to consider." Taivana had been pretty straight with us, from the start, but he was porracci, and he outweighed me by two hundred pounds. An annoyed swat from him could have been . . . discouraging, and I knew that it was something he might be perfectly capable of under the stress of a campaign.

The expression on his face eased. "Your observation is noted, Sergeant," he said, his voice a muffled growl, almost a normal tone. "I made the same observation to Captain Fusik."

"Yes, sir. I did not mean to imply that you would miss such a thing, but I felt it my duty to make the observation." In case he *had* missed it—but you have to be careful with porracci officers, and I was still feeling my way around, testing how far I *could* go. That's the trouble with aliens; you have to learn whole sets of new rules; they don't think like we do. I did know that porracci consider insubordination an even worse offense than human officers do, and Taivana was in a position to make life hell for me if I made him too angry.

"Keep your eyes open, Sergeant," Taivana said. "Perhaps we will find an opportunity."

WE FOUND A SPOT THAT TAIVANA AND TONIO

liked for our ambush. They posted my squad a hundred yards farther from the city than the rest of the platoon—covering the back door, in case the enemy came from the opposite direction. So far, with all the men we had on the ground and all the eyes we had looking in from space, we had not located the enemy's main force. We were in the trees to either side of the road, at approximately a sixty-degree angle. I sent Oyo and Iyi out farther, another two hundred yards, to plant electronic snoops and a couple of command-detonated land mines to make it difficult for anyone to come on us by surprise. The mines were closer than the snoops, less than a hundred yards from the outside ends of our ambush.

The two biraunta came back to report to me face-to-face before taking their places in the squad. "Find yourselves spots in one of the trees over on this side," I told them, pointing in the direction I meant. "Past McGraw's location, halfway between him and the mines." Robbie was holding down the far end of our fire team. "Where you can see the location of the mines. I'll want one of you to detonate them, if the time comes—but on my order. We won't waste them on civilians or a small patrol."

They nodded in unison, then scampered off to find a tree to climb. The rest of us remained on the ground, with only what cover the terrain offered—trees and a few low rocks. We did not dig in, though that was tempting. If trouble found us there, we were more likely to move than try to stand against any significant enemy force. We might try to draw them into the ambush waiting with the rest of the platoon or try to get them heading off in a different direction so the platoon could hit them from the side, or from behind. It depended on how large a force . . . and what the lieutenant or the higher-ups wanted.

I was on my stomach, looking around the side of a tree whose trunk was fifteen inches in diameter, facing out along the road. I didn't have much to do but keep my eyes open while I listened to the battle reports over the radio . . . and wonder how much time we were going to waste where we were. It's not that I was eager for combat—I'm no bloodthirsty action-vid hero, and I had already seen enough fighting and death to last a couple of lifetimes— but I couldn't see that we were contributing to the effort where we were. We had an army to beat, and we needed to do it before the enemy brought in massive reinforcements. That might not take more than a few days if they had a force available for deployment immediately upon learning that we had landed.

We had been on the ground less than two hours.

MAYBE IT WAS TOO SOON TO EXPECT HEAVY OP-position. It might have taken us more than a few minutes to respond if Earth had been invaded and the landings hadn't been in the middle of one of our bases. Troops in garrison away from any war zone do not normally go through the days and nights with combat gear on and ammunition readily to hand. At Fort Campbell, our rifles would have been locked in the armory except while we had them out for training purposes. Ammunition would have been in another building, also well secured.

From what we had been able to observe, the tonatin regiment on Olviat had organized at least as rapidly as we would have if our positions had been reversed. When our aerospace fighters attacked the known military camps—

while Ranger Battalion was riding its airsleds in—they apparently blew up nothing but empty buildings. The men, their personal weapons and ammunition, and the attached field artillery and armor had all been moved out, and we were having difficulty finding where they had gone. Our ships had not detected any major troop movements since we landed, and we did not know where any of their forces were—except for the small patrols we had encountered.

Tonatin field uniforms were at least as effective at thermal camouflage as ours were, and the tonatin were observing electronic silence for the most part. Their heavy weapons had been dispersed and—as long as they weren't used—kept undetected, camouflaged or under cover.

What the hell are they waiting for? I wondered. I had heard reports of the landings of all of our strike force. The rest of the 1st Combined Regiment and its attached porracci battalion, the other units—we were all on the ground, no reserve held aboard the ships, and the landings had been virtually unopposed. It didn't make sense. While invading troops are boxed up in their shuttles or airsleds, *that* is when they're most vulnerable. They can't defend themselves. Every shuttle you blow out of the air or destroy as it's landing means a platoon of troops you don't have to face on the ground. That's always important, but never so important as when you're massively outnumbered.

None of our spec ops squads on the ground had encountered an enemy force larger than a single platoon—about forty men—and there hadn't been many of those; most of the patrols had been single-squad or less. We had teams scattered all around the capital city and near the military bases that had been identified in advance. Nothing—or next to nothing. With all of our line units also on the ground, assembled, and moving, the enemy had to show fairly soon.

"Come on; where are you?" I muttered. The one place we had not yet looked was *inside* the city. *Is that where they're hiding?* I asked myself. *Hiding among the civilians?*

I wasn't sure whether that would be good or bad, but you live a lot longer being a pessimist. We expected trouble from the civilians, but there might be political hell to pay if we caused a lot of civilian casualties trying to get at their military. Worse than that, if we had to go in and try to clear the enemy out a building at a time, we would lose a lot of men, and that could cause more trouble at home than the death of noncombatant enemy civilians.

THE TIMELINES ON OUR HELMET HEAD-UP DISPLAYS had been adjusted to local time. It was just short of 2500 hours, about two hours before midnight on Olviat, when orders came to abandon our ambush and start moving away from the city. That put my squad on point, and we maintained about the same gap from the rest of the platoon as we had in the ambush, a hundred yards.

We picked up our snoops and mines; we might need them later. I had Iyi and Oyo on point, flanking the road, thirty yards ahead of the rest of the squad. They were the best men in the squad for scouting. They almost always drew that duty—and never complained about it. I kept the rest of my fire team on the right side of the road and put Souvana's team on the left—*off* the road, under the cover of the regularly spaced trees that flanked it. It's not that I thought there was any great chance that the road would be mined or booby-trapped, it's just that it's better not to take chances when you don't have to.

Tonio had not said where we were headed or why, trying to minimize his time on the radio to keep down the chances that the enemy would pinpoint our position. I was beginning to think that maybe the bulk of the tonatin troops *were* inside the city, which meant—if I was right— that we were moving away from the enemy, away from the greatest danger.

Maybe the lieutenant heard something I didn't, I thought, *maybe we know where the enemy is.* I kept my eyes open, kept moving my head, looking for the enemy. I had to force myself to pay attention, to not let my mind wander too much. Carelessness can get you killed in a heartbeat—your final heartbeat.

We had gone about a mile and a quarter when Tonio called me with a one-word message. "Halt." I gestured for my men, and used the radio to stop Oyo and Iyi. We went down, taking what cover we could, and waited. It took Tonio nearly two minutes to come up to my position and sink to the ground next to me. He lifted his faceplate and leaned close to whisper to me.

"We're turning to the right, back almost due north. We're to head to the river then turn east, back toward the city. CIC thinks they've spotted a concentration of enemy forces. We're closest to that location so it's up to us to confirm or . . ."

He didn't finish that sentence. The battle finally erupted, and it was a lot closer to us than we expected. Or wanted.

NO, WE HADN'T WALKED NEATLY INTO THE MAIN tonatin force on Olviat—that might almost have been a picnic compared to what we *had* almost walked into. We had nearly stumbled into several batteries of tonatin artillery—about a dozen big self-propelled rocket launchers, remote-controlled units. Iyi and Oyo must have come within sixty yards of the nearest launcher before we stopped. There were apparently no infantry units guarding the launchers, but there wouldn't be—not close. Artillery units, rocket launchers or howitzers, are magnets for trouble. That's why they're unmanned, directed by remote control.

Then those launchers started firing their missiles in volleys, the carriages moving almost before the tails of the first rockets cleared the rack. Fire and move. That's the only way to hope to escape counterbattery fire. Our ships would pick up the launches and the return fire would be in the air in less than ten seconds. The problem is that the only way you can hope to knock out moving launchers like that is to saturate the area around them, in every direction.

Which put us in a highly untenable position. It didn't matter that there were apparently no enemy *troops* in our immediate vicinity. If we didn't move in one hell of a hurry, our own people would dump rocket and howitzer fire all over us.

"Move it! Everyone, straight north to the river. Run for it!" I couldn't blame Lieutenant Taivana for yelling over the radio. I felt like screaming myself.

I got up and started moving, looking around for my men. Tonio was at my side, but not for long. He was moving north, and angling toward the east, in the direction of the rest of the platoon. Our only hope was to get out of the line of fire, and out of the path of rocket launchers that were racing to get somewhere they weren't when they last fired. Somewhere, most likely at a relatively safe distance, there would be tonatin controllers moving those launchers. They might not see us, or even suspect that we were in the vicinity, but that wouldn't help if one of those pieces of heavy, tracked equipment rolled over us at thirty or forty miles per hour. The result would be as deadly as getting shelled by our own people, who were trying to knock out those launchers. It's a no-win situation, which was why we had no choice but to get the hell away as quickly as we could.

I hoped that our men with the shoulder-operated rocket launchers had their tubes loaded, just in case any of the enemy vehicles rumbled into view, but I didn't have air to spare to say anything—either directly or as a suggestion to Tonio or the lieutenant. Our rifles wouldn't dent the minimal armor of a big self-propelled launcher, and I doubted that an RPG would do much more damage . . . unless a lucky hit cooked off the warhead of an enemy rocket in its rack.

Run. Part of my attention was devoted to listening for the different sound of incoming rockets or howitzer rounds amid all of the outgoing crap. The sound is different, but there was so much tonatin stuff being launched around us that it might smother the sounds of our stuff coming in.

I tripped over something—maybe my imagination—and went flying face first into the ground, stunned for a few seconds, the air knocked out of me. Before I could suck in fresh breath, Nuyi was trying to pull me to my feet.

"Keep going," I shouted. "I'm okay. Move it!" Nuyi hesitated for no more than two seconds, and I was almost back on my feet by then. He nodded and started running again.

Divotect aren't build for speed, but they do have endurance. I could take Nuyi in a sprint any day of the week, but once distances got up to a mile or more, we were fairly even, and I wouldn't have wanted to try to take him in a marathon . . . if I was crazy enough to try a marathon under any circumstances.

I was wondering how far away the river was and couldn't recall, and I couldn't take time to check the map. All I could do was keep running, trying to make certain that none of my men fell too far behind. I had been looking over my shoulder when I tripped. I didn't have to do that after I got back up. Everyone but Nuyi had gone past me while I was on the ground.

Beyond the sound of rockets being launched—and the first explosions of Alliance counterbattery fire coming back—I heard the rumble of a big engine, and I had to look back over my shoulder again. One of those launchers, six feet wide and more than twenty feet long, with a dozen rocket tubes on top, was heading directly toward me, too damned close for comfort. I veered left, trying to get out of its path.

I saw Nuyi moving in the other direction, but I didn't really register the fact that he was maneuvering his rocket launcher around until I saw the jet of fire come out the rear of the tube as he fired at the self-propelled rig behind us—really too damned *close* behind us.

"Down!" I think it was my squad frequency that my transmitter was set to, but I can't guarantee that. I threw myself down and saw Nuyi going down just a fraction of a second before that tonatin SP launcher erupted in bright orange flame and dirty orange and red smoke. Nuyi must have hit it perfectly, burning through to the fuel tank or something. There were several secondary explosions as the ten-foot-long rockets the rig carried exploded—either fuel or warheads. Or both.

The first thing I felt—completely overriding any sense of slamming into the ground—was a wave of intense heat, as physical a buffeting as if the flame and heat had been solid object. The heat rode up under the rear flap of my helmet and scorched my neck. It felt as if the skin on my neck must have blistered instantly. Our uniforms are fire resistant, but no one dares to call them fire*proof*. Subjected to enough heat, almost anything will burn, melt, or something.

Debris started pelting everything. Luckily, most of the debris from the vehicle and its cargo went past us, not curving back to the ground soon enough to hit us. That would have been as deadly as shrapnel at that range, and some of the chunks were a lot bigger. But a lot of the metal and composites did hit the trees around us, severing branches, felling whole trees. Some of that secondary debris did hit us. A branch came down on my left shoulder and upper arm with enough force to bring first pain and then numbness to the affected area.

I pushed up off the ground, got as far as hands and knees. My left arm didn't want to support any weight, so I leaned the other way. I had been stunned and wasn't thinking completely straight, but I did take a quick look around. There was a fire where the tonatin SP launcher had been, bright enough to hide whatever remained of the vehicle, and the fire had spread to the trees and grass—both right around the carcass of the vehicle and off where flaming debris had started additional fires. Some of those were picking up, whipped around by a growing breeze. The entire area might get untenable very quickly.

"Anyone hurt?" I asked on my squad channel. "Check

on those around you." I was looking for Nuyi. There was a
tree down between us, but I eventually saw him get to his
feet, looking my way, then in the other direction when he
saw that I was able to move on my own.

"We're okay in this team," Robbie said. Five seconds
later, Souvana said much the same thing, in half as many
words. I switched to my link to Tonio and let him know
that my squad remained intact, that no one was complaining of injuries.

"Get your people moving again," Tonio said. "Most of
the others are already at the river. You've got another seventy yards. Hurry before more stuff hits. Was that blast incoming?"

"Hell, no. Nuyi got that one," I said. My breathing was
finally back in order, and the squad was moving. "He cut it
a little too close though."

Tonio didn't bother to respond.

WE DIDN'T GO *INTO* THE WATER, JUST STAYED AS
close as we could, ready to get wet if we had to. The
enemy's self-propelled artillery wouldn't be going into the
river, so our counterbattery fire wouldn't be aiming that
way. That was the logic behind our move—beyond the fact
that we had been getting ready to head in that direction before the artillery barrage started.

The lieutenant seemed to be in no hurry to get us moving back toward the city—to the east. Maybe he was
weighing the possibility of going back after those launchers with our own shoulder-launched stuff. That wouldn't
have surprised me, and, if we could get the incoming
heavy stuff stopped, it might even be a smart move, give
us a chance to do some good.

Lieutenant Taivana made the rounds, checking personally on each squad, with Tonio staying at his side. He
asked about rounds for the rocket launchers, but only after
he had asked about injuries. My people had been closest to
the explosion, but the blast effects had scattered far enough

that none of the squads had completely escaped. There had been a few minor injuries—burns, cuts, bruises—some of which had not been recognized by the men who suffered them until we were resting at the bank of the river. I had a moderate burn on the nape of my neck, but a little salve from my medical pouch soothed the pain.

The lieutenant had much of the fur on his left forearm singed away, and he had been quite a distance from the explosion. It was Kiervauna who pointed to the lieutenant's injured arm and said something about putting a patch on it. The lieutenant nodded and let Kiervauna apply the medical patch.

We had come out of the incident far luckier than we had any right to. Hell, that blast might easily have taken out my entire squad, but we didn't have anyone hurt badly enough to slow him down. I got the impression that we weren't going to be moving immediately, though, when the lieutenant sat down, lifted his helmet faceplate, and took a long drink of water. That seemed like a good idea, so I took a drink myself. I was already sitting, squatting rather, one knee on the ground.

The artillery duel had not ended, but the near end had moved farther away from us, and farther away from the capital. *Okay, that means we probably can't get close enough to knock out any more of the enemy launchers,* I thought—with a certain amount of relief. My hearing was starting to get back to normal, though I still had a bit of a ringing in my ears. I had been around long enough to know that it might be a day or two before the last of that was gone. Shaking my head several times didn't really help, but it was an instinctive reaction. I took another drink, then put my canteen back on my belt and went over to where Tonio was resting, on both knees, and I crouched next to him.

"Next time somebody asks if I believe in miracles, I'll know what to say," I said. "We could have been slaughtered back there." Tonio nodded slowly. His breathing was a little forced, a little fast. "You have any idea what's going on now?"

"Not in any detail," Tonio said after sucking in extra air. "But that artillery barrage was the start. The hide-and-seek is over. The tonatin have decided to come out and start fighting."

CHAPTER 9

LIEUTENANT TAIVANA RADIOED TO ASK CAPTAIN Fusik if there were new orders for us, then the platoon moved several hundred yards east along the bank of the river—simply to put distance between us and the location where the lieutenant had broken electronic silence. No immediate answer came, so we rested a few minutes longer. I took a few minutes to talk with each of my men to ask how they were doing and remind them what we had to do, then resumed monitoring the CIC channel as we finally started to make sense of what the enemy was doing. The tonatin defenders had mounted a three-pronged counter-attack. Each element was roughly one battalion in size. Two had come out of the capital a third of a mile apart and the third had moved up from the south, aiming toward the gap between the two battalions coming out of the city. That put about a third of our force in the middle.

All of the action appeared to be on the south bank of the river, the side we were on, which meant that the two battalions of troops we had landed on the north side were completely cut off from the action, as ineffectual as if they had landed on the wrong world. It would take two hours to get them moved, more if the enemy had anyone in position to harass them. With the bridges we had blown, hoping to isolate some of the tonatin force on the north bank, we had complicated matters for ourselves. It might be necessary to bring in shuttles to move them, and shuttles would be vulnerable to enemy artillery, even to shoulder-launched missiles.

The tonatin artillery we had stumbled on was not the only unit that had joined the fight. There were two other groups of self-propelled rocket launchers and a full battalion of self-propelled howitzers, all located well away from the city and their ground troops, moving as quickly as they fired, changing direction and speed in what was supposed to look like random patterns. That was a lot of firepower, nearly matching what we had brought in with us. Although we had knocked out all of Olviat's orbiting satellites, their artillery was still getting targeting data good enough to do a lot of damage to our people on the ground.

It was a few minutes later before I figured out that at least one of our spec ops squads had stumbled into the enemy battalion coming up from the south and been destroyed before they could radio news of the encounter to CIC. A squad from D Company had gone missing, in any case, and their last-known position had been somewhere in the vicinity of that enemy column.

Finally, new orders came through for us. We were to continue toward the city, along the river. *Infiltrate. Attempt to get behind the nearest of the enemy battalions coming out from the city. Do what you can to slow down and disrupt their attack.*

"Sounds like they're not thinking straight in CIC yet," I whispered when Tonio gave me the orders. "Send ten men into the middle of half a million hostile civilians and a couple of battalions of troops and tell them to do what they can. Recipe for suicide."

"They'll refine the orders before we get there. This just gets us moving in the right direction," Tonio said. "We're not the only ones going. Half the battalion has the same general orders. Infiltrate the city and cause enough ruckus to make them turn their attention to their backs. Most of the rest of the battalion is going to try to harass the other tonatin battalion. Give our line companies a break, a chance to take care of the main enemy force."

Yeah, I thought. *"Give our line companies a break."* Put *that on my tombstone.* We started moving. This time, we had the rear guard. Third squad was on point, with the lieutenant and Tonio positioned behind them, in with the men of fourth squad.

We moved slowly, well dispersed, taking as much care as we could with staying under cover. *Infiltrate* means don't let the enemy see you before you get into position and clobber them . . . and don't let them *see* you then. Get in, raise your hell, and get out. That's one of the things we're supposed to be the experts at.

If you're careful—and lucky—it's not as difficult as it might seem, especially at night, even when the enemy has night-vision gear every bit as good as your own. You move slowly and make use of the available cover. Since our uniforms provide thermal insulation to minimize the advantage of infrared detectors, rapid or jerky movement can be the fastest way to give yourself away to an enemy watching through night-vision gear. As long as you don't physically trip over the enemy or come within range of an electronic snoop you have a good chance of getting almost within spitting distance without being spotted . . . if you know what you're doing.

Our biraunta could move like ghosts in a forest, not just up in the trees, but on the ground. The porracci, despite their size, were almost as stealthy, and so were the ghuroh. All three species are, in some ways, closer to their prehistoric roots than humans are. Sentience and civilization have not so completely robbed them of the basic survival skills of their precursors.

For the rest of us in the unit—humans, divotect, and abarand—the skills were far more completely learned than instinctive. The presentient divotect had been masters of their environment, with no significant predators, little need for these talents. Primitive abarand had been able to fly away from any threat; some of them still consider the loss of the ability to truly fly, rather than just glide, too high a price to pay for sentience. It's a long-ranging nostalgia for them; for some it becomes an almost pathological obsession.

The battle was audible now, the distant explosions of artillery like the rumble of thunder, each blast lightening the sky over its point of detonation for an instant before it faded, blossoms of light that rose then failed, only to be replaced by the next explosion's glare. Only rarely was there any rifle fire near enough for us to hear, and none of it was close enough to affect us. And none of the artillery fire was directed near us.

Fang, Claw, and Kiervauna hung back thirty yards behind the rest of us, and a little to the sides—trailers to catch any enemy patrol that might try to take the platoon from the rear. I had Oyo and Iyi on the flanks as well, a little ahead of my position near the front of the squad. The rest of us were in two staggered columns, five or six yards between men so that even if we walked into an enemy ambush the enemy would be unlikely to take us all out at once before we could respond.

Until we got very near the edge of the capital, there was no indication a city was anywhere near. There were no fields or pastures close to the urban area. The farmland was farther out, much of it on the other side of the river. Closer in, the tonatin preferred to keep the terrain in parks and woodlands, though those showed signs of careful husbandry and planning. Little was left really *wild* near the city. Most of the trees and shrubs were imports, not the native flora of Olviat—though I had only the briefing material we had been given to support that. I hadn't seen any fauna yet, except for a few small birds—and I hadn't really *seen* them. They had been momentary disturbances amid the trees as they flew away.

Lieutenant Taivana stopped the platoon after forty minutes. The signal was passed back to move into a loose defensive perimeter and take ten. The city was not far ahead. Through breaks in the trees we could see the outlines of some of the taller buildings—all dark. I guessed that it meant that no power had been restored to the city, though if there was an alternative source to the center we had knocked out, the city might simply be observing blackout conditions, or husbanding any available power for essential defense purposes.

No need to backlight any troops they've left guarding the city, I thought. Turning out the lights would be sound from a tactical standpoint. *Let the civilians hide in the dark, take what false comfort they can from that.* I didn't know that any civilians would be hiding. They might be as actively hostile as their army. We had been warned not to take tonatin civilians lightly, or to assume that they would be noncombatant.

Ten minutes passed, but the lieutenant did not give us a signal to get up and start moving again. Maybe he was trying to get a better idea of exactly where we should try to infiltrate, or what we might be able to do when we did. There was no call to go running madly into the middle of a situation until we had *some* idea what that situation was going to be and what we could do to affect it.

I had been listening idly to the reports from CIC, the volume low enough that it would not keep me from hearing a threat nearby. I had the external pickups on my helmet cranked almost to their maximum; the snapping of a twig thirty yards away would sound louder than the radio reports. There was little new in those reports now, beyond the fact that the infantry battle had been joined and the artillery duel was continuing. The tonatin had unleashed their antiaircraft batteries finally—mobile rocket launchers—which were giving our air cover difficulty, cutting down on how much attention they could give to attacking the enemy infantry.

Fifteen minutes. Tonio signaled for me to move forward to join him. The other squad leaders were also gathering.

Conference time, I thought, trotting over to where Tonio and Lieutenant Taivana were. We all got in a neat little circle, as close together as we could get, kneeling or squatting low, to present the smallest targets possible in case the enemy stumbled on us. Tonio and the lieutenant had their faceplates raised, so the squad leaders did the same.

Lieutenant Taivana opened up his electronic map and laid it on the ground in the center of the group. The dimly backlit map was adjusted to show the western half of the city and the forested area outside it. Taivana tapped a small cluster of light-blue blips. "This is where we are. There are other spec ops teams, scattered almost all the way around the city, except down near the southwestern corner, where the major battle is going on. The idea is to get as many of us between the civilians and the tonatin army as possible, work against the rear of the two battalions thrusting out against our force. We interfere with any attempts to resupply those battalions, cut into any traffic at all, and attempt to hit their command centers behind the lines—if we can locate them."

That was going to be fun. It didn't take a habitual pessimist to guess that our brass was sending as many of us as possible in on the hope that enough squads would survive the infiltration to actually do some good before we were trapped. There were red blips indicating the known positions of tonatin military units, but we couldn't expect those blips to show all of the enemy; any that were observing electronic silence would most likely not be known.

The lieutenant stopped and looked around the circle, meeting our gazes one by one. The stare of a dominant porracci can be unsettling. "We treat the area as a free-fire zone. We assume that any tonatin in the city are potentially armed enemies."

"Shoot first, ask questions later?" I whispered, almost under my breath—but the lieutenant heard. I guess he had the volume on his audio pickups turned way up as well.

"Shoot first and no questions asked, now or later," he said. "This directive comes directly from General Ransom."

"Yes, sir," I said. "It's better not to have our hands tied.

I'm just surprised that we're being allowed to operate so freely."

Taivana bared his teeth in a grin. "Yes, Sergeant, there is that. Now . . ." He started laying out our route, which would include getting wet, wading along the edge of the river—assuming there was any water shallow enough for wading—to avoid sentries watching the direct routes into the city. The river wasn't what you would call a major waterway. It wasn't like the Mississippi or the Amazon. Where we were, the river was nowhere wider than forty yards and according to the data fed to our electronic maps barely fifteen feet deep at its deepest points. But fifteen feet or fifteen fathoms, it was too deep for soldiers toting half their body weight in weapons, ammunition, and other gear to swim or wade.

"We have considerable night left to work in," Taivana said, "so let's get some work done." He got to his feet to signal the end of the conference. "Get back to your squads. We start moving in exactly three minutes."

I GOT BACK TO MY MEN QUICKLY AND REPEATED the essentials. "Save your questions," I said. "I've given you everything I know. Keep your eyes open, and be certain of your targets if we get into a shooting situation. We don't wait to let any enemy have the first shot, but there are going to be other spec ops teams trying to work their way in. We don't want to squirt our own people by mistake."

After that, there was barely time for each man to take a quick drink of water before the signal came to start. We moved down to the lower ground along the bank of the river almost at once. The parklike area we had been walking through was nine feet above the water and almost flat, offering minimal cover. There was a narrow ledge of rock and mud between the water and the embankment, which was fairly steep and slippery except in a few spots. Once we were down at the water's edge, we would be out of casual view of anyone up above us on the south side of the river. Unless they were fairly close and looking down, we would be practically invisible to anyone in the city.

Before we had gone far, we learned that there was more mud than rock, and the rocks tended to be slippery, covered with wet moss. Keeping our balance—not falling into the river—and trying to move silently required concentration. The physical effort brought aches to legs and ankles, an occasional cramp that could be extremely painful and momentarily disabling. It required that we go slower than the lieutenant wanted, but he had to give up on the quicker pace or face the strong possibility that we would have to fish some of our people out of the water or maybe even lose someone to drowning.

We had to walk single file. The ledge was too narrow for anything else, never more than three feet wide and often less than eighteen inches. That strung the platoon out over a considerable distance even though we lessened the interval between men. If someone opened up on us with automatic weapons from the north bank of the river, we might be in big trouble, so we kept our eyes open for any hint of an enemy presence over there, looking for visual, infrared, or electronic clues.

Somewhere in front of us, inside the city, there were two piers jutting out into the river and two bridges crossing it. The bridges had been destroyed—the central portions of the spans bombed—but the shore-ends of both were still standing, as were the piers, where there might be a few small boats tied up. The plan the lieutenant had dreamed up called for us to go past the first pier before we looked for a place to climb back to higher ground. That would put us inside the first line of buildings on the west side of the city. We hoped it would put us behind any defenders looking for us.

It took twenty-five minutes to reach that pier. There wasn't room for the entire platoon to get under the structure, which would have put us out of sight of anyone not on the narrow strip of mud and rock with us. Most of us simply had to lean against the embankment, rifles ready to meet anything that appeared right over our heads, until Sergeant Aytah Vul Nenmi, the biraunta leader of third squad, took his fire team up the wooden ladder on the east side of the pier to see what might be waiting for us.

Two minutes that felt longer than the twenty-five we had spent getting there: that was how long we had to wait before Aytah signaled that it was safe for the rest of us to come up. The other fire team from his squad was next to climb the ladder. After third squad moved to cover twenty yards away from the river, spread out in an arc, Tonio went up with second squad. Then Lieutenant Taivana came over and whispered to me that my squad would go next, and that he would be with us.

"Yes, sir," I whispered back. I waited until the lieutenant signaled that it was time, then sent Oyo and Iyi up the ladder. I followed them because I was getting antsy below— and I didn't want Lieutenant Taivana going up ahead of me. The lieutenant was right behind me. Within another thirty seconds, the rest of my squad was up top and we were moving toward the base of the nearest building— twenty yards farther out than the first squads—while fourth squad came up behind us.

We had been told that the city had about half a million residents, an estimate based on the size of the community, the number of buildings, and so forth rather than on census data. Anywhere off Earth or the homeworlds of some of the other sentients, half a million people is a *huge* city. Settlers generally remain well-dispersed on any colony world for a considerable number of generations. When usable land is plentiful and there are no serious natural threats to colonists, there is no incentive to crowd together and build tall buildings. I didn't know if the tonatin generally preferred to stay close or if Olviat was an aberration, but half a million of them lived in an area about three miles by two miles—sort of a D-shape, with the river the almost straight line.

Where we were, along the riverfront, the only buildings we could see were high-rises, six to ten stories, well separated, with paved streets and extensive green areas between them. From the map view, it was almost a checkerboard effect, buildings and parks. From where we were, it wasn't easy to guess which buildings were dwellings and which were commercial—if the tonatin made that distinction. I wasn't certain about that. There was too much we didn't know about the enemy.

Ignorance might be bliss for some, but not for a soldier in a combat zone.

WHAT WE DIDN'T SEE WERE ANY LIVING, BREATH- ing people. For all we could tell, our platoon might have been alone in the capital of Olviat. It was a ridiculous thought—the tonatin had certainly not evacuated the city—our observers would have seen movement on that scale. Still, I couldn't help the feeling, a prickling at the back of my neck, wondering where in hell everyone had gone. There wasn't even any trash visible, not a single sheet of paper blowing along a street in the wind. The city might almost have been brand-new, built all at once, waiting for its first inhabitants to move in. Spooky.

We took our time checking the area, with the platoon broken down into squads. We spread across three blocks of the riverfront, searching carefully for any hint of the city's inhabitants or soldiers left to guard them. We looked down each avenue, sent scouts to the next intersections, looked in the darkened doorways of buildings. Nothing moved, anywhere in sight, but the forty-two of us. Tonio and Lieutenant Taivana huddled together twenty yards from the corner of a building that I was peering around, trying to decide what to do next. I was just as happy not to be part of that conversation.

It can't be as deserted as it looks, I thought. *They had to leave* some *defenses behind. We* wouldn't *leave a major city unprotected. There's no reason to think the tonatin would be more cavalier about their civilians.* The tonatin hadn't built themselves up to being one of the two most numerous peoples in the Galaxy by being wasteful of lives. Thought processes did not detract from my alertness. I had switched off the radio feed from CIC to help me concentrate on what I was doing. *Where were the civilians? Where were the soldiers who should have been protecting them from the likes of us?*

It might have been fifteen minutes before the conference broke up and Tonio came over to where I was. He tapped me on the shoulder and gestured for me to pull away from the corner, then he lifted his faceplate. I did the same.

"The lieutenant wants to move farther from the river before we start anything," Tonio whispered. "We're going to split into squads to cover more ground and, uh, limit our vulnerability. I think he's annoyed at the lack of any enemy response. And, porracci or not, he's a little . . . reluctant to simply start setting off explosives in buildings that might contain nothing but frightened civilians. Women and children."

"We just gonna sit around and count our toes then?" I asked. "I thought we were sent in here to raise some hell, make the enemy put some soldiers to the task of protecting those women and children."

Tonio's snort was almost soundless. "But we don't want to start anything against civilians, without provocation. We figured there would at least be military outposts we could strike, use that to draw more of them in. Or we thought that maybe some of those civilians would start something that would make them no longer noncombatants."

"What happened to all that free-fire crap? Shoot first and no questions will be asked?" I demanded, letting my voice get a bit louder than I should have. I caught myself and started whispering again. "Why do we start pussyfooting around now? We've got half a battalion of rangers sneaking into this city. There's gonna be fighting. That was the whole point of this. Why don't we stop tiptoeing around the crap and get on with it. Hell, if the lieutenant doesn't want to blow up buildings with civilians in them, why not blow up a couple of these damned trees just to make some noise and let the enemy know we're here."

Tonio got a startled look on his face and his mouth dropped open about half an inch. "Hang on," he said after a moment. "Let me check that with the lieutenant." He got to his feet and ran back to where Taivana was. They only talked for a few seconds this time before the lieutenant nodded and Tonio trotted back to me.

"Nice to know that brain of yours hasn't rusted completely," Tonio said. "That's what we're going to do, make some nice, safe noise to let the enemy know we're here. Once anyone starts shooting at us, we don't have to worry about the niceties any longer." Tonio sucked in a deep breath before he continued.

"We split into squads. I'll stay with you, after I give the other squads their assignments. We go one block south and find a couple of likely trees in the next park, the bigger the better. The other squads with go south or east, fanning out to spread the joy. We'll work on a schedule—fifteen minutes after we leave here. That's to give the squads that have farther to go enough time to get there and get their targets wired. We set up the explosives and wait. The lieutenant will break radio silence to give the order, and each squad leader will acknowledge the order. Make sure the enemy knows we're here if they're monitoring for active electronics. Then we set off the charges and move—deeper into the city."

I chuckled. "Sounds good to me."

Tonio nodded. "Maybe enemy units moving to get at us will stumble into some of the other spec ops teams where they're not expecting them. We might open this city right up. Brief your men while I take the orders to the other squad leaders."

As soon as Tonio left, I gestured to bring the rest of my squad over. Along the side of the building facing the river, with no windows along the lowest stretch of the building, there was little chance that anyone would see us, but we stayed low while I told my people what we were going to do. The only one in the squad who made any comment was Souvana, and all he did was grunt in what seemed to be disdain at the way we were trying to avoid causing casualties among noncombatants. For once, his sentiment seemed to echo my own reaction, but I stared at him a second longer than necessary to remind him that what he thought didn't count for a whole lot. We obeyed orders.

Three minutes later, Tonio was back. "We wait for the lieutenant to signal, then move out. Fifteen minutes later, we set off the fireworks."

We didn't have long to wait. Lieutenant Taivana pumped his right arm up and down twice, then pointed deeper into the city. He headed east with second squad.

"Okay, let's move," I said, starting around the corner of the building with my squad. "Let's get into this fight."

CHAPTER 10

"**JUST USE ENOUGH EXPLOSIVE TO MAKE A LOUD** bang," I warned Robbie. "We want to save as much as we can for later, when it might do some real good." I had already given Claw the same order. He would be the other one planting a little package of sticky-boom—what we called the general-purpose explosive we had been given.

"I know what to do," Robbie replied. "Doesn't take much of a charge to bring down trees this size, if you know where to put it. And I do. Got in trouble once when I was a teenager, using homemade black powder to fell trees one Halloween."

"I don't need your life story," I said over his subdued chuckle. He was already working the charge into shape, as casually as if it were dough for biscuits. "Just get the stuff planted and get back here out of the way."

We really weren't rushed for time, but I didn't want to give Robbie the idea he could slack off. My squad had used only three of the allotted fifteen minutes to get where we were going and choose the trees we were going to blast. The larger of the two, the one I had given to Robbie, looked like it might fall into the nearest building—a structure with a lot of regularly spaced windows—if the charge was planted correctly. I thought the building might be residential. I had already pointed out the way the tree leaned to Robbie. He had taken the hint with a nod and a wink. We weren't going to start *shooting* at civilians until somebody started shooting at us, and the explosive charges certainly weren't heavy enough to do any direct structural damage to the buildings, but the lieutenant didn't say anything about not giving enemy civilians a *scare*. A tree branch coming in the bedroom window in the middle of the night ought to at least startle anyone inside, especially right on the heels of a nearby explosion.

Robbie hurried off, rifle in one hand, explosive packet in the other. Claw was already at the other tree, thirty yards from Robbie's. Placing the explosives and arming them with small command-control blasting caps didn't take either man more than thirty seconds. They hurried back to their fire teams and we all moved farther back, around corners, out of the way of any loose wood that might fly away when we popped the charges. A sliver of wood propelled with the velocity of a bullet can do just as much damage as if it had come out of a rifle. I was at the corner. I had to be in line of sight to trigger the two little bombs when Lieutenant Taivana gave the command.

I kept glancing at the timeline displayed at the top of my helmet faceplate. We had nearly ten minutes left of the fifteen the lieutenant had set. *What do we do if an enemy patrol wanders in on us before then?* I wondered, surprised that I hadn't thought of that before. Finding things to worry about is one of my strong suits. I glanced at Tonio. He was the platoon sergeant, the senior man on the scene, so it would be up to him. He was nearly a block away, with my second fire team, too far away for me to ask without breaking radio silence.

The men in my fire team were flat on their stomachs, close to the wall of the building, minimizing their exposure, stretching out in an arc behind me—watching for any enemy units that might sneak up on us. Across the way, the men in the other fire team were also down.

Five minutes left. I hadn't heard any sounds of nearby fighting. I wondered where all the other spec ops squads that were supposed to be infiltrating the city were. There were supposed to be a *lot* of us working. We were still close enough to the edge of town that we might have seen *some* of the other teams, even if just as blurred movement hurrying across open spaces. We were keyed up enough that even the merest hint of motion would have drawn a glance.

I put the side of my helmet against the building next to me, the sound pickup over my left ear right against the bricks. If there's any machinery running inside a building—heating, cooling, or just about anything else—you can sometimes feel, or hear, a low-pitched hum if you're in contact with the structure. Even with the power off, there might be *some* sound, though certainly nothing as loud as it would be with electricity flowing to all the machinery. But I heard nothing at all. Maybe the building *was* deserted, as unlikely as that seemed.

I tried to swallow but found that difficult. My mouth and throat were dry. The tension of waiting was starting to get to me. My palms were sweating. I wiped them on my uniform, one hand at a time, always keeping the other hand on my rifle.

Three minutes left. I blinked and looked across the sixty-yard square park—or whatever the locals might call it—in front of us. Little squares of trees, bushes, and flowers spread all around the city. There are a few towns on Earth that try to maintain something like that, parks, greenways, but never so . . . precisely, so completely as the tonatin had managed here. At least not in any town I had seen.

"Squad leaders, mark thirty seconds from now for action. Acknowledge." Lieutenant Taivana's voice over the radio—automatically interpreted by the translator button in my ear—startled me so badly that I jumped a little.

"Drak, Roger," I said, my acknowledgment almost running over the words of Sergeant Chouvana, the porracci leader of our second squad. The other squad leaders got their acknowledgments in. I was staring at my timeline again, waiting for those final thirty seconds to disappear. They seemed to evaporate in slow motion. When I noticed that I had started holding my breath I inhaled deeply, then let it out and took in another.

Silently, I counted down the last ten seconds, lips moving, my thumb on the detonator, hand stuck out around the corner. *Twenty-nine. Thirty.* I pushed the button and dropped flat, my face against the ground, as I pulled my hand back. By the time I remembered that I hadn't cranked down the gain on my external audio pickups, it was too late to rectify the error.

Well, the explosions weren't deafening. We hadn't used enough sticky-boom for that. And only the two charges my squad had planted were really *close*—the nearest thirty-five yards from me. But the blast was loud enough to drag a wince out of my throat, and my ears rang for a minute or more after the trees fell and the last bits of wooden shrapnel stopped showering down. I can't really say that I *heard* the explosions set off by the other squads. They were farther away, no larger than the two we had set, and near enough to simultaneous that they got caught up by the closer noises.

Blast of explosives, crack of wood breaking, glass cracking, limbs scraping against walls, trunks collapsing through their leaves. The smell of explosives and burned wood caught my nose, making it twitch reflexively. When I looked back around the corner, I saw that the tree Robbie had blown had indeed fallen against the structure I had thought it would hit, and there were a lot of broken windows. Apparently, the concussive force of the two explosions—small though those blasts were—had broken more windows than the tree itself had.

I also heard one high-pitched, continuing wail—sort of a drawn-out scream—coming from inside that building. At least we knew that the city hadn't been *completely* deserted. After that first sound of pain or fear, I gradually became aware of other noises coming from the buildings around the park—enough to make it clear that there were people in those buildings, reacting to what we had done, or to what had happened to them.

"Let's get out of here," Tonio said, speaking over my squad channel. He got up and gestured. We had been given a rendezvous earlier. We had to cross the park block we had just bombed to get to the rendezvous on the direct route, and this was the time for directness.

As I got up, I spotted one shard of wood, two feet long and an inch or so thick, stuck into the brick wall just around the corner from where I had been lying. There had been that much force behind the blast. I whistled under my breath. Then I had other things to think of. I saw the ground in front of me suddenly erupt in a tiny explosion of dust—the sort you get when a bullet hits pavement at an angle. Then there was another, a couple of feet from the first. Someone was shooting at us, single shots, not automatic fire. I shouted a warning over my squad channel, then pointed off to the right, the direction the shot had apparently come from.

"On the roof, near the far corner!" It was Robbie who spotted the target. He didn't bother pointing. His rifle did that as he sprayed a long burst in that direction. Three other rifles joined in. I don't know if we killed the sniper, but his rifle fell, bouncing once when it hit the sidewalk.

Each fire team moved in a loose column, men moving at a jog, crouched over, zigzagging, more or less from tree to tree. Connecting the dots. Doing everything possible to make it more difficult for anyone else to target us.

I was about halfway across the park when I saw motion in the doorway to my right—in the building that had been struck by Robbie's tree, the building that had had a sniper on the roof—not more than twenty feet away. I swiveled in that direction, bringing my rifle up to firing position, but I didn't pull the trigger. Two civilians, both women, staggered out of the building, one half carrying the other. One woman was bleeding badly from the face and chest. I could see a splinter of wood, maybe a foot long and nearly an inch in diameter, sticking out below her left shoulder, in

front and behind; it had penetrated completely. The other
woman noticed us and screamed, a noise more piercing
than the explosions had been.

"Leave 'em be," I said on my squad frequency. "They're
no danger to us. Let's just get moving."

THOSE TWO WOMEN POSED NO IMMEDIATE THREAT,
and I figured it would take time before they would have the
opportunity to tell anyone about us. They weren't armed,
and the one who wasn't badly injured looked too hysteri-
cal to think of doing anything. The one sniper had reminded me—all of us—that we had to watch the rooftops
and windows. That sniper might have been a civilian with
a hunting rifle. And there might be others.

In the next minutes, I did start to hear small-arms fire in
the area, nothing directed at my squad, but close enough
that I could pick out the sounds of individual weapons as
they stuttered on automatic or yipped on single fire. Some
of the other spec ops squads had apparently run into tonatin military units, or other snipers. The gunfire was
enough to make certain that we kept our eyes and ears
open, and we were even more cautious crossing open
spaces, where there might be stray rounds flying. We knew
we were in hostile territory, and we had started the blood-
letting inside the city. There might be enemy patrols
around any corner, anxious to get in a few licks of their
own.

Once we were on the move, we went back to electronic
silence. Those two women might be able to tell what direction we had headed in, and there were likely other eyes
that had seen us and the other squads, but we didn't know
how efficient the tonatin military would be in gathering intelligence from their civilians. By the time they found out
where we went, we'd be somewhere else.

We were a quarter mile from the rendezvous when the
enemy found us.

•   •   •

THEY DIDN'T SO MUCH *FIND* US. IT WAS MORE A matter of us stumbling on each other. We were going one way and they were coming in from our right. For an instant we were both exposed—the lead elements of my fire teams and the entire enemy patrol—both caught by surprise. The man on point, Jaibie, was looking the wrong way at the wrong time. That was the bottom line. He should have spotted the enemy and stopped us before anyone else got out in the open.

My initial estimate, made while I was diving toward the ground, was that there were about thirty tonatin coming at us, the nearest no more than forty feet from the point man from my second fire team, over on the right.

For a fraction of a second that seemed to last several hours shock kept fingers from triggers. I wasn't the only one whose first impulse, once that instant of shock released mind and muscles, was to dive for whatever cover an inch or two of grass might provide. That hesitation wasn't noticeably longer for one side or the other. It gave way to a fusillade of gunfire, sprayed rather than aimed. Most of the fire, in both directions, was high. That's a common failing, especially at night.

We were too close to withdraw, or to move to better cover. We had met at an intersection, where there were no trees, and only a few men on either side had partial cover from the corner of the building that had concealed us from each other until it was too late. We hadn't been cautious enough, but I didn't have time right then to think about that. Iyi and Oyo had been just in front of me. At least the enemy patrol had made the same mistake. Small comfort.

Tonio lifted up just enough to toss a hand grenade. I saw his arm snap back unnaturally and made the easy guess that he had been hit by a bullet. Behind me, Nuyi got his grenade launcher around to where he could use it and popped three quick rocket-propelled grenades at an extreme angle to drop them in the middle of the enemy patrol. I heard a bullet hit metal but couldn't turn my head to see what had been hit. I was too busy laying down as much gunfire as I could in the direction of the enemy.

It was the grenades that made the difference—the fact that a couple of our people thought of them before anyone on the other side did. In the instant after the blasts we were all moving toward whatever cover we could find quickly. All we could do was pull back and look for a different route, or try to come on the enemy patrol from a different angle, hope to get the drop on them next time.

One man did not pull back with the rest of the squad. Jaibie, our lone abarand, didn't move at all. He was face down on the ground where he had gone down at the start of the ambush—farther out in the open than the rest of us. I clicked over to check his vital signs on my helmet's display. No heartbeat. No respiration. The last brainwave activity fluttered out. *Well, I guess you can fly now,* I thought. Abarand believed that when they reached the afterlife they would regain the ability to fly freely that their primitive ancestors had lost.

"Jaibie's dead," I told Tonio, switching to the channel that connected me just to him. "How are you?"

"Hurting." I could have told that from the tightness of his voice, the fact that the word obviously came through clenched teeth. "Arm's broke below the elbow. We pull back to the next corner, then head south, try to get out of the way before that patrol pulls itself together enough to come after us."

"You gonna be able to manage?" I asked.

"What choice do I have? Lead with your fire team."

"On the way," I said, gesturing for Iyi and Oyo to start. I switched channels to speak to the entire fire team. "To the corner, then left. We want speed, but let's be more careful this time. I don't want to lose anybody else." I used the squad frequency to ask if anyone else had been wounded. I got back a string of negatives, one for every remaining man in the squad.

I hadn't quite emptied my rifle's magazine during the firefight, but I put a fresh clip in—saving the partial I took out, in case I ran short later. If we ran into more tonatin, or that same patrol hit us again, I wanted to have as much ammunition as possible in the rifle.

We paused before rounding that next corner. Iyi knelt at the edge of the building and peeked around, exposing just enough of his head to get one eyeball where it could see that there was no surprise waiting in the cross street. He signaled the all clear, then he and his brother started south and the rest of us hurried after them. Once around the corner, we moved out into the park area between buildings, where there were at least occasional trees to provide cover.

After I could see for myself that there were no enemy assets in front of us, I glanced back to see how Tonio was holding up. Tonio and my second fire team weren't too far back, and both porracci were behind Tonio, acting as rear guard for the squad. Fang and Claw were flanking Tonio, and one of the ghuroh was close enough to give Tonio a hand, if necessary.

That was all the time I could spare—all the time I was *willing* to spare—on Tonio's condition. I had to be ready to do the leading myself if he was in too much pain to think straight, so I had to start giving some thought to possible moves. The checkerboard arrangement of buildings and parks meant that after one block going south we would have to angle either left or right. Left would take us back toward that enemy patrol, which might well have headed south to intercept us. That meant we had to go to the right, around the building on the south side of the park we were in.

If Tonio couldn't make the decision. He had told me to lead the way, so before we got to the end of that next block, I decided to go ahead and do the leading. I lifted my faceplate a little and whistled to get Oyo's attention. He looked back toward me and I gestured to the right. Oyo nodded. That was almost a no-brainer. I glanced back to see if Tonio had noticed. He gave no indication, so I turned my attention to the front—and to what I assumed was the dangerous side, the left. As long as I eventually got us moving toward the rendezvous again, I doubted that Tonio would complain.

We crossed the last stretch of park, and the street beyond it, as if we *knew* there were enemy soldiers waiting on the left. One man ran across the danger zone at a time while the rest of us had our rifles trained to the left. But no gunfire came. Once my first fire team was across, we took up positions to cover Tonio and my second fire team. Before we started moving again, I went to Tonio. He had dropped to one knee and set his rifle on the ground, the muzzle resting on his foot.

"I've got to get this arm supported before the hand falls off," he said through gritted teeth.

"Here, let me." I pulled a strap from the outside of his backpack to fashion a rough sling and got the arm in it. "You slap a pain patch on?"

"Two. It still hurts. You run the squad. I'm not thinking straight. Get us to the rendezvous."

"Are we going to have to carry you?"

He hesitated for maybe five seconds before he answered. "I don't think so. Not yet. I'm hurting, but my legs still work. Fang got the bleeding stopped, and I don't think I lost so much blood that I'm likely to pass out. Come on. Don't waste time. I'm sure we didn't wipe out that enemy patrol. They're gonna be lookin' for us."

I couldn't argue with that. "Just the same, if you need help, don't wait too long to ask. We've got enough big guys to handle you."

I HAD COME UP WITH ONE POSSIBLE ALTERNATIVE to the cut-and-run we were doing. If Tonio lost consciousness, or got too weak to keep up, we could consider going into one of the buildings—hole up with enough civilians to give the tonatin military cause to hesitate before they blasted us—and hope that our people got to us before the enemy could dig us out.

Despite all the propaganda we had been fed about how

utterly ruthless the enemy was, I was fairly confident that the tonatin military would not recklessly endanger their civilian population to get at us. I didn't mention my alternative to Tonio, but . . . if it came to it, it was something to think about, even though I didn't like the idea of backing us into a corner we might not be able to get ourselves out of unless there was no other way. The key to spec ops is to stay mobile.

AT THE END OF THE NEXT BLOCK WE ANGLED BACK to the left. Going any farther right would have put us too close to the edge of the city. That would make it more likely that we would run into other tonatin units, or get into crossfire between the enemy and some of our own people. We went to the ground again about a minute later when we saw movement to the south of us, but we had merely run into another spec ops squad. I got a recognition blip on my head-up display and an identifier showing it was someone from the second squad of fourth platoon. They waited in place for us.

I went to talk to the squad leader, a biraunta sergeant named Ikai. Tonio had merely sat down when we stopped, slumped over, his chin hanging down to his chest, concerned only with keeping himself going until he could get medical treatment. I told Ikai about our skirmish, and where it had been.

"We, too, have tasted the enemy," Ikai said. We were whispering, faceplates lifted. "I lost two men, but we took fivefold payment from the tonatin. None of them escaped us."

"Good for you. Look, my platoon sergeant is hurting pretty badly and we've got to get back to the rest of our platoon. Can you take a couple of minutes to cover us through the next block or two—until we know we're away from what's left of that patrol we fought with?"

Ikai clicked his teeth together twice and winked, the biraunta equivalent of "Can do."

"Thanks." I grinned and gestured for my men to start moving. Tonio almost couldn't stand by himself. I didn't ask him if he wanted help. I just told Kiervauna to pick the platoon sergeant up and carry him. Kiervauna nodded and handed off his extra weapons—the rocket launcher to Souvana and the grenade launcher to Fang—and scooped Tonio up as if he weighed no more than one of those weapons. I picked up Tonio's rifle. There was no call to leave anything an enemy civilian could use against us.

I waved to Sergeant Ikai as we left. He waved back. Ikai had already started deploying his men. It felt good having someone watch my back for a few minutes.

CHAPTER 11

TONIO LOST CONSCIOUSNESS NOT LONG AFTER
Kiervauna started carrying him. I figured that was a break
for Tonio. It would save him some pain since the patches
he had put on apparently hadn't done the job. That was un-
usual, but not unheard of. It might mean extensive nerve
damage. If Tonio was really lucky, he would stay unconscious until we rendezvoused with the rest of the platoon
and got a splint on the broken arm and better analgesics in
his system, even if we couldn't get him to a medic with a
medtank. When we did reach the rendezvous, the third
squad to arrive, Tonio's right arm was swollen from above
the elbow right out to his hand, and the skin was turning
dark. Robbie did what he could, fashioning a splint and
pumping extra medical nanoagents into Tonio. I knew
Robbie had never taken the medtech courses, but he oper-
ated as efficiently as if he had been doing that kind of work
for years.

I had to report to Lieutenant Taivana. He listened while
I summarized what we had done and how we had been
caught by the enemy patrol through our own carelessness.
I didn't try to gloss over that. If I had, Taivana would have
jumped all over it, and he would have made a bigger deal
out of it.

His growl and scowl signaled his displeasure, but he did

not interrupt. "One man dead, another temporarily in-capacitated," he said—very softly—after I finished. "Through a lapse of concentration. That is not good."

"No, it isn't, sir," I said. "And it isn't enough that the man on point paid as heavily for his mistake as any man can. But I think the example will ensure that no one else in the squad makes the same mistake in the future. What do we do now, sir?" I gestured to the side. "Wait for fourth squad to arrive, then what?" I wasn't simply trying to change the subject, though I did want to do that. We had to think about whatever we were going to do next. We were near the middle of the enemy's capital city, with perhaps half a million enemy civilians and several thousand hostile soldiers between us and the majority of our force. It was not the place for a lengthy critique of mistakes.

"We don't wait," Taivana said. "Fourth squad has run into a little difficulty. We go to them, as soon as Sergeant Xeres can be moved." He nodded toward Tonio. "Once we relieve fourth squad, we all move back to the river. Our or-ders are to cross it before daybreak." I looked at the time-line on my helmet display. We had about two hours of darkness left.

OUR FOURTH SQUAD HAD ALSO ENCOUNTERED A tonatin patrol that outnumbered them. The ghuroh squad leader, known as Sergeant Slash—ghuroh proper names were incredibly difficult for any of the non-ghuroh species to pronounce, so they all had simpler, and usually rather evocative, nicknames—had taken the alternate choice I had not. He and his men had taken shelter in one of the buildings. While they had been able to keep the tonatin military from getting at them—and the civilians who lived in the building had been no problem—the squad had not been able to get out.

Lieutenant Taivana split the platoon again as we neared the location of fourth squad. Kiervauna stayed back with Tonio and two wounded men from second squad. First and second squads moved around on the left. Third squad moved in on the right. We took the tonatin unit, about a platoon, under fire, getting a lot of rounds off, including a few grenades, before they were able to turn to meet the new threat. And as they did start to turn their attention to us, Sergeant Slash led his squad out of the building, catching the tonatin in the middle.

This firefight lasted less than a minute, and we did not suffer additional casualties. It was as one-sided a fight as any I had been in. I was thankful that I wasn't on the short side this time. Not all of the tonatin soldiers were killed, but we didn't waste time seeing to the wounded, and of the survivors, not one was unwounded. At the moment, we were only interested in making sure that they were no threat to us. We stripped the enemy soldiers of weapons and helmets. There wasn't much we could do about the weapons—no one in our platoon knew how to field-strip and disable the tonatin rifles—so we collected all the ammunition to dispose of it once we got to the river. The helmets we could take care of, disabling the electronics.

We gathered our wounded and Kiervauna, then started north. We left the tonatin wounded where they lay. Any help for them would have to come from their own forces or from civilians. Until we moved out, I stayed fairly near the enemy wounded, mostly to make certain that Souvana or one of our other porracci didn't decide to end their suffering prematurely.

The river was only four blocks past where fourth squad had been pinned down. It didn't take long to reach it. We pitched the tonatin ammunition into water that was deep enough that no one would see it while second and third squads went along the waterfront to find boats.

There weren't enough nearby to carry all of us, so it took two trips. But we made those trips safely, with the wounded going in the first relay. We were all on the north shore an hour before sunrise.

•　　•　　•

WE DIDN'T SIMPLY CROSS THE RIVER AND SIT ON
the bank watching the city. Our orders were to move farther north, about a mile. That put us in a wooded area—
wild, left to its native flora and fauna, unlike the areas right
around the city. We rendezvoused with a company of one
of our line battalions that had landed north of the river.
That meant that we were able to get proper medical attention for Tonio and the two other wounded men. The line
companies had medics and medtanks.

As soon as our wounded were being taken care of, Lieutenant Taivana called all four squad leaders to him. "Drak,
as senior squad leader, you will act as platoon sergeant
until Sergeant Xeres returns to duty. Your assistant squad
leader will take over for you."

"Yes, sir," I said. "Shall I have Corporal Souvana join
us?"

"Yes." Taivana waited while I went over to my squad. I
brought Souvana back, telling him about the new command arrangement on the way. I couldn't see the expression on Souvana's face, but I assumed it was something
approaching glee. At least for a short time, Tonio's wound
moved Souvana up in the dominance chain, something that
nearly every porracci lusted for routinely. And Souvana
had never been shy about pointing out anything he would
have done differently than I did it. He felt he was more fit
to be squad leader.

"I have been in contact with Captain Fusik," Taivana
said as soon as Souvana and I joined the group, "and I have
received the latest status reports from CIC. We will return
to the river to assist other teams from our battalion to
cross, providing covering fire and any other support possible. Once as many of those teams as possible are on this
side of the river we will withdraw to provide security for
an LZ. The two battalions of line troops that were brought
in north of the river will be picked up and moved south
where they can be employed more usefully. Until sunset,
all elements of Ranger Battalion north of the river will stay

on this side, moving back to the shore to make sure no IFers"——Ilion Federation soldiers—"cross, and to harass any who come out in the open on the south bank."

"Overall, how is the fight going?" I asked.

Taivana hesitated before he answered. "CIC says that the situation remains 'fluid.' In this situation, I believe the word is probably uncommonly accurate since the major units of both armies are maneuvering freely to the south and west of the city. The one significant piece of new intelligence we have is that the enemy have apparently armed a portion of their civilian populace in a militia-type organization. It is no longer simply isolated snipers. Several units of between fifty and one hundred individuals have been spotted. So far, although they have demonstrated considerable eagerness for the fight, they have not shown much skill. They have suffered heavy casualties in two firefights. It does call for an added degree of caution for our teams." He paused, staring at Slash. "I don't want any of us attempting to seek shelter in any building that might harbor armed enemy—military or civilian—personnel."

Slash gave no response.

THE TWO BATTALIONS OF LINE SOLDIERS FOUND their own landing zone and put guards on the perimeter until the shuttles came in and they started loading. For a time, we returned to the river and helped a couple of spec ops squads get across, ferrying them with the few boats we had found before. Then we went back to the LZ. By that time, the sun was peeking over the horizon and any additional river crossings would be more hazardous.

Six shuttles landed at a time—all the LZ would hold comfortably. As soon as each shuttle was filled, it took off. Then the next batch started coming in. The pilots didn't want to waste a second more than they had to. It was daylight, which made them more vulnerable to attack. They wanted to get high enough to be out of reach of enemy anti-aircraft artillery and rockets and shoulder-launched rockets. Halfway through the process, we took over perimeter security—two squads at each of the cardinal points of the compass. It wasn't just our platoon any longer, or the few squads we had helped across. Several other ranger platoons—odd squads from different platoons—had made it across the river on their own, some of them from considerably farther east, and were added to the perimeter.

Lieutenant Taivana was the only officer from Ranger Battalion on site, so he took tactical command of all the spec ops squads. There must have been close to a hundred of us, quite a command for a junior lieutenant. Once the last shuttles had taken off, some seventy-five minutes past sunrise, Taivana started moving us back toward the river to help any other teams from the battalion to get out of the city. One squad from C Company was left to guard the wounded, after they were moved a couple of hundred yards from the LZ. That squad got picked because they were short four men, almost half their strength. It would be another two hours or more before the last of the wounded came out of the medtanks, ready to return to duty.

The sun was well above the eastern horizon before we took up positions along the north bank of the river again. Anyone who tried to cross was going to have to do it in full daylight—exposed to anyone who wanted to cause them grief, or who might pass intelligence to the enemy's commanders. I felt a lump grow in my middle. It was a situation I wouldn't want to face, trying to paddle a small boat across that river in daylight. *They'd be better off staying on the south side, hiding until sunset,* I thought, wondering how firm the orders had been for the rest of the teams to cross the river. How much leeway had team leaders been given? Had I been leading one of those teams and not been able to cross before dawn, I would have been sorely tempted to disobey orders regardless of risk—or, at least, to move back to the west, clear of the city, before I made the attempt. Better to give men a chance to get back alive and risk the consequences of disobeying later.

The boats we had used to cross during the night were all on the north bank, pulled out of the water and out of casual sight of anyone looking from the south side. *Anyone comes out looking for a way across, we're going to have to ferry the boats to them,* I thought. Someone would. I felt a guilty relief in knowing that my squad wasn't closest to the boats.

According to Taivana, there had to be about a company of our people inside the city, around two hundred men, separated in teams from one squad to a full platoon. Minus any who had been killed. Two hundred men were more than we could hope to get across the river if all we had were the few boats we had commandeered. I spent a few minutes scanning the south bank, mostly to the east, looking for other boats, but didn't see any. The river did bend south off in that direction, so I couldn't tell. There might be a whole flotilla of small craft just beyond the section I could see.

Once we were settled in, I started listening to the regular data feed from CIC again, hoping for advance warning if any of the other teams did manage to reach the river—and to see if I could make sense of how the rest of our people were doing.

The voice from CIC never showed any emotion. It might almost have been a synthetic computer voice speaking, except that it sometimes made mistakes, changed direction in the middle of a sentence as new information came in. Occasionally, an "er" or "ah" slipped in. The situation on the south and west side of Olviat's capital was confused. There was a major battle in progress, but no firm battle lines. Both sides were maneuvering freely, the pattern of unit positions changing constantly. That limited the use of artillery and air cover. There was too great a chance of hitting friendly forces. The two battalions of our people who had been shuttled closer to the battle had not joined the fighting. They had been landed several miles out to minimize the chance of having shuttles shot out of the air, so they had to hoof it before they could take part.

Casualty reports were the slowest to hit the feed, and I had to listen between the words to get a good picture of what was happening. I gathered that we were losing people faster than the general staff had projected, but that our losses had not hit the critical level—the point at which the commander has to start thinking about withdrawing. Just what that point was had not been shared with us common types. Probably only the commanding general and his senior staff officers had that information.

I did gather that, as usual, we had underestimated the size of the enemy force. The projections of military planners are almost always overly optimistic. We did not have the serious numerical superiority we had been told we would have. Even not counting the civilians the local garrison had armed, we did not come in with more than a five-to-four advantage. We did have air superiority though, and that counted for a lot. Olviat had not been able to put up more than a couple of aerospace fighters, and those had been shot out of the air almost immediately.

LIEUTENANT TAIVANA PUT US ON HALF-AND-HALF watches. That gave everyone time to eat battle rations and get a little sleep. We started out an hour at a time, then stretched the cycle to ninety minutes the second time around. I alternated with Lieutenant Taivana, though he really didn't try to sleep. He took his command too seriously. Maybe he knew his own limits. Porracci seem to have more endurance than humans—at least, they do whatever it takes to make us think they do. Me, I was grateful for a chance to get even thirty or forty minutes of sleep at a time.

In five hours, only three of our men reached the river and had to be ferried across, one at a time. All were men who had become separated from their squads. Taivana questioned each of them to pass the information to CIC.

All the stories were similar. The squads of each of the separated men had been in firefights and had been forced
to scatter to avoid capture or death. Capture might have
meant death in any case. The war had seen numerous in-
stances of tonatin soldiers killing prisoners—not merely
isolated events like one porracci putting two soldiers who
were probably doomed anyway out of their misery. One
man thought he was the only survivor of his squad. The
other two didn't know what had become of the rest of their
teams. They had simply done what they had to in order to
return.

"Looks pretty bad for our guys, doesn't it?" Robbie
asked, about noon. He had crawled over to the slit trench I
had dug for myself among the roots of sprawling vines
above the riverbank. "You'd think anyone who could get
out would have by now."

"Not necessarily." We both had our faceplates up. We
weren't using the radio. "I can imagine a lot of reasons
why they haven't come over, not all of them bad. Some
teams simply may have had to hole up where they could.
Some might have worked their way farther east or west,
out of the city. Or even moved south, following the tonatin
army out on that side. We haven't heard all the orders
going out or all the reports going up the chain."

"They'd have pulled us off this watch if they didn't hope
there'd still be people to get across the river," Robbie said.

I shrugged. Robbie hadn't said anything that hadn't run
through my head at least once. I had the arguments down
cold on both sides of the question. "Don't borrow trouble,
kid," I told him, but gently. Robbie McGraw was showing
more promise than I had expected. "It finds us fast enough.
As long as we're here, we can function. We're accom-
plishing something. We know that no enemy units have
crossed back to this side in the stretch we're watching—
most of the city's shoreline. If the general figures out
someplace we can be more useful, I'm sure he'll tell us.
Just get back to the squad and keep your eyes open."

• • •

I FOUND MYSELF WONDERING HOW MANY HUNDRED pairs of eyes were watching from the buildings facing the river on the other side. I could imagine all those civilians, maybe mostly women and children if the tonatin had armed the men, peeking around drapes, looking for any hint of us on the north bank, counting how many men they could see, somehow getting that information to their military. Maybe the tonatin army would start sneaking sharpshooters into some of those buildings, snipers ready to pick off any of us who got careless and showed ourselves.

The longer we stayed, the greater the temptation to get careless. A couple of times during the morning I warned everyone in the platoon to be careful, and after Tonio returned from his medical treatment it wasn't five minutes before he did the same thing. I was back with my squad then. Souvana managed to hide his disappointment at being merely a fire team leader again.

The medics had pronounced Tonio fit for duty, but it was clear that his mind hadn't yet thrown off the memory of pain. That can be the hardest part of recuperation. Maybe the speed of physical healing has something to do with that. Back in the days when a bullet wound or other injury might keep a soldier off duty for days or weeks, they had time to gradually readjust. Now, some men never make it all the way back. The memories intrude. A soldier loses his confidence, his daring.

We spent a few minutes together right after Tonio got back. I briefed him as fully as I could on what we had done and what we were supposed to be doing. Although I'm sure Taivana also briefed him, Tonio listened to me with no show of impatience, nodded at the appropriate time, then sent me back to my squad. He didn't look or sound like the Tonio Xeres I had known for years. His wound during the night hadn't been nearly as serious as the wounds he had experienced the first time we had been on the divotect world of Dintsen together—where the tonatin had surprised everyone. That had been the invasion that started this war. Tonio had barely survived that fight. There had been serious doubt whether any of us would survive that fight.

"You sure you're okay?" I asked him before moving away.

He hesitated, then nodded. "I will be," he said, very softly. "I've still got a little of the pain left in my mind. Once we get busy, I'll be okay."

I had no choice but to take him at his word. As long as I had known him, his word had always been good.

TWO MEALS. THREE SHORT PERIODS OF SLEEP. Noon came and went; the afternoon started dragging. We were still stretched out along the north bank of the river that marked the northern boundary of the capital of Olviat, under cover of the trees and bushes behind the shore. As the day warmed up, getting near sixty degrees by the time the sun was overhead, I found it harder to stay awake when I was supposed to. I occasionally made the rounds, moving behind the positions of my men, making certain that the people who were supposed to be awake were. That was as much to help stay awake as to make sure the others were.

I found myself wondering if command had forgotten us. The general and his staff certainly had enough to worry about keeping all the facets of the battle in focus. A few dozen men on the side wouldn't have been important. Not that I objected to every possible hour of sleep and relative safety. I was never a fanatic. I would fight when I had to, but I wouldn't look for ways to volunteer for anything I didn't have to. I had already had one man killed in my squad on this operation. When I closed my eyes I could still see Jaibie lying on the street, life signs gone. I didn't like the fact that we had been forced to leave him behind, but there had been no chance to bring him along—not without risking more lives. If he had merely been wounded, we would have done everything possible to bring him out with us, but we wouldn't risk lives for a corpse. Later, we would go back to recover our dead. After the fight. Of course, if we lost, there was little chance that we would be able to recover anyone.

I got up to make another of my periodic rounds, staying low, out of sight of anyone across the river. We were far enough back in the trees that it wasn't difficult. I slipped into the slit trench next to Nuyi. Divotect tend to be sluggish when the weather is cool, a remnant of their reptilian ancestry, so I made a point of checking on him more frequently than I did the others. He lifted his head and turned it as I came in, showing me that he was awake.

"How long do we lie here, Sergeant?" he asked.

"Until they tell us to do something else."

"I cannot see how we contribute to the effort here. We should be over there, somewhere, helping to defeat the tonatin." The war had started when tonatin invaded a couple of divotect colony worlds, and the divotect casualties had been extreme. There were rumors that the tonatin were on a genocidal quest to eliminate the only sentients who had not descended from mammals. That was probably why all the member worlds of the Alliance of Light had so quickly responded to the initial attacks by the tonatin who controlled the rival Ilion Federation. There was prejudice against the divotect among the other species, but no one wanted to sit back and let them be exterminated. The divotect themselves were in the fight totally, knowing that it was a life-or-death matter for their race. Nuyi was bloodthirsty when it came to fighting tonatin.

"We'll get our chance. This campaign isn't going to be over in a single day."

"If it takes too many days, the IFers will reinforce the garrison here."

"Leave that worrying to the general and his staff," I advised. "That's what they get paid for. Anyway, we work better at night, and sunset is a long way off." I gave him a thumbs-up gesture, then started sliding along to the next slit trench.

• • •

Sᴜɴꜱᴇᴛ ᴡᴀꜱ ᴛʜʀᴇᴇ ʜᴏᴜʀꜱ ᴀᴡᴀʏ ᴡʜᴇɴ ꜱᴇᴠᴇʀᴀʟ squads were pulled out of the line along the river. My squad was the only one from our platoon. We were told to report to the LZ that had been used that morning and wait for transport; we were going to be dropped at several locations near other towns within thirty miles of the capital. We were to hit power stations and public buildings, raise enough hell to—it was hoped—give the IFers more problems, maybe pull some of their troops away from the capital to meet the new threats. Give them something new to worry about.

"They will not rise to the bait," Souvana said while we were waiting for the shuttles. We had been at the LZ more than two hours, and we were all a little antsy, wondering how long it would be. Sunset was only an hour off. "They would be foolish to risk their capital and the major concentration of their civilian population to respond to flicker bites elsewhere." *Flicker* was how my translator button interpreted the name of a bug from Souvana's homeworld. "We should simply mass our forces and bring the campaign to a conclusion as quickly as possible."

"You know they probably won't respond and I know it—and the general probably knows it as well," I said, "but we do what we're told. Maybe we'll scare up a few enemy units the brass doesn't know about. There may be garrisons at these other towns, and we could still get in deep shit, so pay attention to the work you're supposed to be doing."

Souvana's answering growl was long and deep. I had probably insulted him so badly that he would have felt compelled to challenge me for leadership of the squad if we had been in a porracci unit. After a moment, he turned and walked away. That was fine with me. Besides, I had just received an alert. The shuttles were making their landing approach.

CHAPTER 12

"AT LEAST WE'RE NOT GOING BACK IN ON AIR-
sleds," Robbie said as we boarded our shuttle. I grunted a
reply and gave him a shove through the hatch. I had
thought the same thing myself. I've yet to meet anyone
who enjoys an airsled insertion. For most of us it's a matter of something approaching dread, made acceptable only
because it can increase our odds of getting in alive on some
operations.

I was the last man from the squad through the hatch. The
shuttle's crew chief closed and sealed the door behind me,
then headed for his cubicle at the front of the passenger
compartment. I got to my seat and strapped in, then un-
folded my map to go over the details of the squad's assignment—for the tenth time. I had our new zone of
operations almost committed to memory. That's part of *my*
way for dealing with the tension—get as well-prepared as
humanly possible.

On Earth, the little town we were going to be inserted
near would have been called a bedroom community—a
place away from the city and jobs where commuters lived,
sort of like the place I lived when I was a kid and still belonged to a family. There was no obvious industry in this
town, just farms surrounding it and small-scale food pro-
cessing operations on the edge. It had its own power dis-

tribution center and had apparently not lost electrical power when we blew the main station in the capital. CIC estimated that the town was home to a maximum of ten thousand people. There was no information about whether it had any soldiers defending it.

By the time I had my map open and powered up, the shuttle was starting its takeoff run. The noise in the cabin increased to a point that would have been deafening without the insulation of battle helmets. I braced myself—feet out, one hand gripping the arm of my seat, body pressed against the web seating by the acceleration. The shuttle hurtled across the clearing, achieving takeoff speed in a hundred yards. The craft tilted back, first at a thirty-degree angle, then at something close to ninety degrees.

We weren't going to make just a quick hop, up and down, landing within thirty miles of where we took off, a flight that would have lasted just a few minutes and never taken us more than two thousand feet up. For some reason that wasn't explained to us grunts, the shuttle was to do a complete orbit, coming in near our target from the southwest. It would take about ninety minutes, with us strapped in the whole time. We would be in near-zero gravity for most of the flight since shuttles aren't equipped with artificial gravity generators.

I studied my map for a few minutes, though it was hard to pay attention during acceleration with the noise and vibration of the shuttle, and the feeling that all my blood had drained to the back of my head and body. Shortly after the rockets were turned off, I linked through to my men on the squad radio channel to go through another briefing on what we were going to do when we landed, concentrating more on the vulnerable first few minutes on the ground than on our mission. It was the fourth time I had put the squad through a run-through, enough that some, if not all, of them had to be thoroughly tired of hearing the same thing, but no one voiced a complaint; there wasn't even a low growl from Souvana.

Souvana had one empty spot in his fire team. There had

been no replacement for Jaibie. But Jaibie had always been the weak link in that team. *Sorry, Jaibie, but it's true.* The porracci and ghuroh had all been bigger and far stronger than the abarand. Not to mention more . . . durable. Abarand had bones that were less dense, almost brittle. Jaibie's talents had been in his marksmanship and in his ability to get up in a tree and glide. In the city, he hadn't been able to use the latter talent at all, and he hadn't had enough of an opportunity for the former on Olviat. In the end, all he had time for was one careless mistake.

I talked the squad through what we would do when we landed, but didn't go beyond the takeoff of the shuttle after we unloaded. We would set up a preliminary perimeter to cover the shuttle until it got high enough to outrace any rockets that might be launched at it—if there were enemy troops with rocket launchers close. Once I finished boring my people, I turned my attention back to the map, setting the scale to show as much detail as possible, going over possible routes from the LZ to our target—roundabout routes so they wouldn't be able to simply wait for us to take a straight line from LZ to power station.

It wasn't until then, halfway through our orbit, that it occurred to me that maybe the single orbit was designed simply to put us on the ground after sunset. The quick up and down wouldn't have done that, and maybe the big shots didn't want us sitting where we had been until after dark before making the jump. For staff types, it might sound logical. This way, it would be forty-five minutes after sunset when we emerged from the shuttle—not quite total darkness, but close enough in a forested area.

We would form our perimeter, wait for the shuttle to take off, then get away from the LZ as quickly as feet would take us, and hope we moved in a direction the enemy would not anticipate. Then we could angle toward the town and its power station . . . and do what we were supposed to do.

Ten minutes before we were due to start our powered descent, I had everyone put fresh magazines in their weapons and gave the "lock and load" command—a round in the chamber and the safety on. Then we waited. It was a time for each man to be alone with his thoughts, a silence I would not breach without considerable need. Give everyone a chance to make his peace with whatever God he believed in, or simply to think about family, fears, or . . . whatever. Maybe we wouldn't have any trouble waiting for us when the shuttle touched down. Maybe we would. Despite the care being taken with our around-the-world approach, and the stealth characteristics of the shuttle, the enemy might shoot us down on our landing approach, kill us before we had a chance to get out of the can where we could defend ourselves. I've had nightmares about that, but there was absolutely nothing I could do about it. If it happened, it happened—and I probably would never know it had.

The pilot gave us a warning thirty seconds before he switched the rockets back on and we started diving toward the surface. Gravity isn't enough for shuttle jockeys. They add the full power of their rockets at the start of an approach, and reverse thrust at the last possible instant, pulling sharply out of the dive, subjecting themselves and their passengers to the highest gee-forces people can stand without blacking out. The idea is to be in the vulnerable range for as few seconds as possible. Get on the ground before the enemy has a chance to line up a rocket and get it off.

When the pilot reverses thrust to start braking, that is a particularly nasty time. Anyone who is going to get sick usually does it then, when apparent gravity is suddenly reversed. It can happen to anyone. This time, I was one of them, and I barely got my faceplate lifted in time to avoid keeping the mess inside the helmet. At least we don't have to clean up after ourselves in the shuttles.

OUR REFLEXES HAD BEEN HONED BY MONTHS OF training, and the adrenaline of a combat landing did the rest. As soon as the shuttle came to a halt, we slapped open our safety harnesses and started toward the two hatches the crew chief opened. We were all outside, running and spreading out to form our initial perimeter, less than ten seconds after the shuttle stopped moving forward. At a time like that, you don't notice the seventy to eighty pounds of gear you're carrying. You move as if you were wearing only track shorts and running shoes.

With only nine men, we couldn't put a complete perimeter around the LZ. All we could do was fan out on either side, by fire team. If a hostile force showed up, we couldn't do more than distract them for a few seconds. We moved thirty yards from the shuttle and dove to the ground, landing in prone firing positions, five to eight yards between men. By the time I got down, the shuttle was already turning around. As soon as it was pointed back the way it had come, the rockets cycled up and it jumped forward again. Its total time on the ground was under thirty seconds.

A man can't completely ignore the racket coming from a shuttle taking off, not that close, but it was only a minor distraction even though it was too much for the insulation in my battle helmet to block completely. My external audio pickups were off, or the noise would literally have been deafening. This time I hadn't forgotten to shut the audio off.

I had started scanning my side of the perimeter while I was running, night-vision system switched on, rifle safety off, ready to take any enemy under fire instantly. Once I was prone, I kept scanning, looking over my rifle at the edge of the clearing, searching mostly for any infrared signatures that might indicate people-sized targets. Any target in our area would almost certainly be tonatin. If, by some wild chance, any of our people had gotten this far from where they were supposed to be, we would pick up recognition blips from their helmets . . . if they were functional.

There weren't any targets near the proper size anywhere close. There were virtually no warm spots that could indicate anything other than plant life—even the birds and small animals had been scared away by the noise. Once the shuttle was fairly gone, the area was unnaturally silent. I turned on my audio pickups and cranked the gain up to maximum. Except out in the open, hearing can be as important as sight.

I looked over my shoulder toward Souvana's fire team, to see if they had spotted anything. Souvana gave me a negative sign with his left arm. I returned it, then gestured for everyone to get up and start moving. We were observing electronic silence, but once Souvana and I got to our feet, the others noticed the movement and got up as well. We got into a loose patrol formation and started toward the southeast, on a course that would take us slightly farther from the town.

ONCE WE WERE AWAY FROM THE LZ, I STEPPED out of the line and gestured for the others to keep moving. The squad was in a loose column, three to five yards between men, with Oyo and Iyi thirty yards ahead scouting our route, angling back and forth across our base course to take advantage of the terrain.

The biraunta, identical twins, were by far the smallest members of the squad. They were high-strung, nervous, tails twitching, coiling and uncoiling, agitated all of the time—except when it counted. On the job, in a combat zone, they were cool. In forested country, biraunta were as comfortable traveling from branch to branch up in the trees as the rest of us were walking. The trees here weren't thick enough, close enough, for them to do their scouting above. They were on the ground like the rest of the squad.

Robbie McGraw was next in line. I hadn't seen enough of him in action to make a final determination of his value, but what I had seen impressed me; he knew his job and had fit into the team from the start. He didn't have the open bigotry of his predecessor.

Nuyi was between Robbie and me. The divotect wasn't

the fastest or the strongest man in the squad, but his heart and soul were so completely in the war that it made up for a lot. If there was a bona fide hero-type in the squad, it was Nuyi.

Souvana's fire team was behind mine, with Fang and Claw as the rear guard—ten yards behind Souvana. Kiervauna was the first man in second fire team, not far behind me. The two porracci were physically the strongest in the squad, though it was a near thing between them and the ghuroh. The two porracci still had little to do with each other except on duty, when it couldn't be avoided. Both did their jobs, and did them well. Both weighed in at well over three hundred pounds, though they were shorter than I am, and I'm barely average height, if that, for a human.

The ghuroh, Fang and Claw, worked well as part of the team. Their traditions were those of pack hunters, cooperative, putting the pack over personal survival. Their faces reminded me of dogs, greyhounds or mastiffs, maybe, though there could be no real genetic connection between ghuroh and any terran species.

Altogether, the squad stretched over about a hundred and ten yards. I stayed off by the side until I could see the two ghuroh clearly—when they were about fifty yards away—then hurried along the side of the column until I was back in my proper place, in the middle of my fire team.

The terrain was native forest, untouched by the tonatin. But trees and other plants are rarely radically different from one terrestrial world to the next. The specifics change, but most vegetation is still primarily green. Photosynthesis drives plant life everywhere on worlds we can operate on without carrying our own oxygen. Despite the differences, the similarities in life from world to world are far more imposing.

There was a fairly decent chance that no sentients of any species had ever walked this route. There *were* animal tracks. We saw signs where grazers and browsers had eaten grass and leaves, but we didn't see any animals up close. A couple of times I spotted warm spots at some distance—four-legged animals, perhaps the local equivalent of deer or antelope. The important thing was that we saw no sign of enemy soldiers. Seeing wildlife is always reassuring. It means no one has come along to spook them. It means that *maybe* there's nothing out there to worry you, but you stay cautious.

Thirty minutes after we left the LZ, I stopped the squad for a minute while I looked at my map to check our position and verify the heading for the next leg of our trek. It was time to angle back toward the town and its power station. I also looked for any indication of active electronics between us and the town and found nothing. That did not necessarily mean that there were no enemy troops, just that no one was using active electronics.

There shouldn't be enemy troops, except maybe right in the town or guarding the power station, but we can't take that for granted, I reminded myself. Logically, there shouldn't be more than perhaps a single company of troops guarding the town and power station—if that. Even with the revised estimates of enemy military strength on Olviat they didn't have enough trained soldiers to guard every little town, every power station, and the enemy had hardly had time to move troops even if they had tracked the shuttle that moved us.

I went up to Iyi and Oyo and gave them the new heading, whispering from habit. "It's two and a half miles, direct line, from here to the power station," I added. "We'll stop half a mile out, then I'll want you two to sneak closer to have a direct look. You'll come back and report what you find. Don't use the radio unless you're under attack." They nodded and I told them to get started. As soon as they were the proper distance out on the new heading, I gestured for the rest of the squad to get up and moving again, and fell back into my position in the line.

Stealth was more important than speed. With most of the night in front of us we would have plenty of time to hit and get away and probably hit the town again from a different direction before first light, with time left to thoroughly lose ourselves in the forest. We moved carefully, as if there were a strong possibility that we might run into an enemy ambush at any moment. That wasn't out of the question, and even if it had been, it still made sense to operate as if it was a virtual certainty. Keep the men thinking about the possibility of trouble, don't let them get careless. Carelessness can become habitual, and the next time we might not get away with it.

I had a tracing of our course and a record of the distance we had covered on my head-up display, so I knew when to slow us down and when to stop the squad so we could wait for Iyi and Oyo to scout the power station. If there were any defenders around it, I was sure that the biraunta would spot them, and the odds were strong that they would escape detection themselves.

We moved out of line of march formation and into a defensive perimeter—sort of a football shape, with four men facing the town and three looking back the way we had come. Once we were on the ground, in position, there was time to take a drink and stretch. It got us off our feet and put the strain on different parts of our bodies as well as serving as a sort of mental punctuation as we switched from one mode to another.

My guess was that we would have at least fifteen minutes, more likely thirty, before Iyi and Oyo came back. They would take whatever time they needed to be certain what we were going to find. I lifted my faceplate and said, "Might as well eat a ration bar or something," in sort of a stage whisper—loud enough for my men to hear, not so loud that anyone more than a few yards past our perimeter would.

Eat when you've got the chance. You don't know when the next opportunity will come. I pulled a ration bar from a pocket, unwrapped it, and ate methodically, not taking my eyes off the forest. Except for the few seconds it took to get the wrapper off, I kept my right hand on my rifle, finger over the trigger guard, ready to go from eating to shooting in less than a heartbeat if necessary.

No enemy came to spoil our meal. It was close to thirty minutes before Iyi and Oyo returned. They came in and crouched on either side of me. Iyi did the talking, whispering.

"We got within fifty yards of the power station," he started. "There was one man, unarmed, doing something in one of the buildings, the smaller structure. He left and started back toward town, riding something similar to a human bicycle, whistling. We waited until he was out of sight, then went all the way around the power station. There were no soldiers, no electronic snoops. We left two snoops of our own, along the two likely routes between the station and the town."

"Good thinking," I whispered. I gestured for the squad to move closer so I could keep my voice down while I laid out the plan of attack, pointing out on my map just where I wanted everyone when we reached the target.

"We'll move in, plant our explosives, then head off at an angle, closer to the town instead of away from it. Take cover, set off the bombs, then move a little farther from the scene and wait to see how the locals react. Once they get involved with the explosion at the power station, we'll worry about hitting that one building in the center of town." I tapped the image on my map. "Intelligence says it's the town hall or something like that. Then we work east, away from town. After I report in, we do whatever they tell us. With any luck, CIC will arrange a pickup."

"Or they'll tell us to hoof it back toward the capital," Robbie said, very softly. "Nice thirty-mile hike to keep our minds active, and try to get there before sunset tomorrow so they can work us tomorrow night."

"No way," I said. "They're not going to let this much prime talent stay out of the fight long enough to hike thirty miles." At least, I *hoped* they wouldn't. Thirty miles of walking cross-country in full field gear almost made more fighting an attractive alternative.

I noted the scowl on Souvana's face at the irrelevant digression, but ignored it. In a way, I enjoyed his annoyance. Anyway, it was better to give the men a few seconds to lighten up than to keep all the tension bottled in. I had everyone take another drink of water before we started, as much to give them something else to think about as to keep them from getting dehydrated. Then I started Iyi and Oyo back the way they had gone before, and the rest of the squad followed, in two columns now, by fire team, thirty yards apart.

When we got to the spot I had decided on, south and a little east of the power station, we went to ground eighty yards out, positioned so we could cover the two men going in to plant the charges, just in case the enemy had brought in a surprise since Iyi and Oyo finished their reconnaissance. I had tapped Fang and Claw to plant the explosives this time. We discussed where they would put the charges—two packets of sticky-boom on the larger building, the one that held the machinery, and one packet on the smaller building, which we assumed held controls—and then I sent them off. The rest of us waited, watching over the barrels of our rifles, scanning two-thirds of a circle. I looked over my shoulder occasionally to check on the remaining third.

As soon as the charges were planted and armed, the two ghuroh started back toward us, moving quickly but taking advantage of every bit of cover along the way even though none of us had seen any indication of a threat. I waited for Fang and Claw to reach us, then moved the squad east, about a hundred yards closer to the town, and told everyone to get down.

There is something about blowing things up that I find satisfying, almost stimulating. Maybe it's unnatural, even pathological, but I am what I am. I looked to make sure my people had their heads down, then triggered the three charges simultaneously. I ducked, but saw the beginning of the blast, the burst of light from the detonation, before my faceplate kissed the grass. Next came waves of sound and heat washing over us, followed by a secondary explosion in the larger building and the beginning of the rain of debris—most of which didn't reach us. Trees came down, or shattered. Branches flew. Bits of the buildings and the equipment inside scattered up and around.

"Okay, let's get the hell out of here," I shouted as soon as there was something approaching silence.

CHAPTER 13

MAYBE I EXPECTED TONATIN CIVILIANS TO REACT the way human civilians on Earth might—running out to stand around and gawk at the fire, or try to put it out. I certainly didn't expect organized response, not right away. The divotect civilians on Dintsen had mostly remained in their houses until the fighting was over during our campaign there. I didn't know how civilians of other species might react to this sort of trouble.

When the power station blew, the town lost lights and communications. I moved my squad toward the location I had picked out, away from the town, but close enough to move toward the building in the center without much delay. Once all the civilians were either doing civilian things like running around asking each other what the hell had happened or hiding in their apartment buildings, we could sneak in close enough to launch our last rockets at their town hall, then make a hasty withdrawal.

For a minute or two, it looked as if my assessment might be correct. A few tonatin did head toward the power station, and I heard a few shouts—too far away for my audio pickups to tell what the words were. I gestured for Iyi and Oyo to start moving, then looked back toward the town.

I had a narrow field of vision through the trees, but I had chosen my position to give me a clear look down one broad street, flanked by apartment houses. As far out as we were, nearly three hundred yards from the nearest building, I couldn't see a lot of detail, but I could see more tonatin coming out of their buildings. Some were carrying weapons.

Civilians or soldiers? I wondered. I decided that they were probably civilians, if only because they were making no effort to be silent and were milling around in the open as no trained soldier would in these circumstances. These tonatin were certainly not noncombatants, not with weapons in their hands. If we had been closer, we could have listened in on whatever they were talking about . . . or planning, since our translator buttons were equipped for both primary tonatin languages.

"Don't trip over the civilians," I whispered. "Let's move." Us tripping over them, or them tripping over us: that was the only way civilians were going to find us at night. The civilians didn't have night-vision or fancy communications gear. If they tried to use flashlights, all that would do is make them clearer targets, or easier to avoid.

We moved, changing course once to stay away from five armed civilians who had ventured a short distance down a grassy lane cut into the forest. Inside the town, the streets were paved, but not even the main road leading toward the capital was more than a cleared grassy lane, suitable mostly for air-cushioned ground effect vehicles. The civilians moved fifty yards beyond the last building on the south side of town and stood in a tight group. One man could have mowed them all down with a single burst from his rifle.

The only defense I have for what happened next was that we were paying too much attention to that one group. Iyi and Oyo had gone ahead of the rest of the squad, as usual, and—like the rest of us—Robbie, the next man in line, was spending as much time looking over his shoulder toward those five tonatin as he was looking where he was going. He didn't *quite* literally trip over the two tonatin who had come into the forest without a light, but it was almost that bad. Before Robbie and the tonatin spotted each other, it was too late to avoid them.

Somehow, one of the tonatin got off the first shots—startled reflex maybe. He missed Robbie, the only one he could have seen, and the rest of us. Even Robbie could have been little more than a silhouette. Robbie returned fire. Nuyi, next in line, also fired when he saw the targets. Those two tonatin both went down, undoubtedly riddled with bullets, but with all the ruckus, the other civilians started firing in our direction.

"Hoof it!" I ordered over the squad channel. We were running before I added, "Let's get all the way around to the east side of town and try to hit the town hall from there."

That meant going nearly two miles. I had Iyi and Oyo angle farther south, so we would be less likely to trip over more civilians, before we got back on course. Once we were three hundred yards from the shooting, I slowed the pace. We went back to stealth instead of simply crashing through the underbrush to put distance between us and those armed civilians.

Yes, we had run from untrained civilians. It wasn't our job to fight them unless we had to. Armed civilians were fair game, but I wasn't going to push that if I didn't have to. I didn't give a damn what the brass might say, only what the voice in my head would say if I did things any other way.

HALF AN HOUR, THIRTY-FIVE MINUTES: I WASN'T exactly sure how long it had been since the shootings. We hadn't seen any more civilians and had moved to within two hundred yards of the east side of the town. I could see the building that was our second target. Tonatin might group together in apartment buildings, but they left plenty of open space between buildings. The last glow of the fires our first explosions had started had faded. We hadn't started a major forest fire—something of a surprise, almost a disappointment, to me. A nice wildfire might have distracted the locals nicely, given them something they might have considered more urgent than us.

"We're not going any closer than we have to," I whispered once I had gathered the squad close enough for everyone to hear. "The two of you with the launchers line up your shots, get them off, and be ready to beat it in a hurry." Fang and Nuyi had the rocket launchers, though each was down to his last two rockets. We would use all four rockets, then make tracks.

We were more careful now. No one wanted a repeat of what had happened before. Fang and Nuyi edged closer to the town, but moved away from each other to get two different angles on the target. The open plan of the town made that easy. The rest of us set ourselves in position to cover them. I had told Nuyi and Fang to coordinate the attack between them—to start firing at the same time. The rest of us waited and watched. I tried very hard not to look at the men with the launchers, but at the forest around us, especially in the direction of the town.

The sound of the rockets igniting in the tubes seemed so loud it startled me. Fifteen seconds later—as the first two were exploding, on target—the last pair of rockets was launched. We didn't stick around for the rest of the show. Fang and Nuyi pulled back and we started moving due east, wanting to put as much distance as possible between us and those civilians, as the last pair of rockets exploded. After hitting these tonatin twice, they might come after us in enough numbers to cause us problems.

THERE HAD BEEN NO NEED FOR ME TO REPORT the results of our two strikes against the town. The cameras and other sensors in the ships overhead would have seen the explosions, and it would not take the computers very many seconds to match that data with our orders. CIC would know we were available for further assignment. That information would be passed through the mill and at some point new orders would be issued for us.

None of that had to distract me from putting distance between us and the town. My responsibility was to keep my command intact, ready for whatever came next. Once we had a decent headstart on any pursuit, I slowed the pace. We changed course several times, generally to avoid crossing farm fields where there was no cover, always moving away from the town . . . and doing our best not to get too near the next tonatin community, four miles southeast of where we had hit.

After an hour, I called for a rest. We moved away from the animal trace we had been following, and arranged ourselves in a loose circle—so we could watch for anyone who might get near. I was breathing a little too heavily. Exertion and nerves. It felt good to get off my feet, but I couldn't relax *too* much. If nothing else, there was always the burden of leadership, seeing to my men and setting a good example.

Not everyone had his faceplate up to get a drink of water at once. Without anyone telling them, they spaced it out so that there were always eyes looking out through night-vision gear. Rifles were pointed outward, ready for action. *A good bunch,* I thought, nodding. *Maybe the best squad I had ever had.* Behind the concealment of my faceplate, I smiled, recalling how dismally pessimistic I had been about the combined regiment project in the beginning. There were still rough edges in our relationships within the squad, but I guess it's like that in the best families—not that I have any firsthand knowledge of the *best* families.

Family. I had been in the army a lot of years before I could say or think that word without feeling bile rising in my throat. Mine had disowned me when I joined the army, and my parents had ruined every relationship I had had with a girl before that. *Girls. Chrissie.* I had been doing a good job of not thinking about her, but she chose that moment to intrude. If I was the marrying type. . . . I shook my head and forced myself to look around; anything to avoid thinking about Chrissie. I didn't need distractions, especially not that kind.

"Meal break," I whispered, loud enough for the others to hear. "Take turns so we've always got eyes watching." Nuyi was closest to me in our little perimeter. I told him to eat while I took care of the looking. For a couple of minutes I was able to concentrate without difficulty. Then, just when my mind was starting to wander again, Nuyi said he had finished and pulled his faceplate back down. My turn to eat.

Army field rations are nourishing and not too tasteless, but it's best to shovel the food in without dwelling on it. I ate, but I started thinking about Chrissie again, telling myself to forget about her. Permanently. If I got back safely to Earth—if the army shipped us back to Fort Campbell, and there was no guarantee of that—just stay away from her. There were plenty of other bars. If we resumed, it wouldn't be long before she started thinking of something more permanent. That scared me more than a tonatin army. I didn't think I could handle it.

BY THE TIME WE HAD BEEN LYING AROUND FOR forty-five minutes, I was getting concerned about the lack of communications. I had gone back to listening to the reports from CIC, but there was nothing about our little piece of the action, and no orders came from Lieutenant Taivana, Captain Fusik, or anyone higher on the chain of command. It wasn't rational, but I started thinking, *What if they've forgotten about us?* I toyed idly with the idea of breaking electronic silence to ask if there were any orders for us, but I did not do that—and wouldn't unless a lot of hours went by without contact. Then I debated whether we ought to simply stay where we were or move on. I could have left that decision to the flip of a coin, but didn't. On balance, we were probably as well-off staying where we were.

"Unless something comes up, I think we'll stay here until command decides what to do with us," I told the others. "Try to get a little sleep. Half-and-half watches, by fire team. Souvana, your people take the first sleep. I'll wake you in an hour." I rearranged my fire team so we could watch all the way around our position more easily while second fire team settled in to grab an hour's sleep.

My brain was too active for sleep, so giving Souvana's team the first go hadn't been altruistic. For a time, I kept my concentration where it belonged, watching the forest. But there had been no hint of locals within a hundred yards—and we would have seen or heard any tonatin civilians who came within that range. We could have planted snoops, but I didn't see any pressing need, not without evidence that there were enemy *soldiers* in the vicinity.

Family. The word came to my head again, but I wasn't thinking of my childhood on Earth. These guys around me were the only family that counted now. Wherever they had come from, whatever their ancestry. *We've made it, I think,* I decided. *Despite all the prejudices, the fighting, and everything else, we've finally made it. We're a team. We're family.*

That made me feel pretty damned good. All I had left to do was get us off Olviat alive. I didn't want to lose any more . . . relatives.

IT WAS NEARLY DAWN BEFORE **I** GOT A CALL FROM battalion operations—from Major Wellman, no less, sent over from regimental headquarters for some unspecified reason. He kept his voice businesslike. For once, there was no sneer in it when he talked to me. "The tonatin are moving two companies of soldiers toward the town you hit. Move your squad along a heading of two-seven-five degrees to intercept and harass them." He had me open up my map and linked through the enemy unit's coordinates. We would have to push it to get to them before they reached that town and got close enough for its civilian residents to get into the act.

The only acknowledgment I gave Wellman was a single click of my transmitter—call it half a second's exposure if the enemy was searching for electronic emissions in our area. I roused the men who were sleeping, and got the squad up and moving. Everyone was relieved at the change, even though the object was to get close enough to attack maybe four hundred enemy soldiers in broad daylight. Souvana might have relished the prospect. He's one of those gung ho, damn-the-odds types you see in phony adventure vids. He liked to fight, never mind the reasons or odds.

We hadn't traveled far before I noticed that the sky was starting to lighten. The darkness wasn't quite so complete. When I flipped up my faceplate there were more shades of gray visible. Birds were moving in the trees. It wouldn't be long before we lost the advantage darkness gives us. Even civilians without night-vision systems would be able to spot us.

Our first concern was to get past the town without getting too close. Armed civilians might be out in the woods trying to defend their homes. I set our course to keep us a mile and a half from the town, hoping those civilians wouldn't patrol that far out.

It took just under an hour to reach a point due south of the town. We moved from tree to tree, doing our best imitations of ghosts. Even in the shadowy half-light early in the day, we can do a fair job of that. I dropped out of the line of march long enough to pull out my map to check on the latest known position of the tonatin detachment. They were still four miles away, and the same distance from the town. It was time to change direction—and pick up the pace.

I got Iyi and Oyo pointed on the new course, angling to intercept the enemy two and a quarter miles from the power station we had blown, and took thirty seconds to let everyone know that we were going to hit the nearest flank of the enemy detachment, then circle to the east, between those soldiers and the town. That might be trickier than the initial ambush.

The demands of moving fast and silent kept my focus where it belonged. There wasn't time to worry about what might happen to me in the fight, and certainly no time to worry about anything extraneous. The only breaks in my concentration came when I stopped to check my map. The blips representing the enemy force had moved. They were either not being too picky about electronic silence or they were visible to the cameras on one of our ships. It's hard to move four hundred infantrymen without showing some sign, even in the moderate sort of forest this part of Olviat was covered in.

Closer. When I figured that we were fifteen minutes from contact, I stopped the squad. We would take two minutes to catch our breath and calm down from the forced march. It's hard to hold a target if your breathing and heartrate are bounding. I went over what I wanted from everyone again, quickly. I didn't need many words to make sure my men knew what I expected.

I sent Oyo and Iyi out to scout the enemy detachment, locate the point and flanking squads, and so forth. I had Fang and Claw plant four land mines where the shrapnel would saturate a section of the logical path for a unit of four hundred men—the broad, grassy lane that connected the capital and the town we had attacked. The rest of us moved toward what looked like a good spot for an ambush—an area with ground cover, bushes, and vines, to conceal while we attacked . . . and give us a chance to break off the firefight before we could get tied down by a force that outnumbered us by forty to one.

Fang and Claw finished their work and took up positions along the line we had established. Then Iyi and Oyo returned. The enemy detachment was less than two minutes away.

CHAPTER 14

WE WATCHED THE POINT SQUAD—TWELVE MEN IN a staggered double column—move past, the nearest of them a hundred yards away, staying close to each edge of the grassy road, near cover. They had their weapons ready and scanned the terrain. We stayed low, almost flat to the ground, not moving at all. Since we had decent visual and thermal camouflage from our battle uniforms, movement was the biggest danger. The eye catches motion that doesn't belong and is drawn to it, which can give a man away.

There was a break between the point squad and the main enemy force of sixty yards. Again, there were two columns, near each edge of the road, and while these men weren't carrying their rifles ready for instant firing, they weren't slacking off either. Rifles were held in front of them, angled across their torsos at what is called port arms. They wouldn't lose half a second getting those weapons into firing position. These soldiers were watching the terrain around them as well.

The flanking squad on the near side was back almost to the center of the column. They came within thirty yards of us. I had decided to hold off springing our ambush until we had those flankers in sight—so our attack would pin them down as well as the main column. That would give us a better chance of getting away. I let the flankers move past, watched while the range between us increased to ninety yards.

Rather than break electronic silence before the attack, the signal for my men to fire would be when I opened up. I had told them that we would not take much time with the initial attack. We would hit with everything we had, then move before the enemy could maneuver to get back at us.

I held my breath the last few seconds. My finger moved to the safety switch, to make certain it was off. Then I squeezed off my first burst, maybe a dozen shots, targeting the flanking squad. After that, it was shorter bursts, three or four shots with each pull of the trigger, moving my aim along the columns of enemy soldiers. Even after they went down, we knew where they were and had clear lines of fire. A few RPGs angled at the main column, a couple at the flanking squad: we loosed as much mayhem as we could . . . for forty seconds, maybe forty-five. Then I gave the command to pull back. Electronic silence was unnecessary since we were in contact with the enemy.

If anyone in CIC was interested, they could monitor all our channels to find out what we were doing, and noncoms and officers have cameras in their helmets, and that feed goes to CIC as well. For that matter, anything we say inside our helmets can be monitored. There have been times when I think they even record our thoughts . . . but that's ridiculous. I think.

We pulled out one fire team at a time, the other covering, fire and maneuver. Move twenty yards and switch over. My fire team moved first, then held our new positions while Souvana's team went back past us and to our right, heading toward the front of the enemy formation. After my team's second move, we stopped firing, trying to break contact—to give the enemy a chance to lose track of where we were as we zigged and zagged. The tonatin kept firing for a minute or more after we stopped.

Because of the way we had been switching back and forth, Souvana's fire team was in the lead as we moved parallel to the road toward the front of the column, 140 yards from the lane. The enemy's point squad was the section most likely to get in our way before we were ready to strike again, and we didn't have Iyi and Oyo out in front to make certain we saw them before they saw us. Kiervauna was in front, and a 320-pound porracci can't be *quite* as stealthy as a seventy-five-pound biraunta. But he did a good enough job, giving us perhaps two seconds warning before the enemy point squad opened up—time enough for us to get behind cover and be ready to shoot back. We didn't hesitate more than fifteen seconds though before I started us off again—more fire and maneuver tactics to get around the enemy point. Nuyi got off a pair of RPGs to discourage them.

We broke contact again and circled north. I set off the mines we had left in the path of the main force. I was fairly confident they wouldn't have been able to move out of the kill zone yet. The need to care for casualties would limit the number of men they could send after us and make it more difficult for them to immediately move toward the town. The longer they were out in the woods, the more chances we might have to hit them.

We crossed the road far enough in front of the column that we couldn't be seen. The enemy's point squad was still far enough out of position that I didn't think they could see where we crossed either. We placed two more mines—the last we had—to catch the main column, then moved into the forest north of the road. The flanking squad on that side would be nervous about follow-up attacks, wondering if they would be next, and they might have strayed farther from the main troop than the flankers had on the other side, anxious not to get caught in the middle.

We found good cover and settled in to wait. It was a nervous time for me. The enemy knew we were around, and might have a decent estimate of our numbers. They would be alert and searching for us, and the sun was up. If the enemy commander reinforced his flank patrol, we might get trapped and be unable to fight clear. On the other hand, I hoped we were doing the one thing the enemy commander might not expect by exposing ourselves that way. Throw of the dice, flip of a coin. There's a lot of that in combat. The best plans can turn sour . . . and the worst turn golden. I think they even out in the long run. It just *seems* that good plans get screwed up more often than the reverse.

Iyi spotted the flanking squad and gave me a hand signal. I turned my head a little to watch as the flankers—two squads instead of one—moved past, fanned out in a series of skirmish lines rather than in line of march. *They've beefed up this patrol, that many fewer men with the main column,* I thought. If the enemy commander spread his men too thin, the unit would be that much easier to hit . . . and that much more difficult to get away from without being seen.

Wait! I told myself. I turned my attention back to the other side, waiting for some sign of the main column moving east again. The road was far enough away that I could only hope to spot men moving across one of the few gaps in the trees. We would hit near the end of the column unless we were forced into action sooner. Hit the end of the main force, then move into the woods again and hope for a shot at the rear guard, assuming they had one.

It was another ten minutes before I saw movement on the grassy lane. The tonatin companies were moving slowly, and every man I saw had his rifle out and ready, muzzle tracking back and forth, looking for something to shoot at—a lot more cautious than they had been when we first saw them.

How many men did they divert to the patrols? How many did they leave with the wounded? How many did we kill? Wound? I didn't have answers to any of those questions. If we had been exceptionally lucky, we might have killed or wounded 10 percent of their force. Any wounded who couldn't be moved would require medics and men to protect them. But I was working from very iffy guesses as I tried to determine when we should hit again—how many had gone past our position and how many were left to come. In a case like that, you have to be pessimistic, assume that you didn't hurt them nearly as bad as you hoped.

Wait just a little longer, I told myself. *A few more seconds.* I was watching the enemy column over the barrel of my rifle. I took a slow, deep breath and let it out just as slowly, then pulled in another, held it, and pulled the trigger. The others in the squad had been waiting for me. They joined in quickly. The tonatin soldiers went to the ground again—more quickly than before—and started to return fire. In the first seconds, very little of that enemy fire came near us, and we didn't wait for them to pinpoint our location. We were up and moving, first due north, then northwest, ready to try to curl in behind them, the one side we hadn't hit from yet.

Then Oyo fell, brought down by a bullet that hit his leg. Nuyi scooped up the wounded biraunta with hardly a pause and kept going, but he moved far more slowly with the extra burden. Robbie and I hung back to cover the others, though we had all stopped shooting when we started to break contact. When Souvana saw what had happened he halted his fire team long enough to let us get by. With a casualty who needed tending, any additional strikes against the tonatin would have to wait. We needed to get far enough from them to take a minute or two to patch Oyo's leg.

Iyi tended his brother when we stopped, but he was so agitated that it took him longer than it should have. His hands were shaking and his tail was coiling and uncoiling madly. The rest of us had spread into a quick perimeter. I thought there was better than an even chance that the IFers would come looking for us in strength. We had hit them too many times for them to just forget us and continue on toward that town.

The squad was in two separate areas, with the biraunta more or less in the middle. Once Nuyi had put Oyo down, he came over and took a position just to my right. Robbie was a bit farther to my left.

Get him patched well enough to move, Iyi, quickly, I

thought, glancing toward the two biraunta. *Anything else will have to wait.* I didn't bother telling Iyi that; he would know it, and he was working as quickly as he could.

I couldn't see or hear any trace of the enemy. I had my audio pickups cranked up to maximum. The tonatin couldn't be *too* far away, certainly no more than two hundred yards— unless they had turned and headed in the opposite direction. I didn't figure the odds of that were very high.

Where are they? I glanced at the biraunta. We had to move. Iyi *had* to hurry and get his brother fit to travel, even if we had to carry him. Biraunta weigh so little that any of the rest of us could carry him for a distance, and either of the porracci could carry him all day and not notice the extra burden.

Iyi turned toward me and gave me a signal with his left hand. We could go. Nuyi and I were just starting to get up when I heard a familiar noise crashing through the leaves overhead—a rocket-propelled grenade. I hardly had time to note the sound before. . . .

LANCE CORPORAL ROBERT A. MCGRAW

We were just getting ready to move after Private Iyi patched up his brother well enough to move. I saw Dragon—Sergeant Drak—start to get to his feet. That meant it was time for the rest of us to get up. I guess the sarge heard the incoming RPG before I did. It wasn't until he started to drop that I threw myself to the ground, and I was on my way down before I heard the grenade. I didn't know if one of the enemy soldiers had spotted us or if it was simply a lucky— for them—shot. You don't think about things like that while the crap is going off.

Nuyi turned toward Dragon, trying to knock him flat, maybe even to cover him. Nuyi took a direct hit from that grenade. Another grenade hit less than a second after the first, and very close to it. I took a couple of shards of shrapnel in my left leg but, to tell the truth, I wasn't aware of it right then. I didn't feel a thing. There was too much else happening.

"The sergeant's hit," I shouted on the squad channel. Sure, I was breaking electronic silence, but Souvana had to know right away. With Dragon down, Souvana was in command. There always has to be someone *in command*. Anyway, someone *on the enemy side* seemed to know exactly where we were.

I needed a couple of seconds to realize that Nuyi and the sergeant weren't the only ones who had been hit, though I still didn't know I was one of the wounded. Iyi was hit; he had fallen across his brother, so I couldn't tell if Oyo had been wounded again. Nuyi—well, he was clearly dead. The best body armor in the universe won't stop a two-inch diameter grenade that explodes against it. The divotect had been literally blown to pieces. His head was no longer attached to his body. His helmet had been blown past me, with however much of his head was left. I couldn't tell about Dragon. He was covered in blood and pieces of Nuyi. He didn't move in the short time I had to look his way. Before I could think about crawling over to check him out, we had incoming rifle fire, and that took precedence.

I started firing at the approaching tonatin on Corporal Souvana's order. There were only five of us able to fight—two porracci, two ghuroh, and me. The rest of the squad was either dead or wounded. I couldn't see any way that the rest of us could avoid joining them for long.

Corporal Souvana must have left the squad channel open, or I wouldn't have heard the call he made to CIC. "We have the enemy on two sides, at least a full company, and we have four men down, dead or wounded. We cannot escape, and we cannot hold without immediate help."

I didn't hear any reply, but Souvana's receiver would have fed any answer directly to his ears, not broadcast it inside his helmet. I couldn't see how anyone could get help to us quickly enough to matter. "Immediate" hardly began to state how desperate our need was. It looked as if almost that entire enemy column was coming at us. There had to be far more than two hundred tonatin. The nearest were 150 yards away, putting down heavy rifle fire as they came. We needed more than immediate help. We needed a full-blown miracle . . . and I had given up believing in miracles a long time before. But . . .

"Get your heads down and keep them down!" I didn't recognize the voice—it wasn't anyone in the squad—but I did as I was told, and our miracle came. It started with an artillery salvo—rockets—with the enemy skirmish line no more than sixty yards from us. It hit all around us. I couldn't tell how many rockets exploded, but it had to be at least a dozen, all within twenty or thirty seconds. They knocked over trees and sent wood and dirt flying so madly that a lot of it passed right over our heads. Then I heard a fighter screaming in. It must have been on its way in when we got in trouble or it couldn't have arrived that quickly. It strafed the enemy positions and fired all of its rockets, making three quick passes. More artillery started going off just after the pilot started climbing out of the way. This time I think it was a mixture of rockets and shells. The guns are slower. It takes their shells longer to cover a given distance.

"McGraw, stay here and check on the casualties," Corporal Souvana said. "The rest of us will make sure there aren't enough of the enemy left to cause trouble."

The enemy was no longer shooting at us. That was certain. The barrage hadn't lasted more than a minute, but it had been intense. Still, I thought the corporal was out of his head to go asking for trouble that soon. There might still be a considerable number of the enemy able to fight.

I was a little shaky as I got to my feet while Souvana, Kiervauna, Fang, and Claw started moving toward the enemy skirmish line. They moved carefully, going from cover to cover, but on their feet, not crawling. They did not draw any fire. The only fire around was the other kind, trees and grass burning from the explosions. There was more smoke than fire though, and an intense smell of burning wood.

The first thing I did was pull Nuyi's remains off Sergeant Drak. Dragon had a hole in his side big enough for me to stick my fist in. I know, because that's what I had to do—after I pulled Nuyi's thigh bone out. That was what had caused Dragon's wound. The jagged end of that bone had penetrated his side, just above the waist—and below the edge of his body armor. I had to reach inside to make sure there were no broken shards of bone still inside, then shoved both of the large bandages in my first aid pouch into the wound to try to stop the bleeding. Sergeant Drak was still alive, but the way he was losing blood he wouldn't be for long. I packed more cloth in on top of the bandages and tied everything in place. I didn't think he had much chance, but I had to try.

It wasn't until I had done everything I could for Sergeant Drak that I went to check on our biraunta. It's not that I have anything against biraunta, or any of the other races in the regiment, it's just . . . well, Sergeant Drak was our squad leader as well as the only other human in the squad, and I could see how bad his wound was, so I took care of him first.

The delay didn't make any difference. Iyi was dead. When I pulled his helmet off I discovered that a hunk of shrapnel had come up under it at an angle from the neck directly into his brain. He must have died instantly. Oyo was alive though, and I couldn't see that he had suffered any additional wounds.

I got Iyi off Oyo and checked Oyo as carefully as I could. He was unconscious, but he had been before. Then I went to see if Sergeant Drak was still alive. He was, but his pulse was so weak that I needed a moment to find it. I started limping while I was going from Oyo to Dragon. That was when I first felt my own wounds. After I sat down and determined that the sergeant was still alive, I looked at my own leg and saw where the bits of shrapnel had hit. The wounds were bleeding, and I didn't have any bandages to put over them, so I had to make do with fabric ripped from my uniform leg. That didn't have the extra medical nanoagents to speed up healing, but I figured I wasn't hurt so badly that it would make much difference. My leg could wait. I did slap a pain patch on.

I called Corporal Souvana to tell him about the dead and the wounded. Just then, I didn't give a damn about electronic silence even though we were apparently no longer in direct contact with the enemy. The corporal listened to my report, then said, "We're on our way back." I was surprised that he hadn't reprimanded me for using the radio. If our positions had been reversed, I might have.

It was another ten minutes before the others got back from inspecting the remains of the enemy attack. "There must be two hundred enemy dead," Souvana said when he got to me—after checking on Dragon and Oyo, and asking how I felt. "CIC is sending a shuttle to pick us up. There will be a medical technician aboard, and several medtanks."

"How long?" I asked. Both of us had our faceplates up. Kiervauna and the ghuroh were watching the forest around us, not ready to concede that the enemy had no force left close enough to resume the attack, even though they had seen no one.

Corporal Souvana lowered his faceplate for an instant, to glance at the timeline at the top of the display, before he answered. "About twenty-one minutes," he said. "We need to move to the LZ, three-quarters of a mile to the north." Understand, the corporal didn't say "three-quarters of a mile." I'm sure he used porracci distance, but the translator buttons they made us stick in our ears translate units of measurement automatically.

Kiervauna picked Dragon up and carried him. I was going to carry Oyo, but my leg wouldn't support the extra weight. It was all it would do to support me. So Fang picked up the biraunta and we started moving toward the landing zone. After the first few dozen yards, Claw moved close to me, ready to give me a hand if I couldn't walk.

It was a near thing. I had a pain patch on, but walking aggravated my wounds until I had tears running from my eyes. I did make it to the LZ under my own steam, but didn't have enough left to hobble onto the shuttle when it landed. I needed help.

I watched while the medic looked over Dragon. He was shaking his head before he slipped the med-tank over the sergeant. "I don't see how he lasted this long," the medic said.

CHAPTER 15

I GUESS I KNOW NOW WHAT IT'S LIKE TO BE dead—some of it. The battalion surgeon told me I had come as close as anyone he had ever treated who made it back. "When you lose a lot of blood quickly, the result of severe trauma, the medical nanobots in your system close down everything but the most essential systems. They make sure that blood and oxygen get to your brain. They fight to keep the heart working. As long as the heart and brain survive, everything else can be regenerated. Everything else is . . . expendable at a time like that. Sometimes it's not enough. With someone who lost as much blood as you did, it shouldn't have been enough. But it was," he said.

There wasn't much I could do yet but listen. I was still woozy, lying flat on my back on a fold-up cot with the surgeon sitting on the edge. The cot creaked noisily every time he shifted his weight a little. There was a roof over my head, the plastic tarp of a pavilion—a tent without sides. It was still light out, but dim under the canopy. They had just peeled the medtank off me, six hours after the surgery. There had been too much torn up in my gut for them to leave it to the medical nanobots. Now, the skin was healed over the wound, and my internal organs were functioning, but there was still a hollow space in my side, a dent that would have hidden a billiard ball. Not all of the meat had been regenerated yet. That would take time, the surgeon said.

"What about the rest of my squad," I asked, appalled at how weak and squeaky my voice sounded.

"I don't know," the surgeon replied. "Just rest now. It'll be another two or three hours before you're fit for duty. At least there's no significant neural damage. That might have laid you up for weeks."

I shook my head gingerly, as if I feared it might come off. Hell, maybe I did fear that. I had spent time in a med-tank before the surgeon got to me, then afterward, and I still wasn't back to full function. That alone said a lot about how serious my wounds had been. *You've used up a lifetime of good luck,* I thought. *Anything after this is gravy.*

There was one hell of a gap in my memory. I didn't remember getting hit, and I had no solid memory of pain, but I could recall the sound of a grenade coming in. Then a shock and the blank that really hadn't broken until a few minutes before, when I woke with the surgeon sitting next to me.

The blank wasn't complete. There were bits and pieces floating around in my head that didn't seem to have any connection to . . . anything I knew about. They started coming together, but not in any coherent order. It wasn't gunfire and explosions, or medics and the surgeon. Maybe it was fragments of dreams. Maybe it was something else. My clearest memory was of an intense white light, impossibly bright, but not painful to look at—sheer illumination that showed nothing but itself. And blackness so complete as to exclude the very possibility of light, or sight. The blackness of a universe in which every star had burned itself out, a universe where light no longer existed. And a strange thought: *A perfect light that showed nothing and a perfect dark that hid everything are essentially identical.*

The memories, or whatever they were, troubled me. I closed my eyes. The surgeon had gone. No doubt he had other patients to visit or new casualties coming in who needed his attention. The extremes of light and dark, some sort of music far in the background, unrecognizable; beyond even categorizing. There was just a memory that *something* had been there in the back of my head. Maybe if I had been more religious I would have built something out of the fragments—I've heard of other people making claims like that—but all I had were troubling bits and pieces, and no hook to hang them on.

The general anesthetic wore off, leaving my head a little clearer. The feeling of living a dream faded, but the memories of what I had seen, or imagined, were slower to recede. I was more aware of sounds around me, but opening my eyes again was too much bother. There was still a numbness to my side, where the medical nanobots were keeping me from feeling any pain. I don't know how much time had passed after the surgeon left, but I started to feel hungry, and I wasn't certain if the repair work on my gut had progressed far enough to allow me to eat.

"Sarge?" The voice was soft, the word hesitant, as if the speaker didn't want to wake me if I were asleep. I opened my eyes. Robbie McGraw was standing next to the cot, but squatted when he saw I was awake.

"I guess I'm going to make it," I said, and my voice sounded stronger than it had when I talked to the surgeon.

"You gave us quite a scare. I thought you were a goner. We all did."

"According to the doc, I should have been," I said. "Tell me what happened."

Robbie hesitated. "Time enough for that after you're back on your feet, Sarge," he said, almost stumbling over the words—something he had never had trouble with before.

"Tell me." I tried to make my voice firmer. This time, I was certain that Robbie was hesitating. He didn't want to answer. He looked around, as if hoping someone would come to his rescue. I told him again to tell me what happened, and he cleared his throat, still stalling. I wasn't going to let him off the hook. The news was obviously bad, or he wouldn't be so hesitant about giving it to me.

"Two RPGs hit, almost simultaneously, within . . . inches of each other, just before most of that enemy force we had been picking at surrounded us and moved in." He stopped, looked around as if for some escape route, then when he continued he wouldn't meet my eyes. "Iyi and Nuyi were both killed."

At first, my mind rebelled, shouted, *"No!"* at me. I lost track of what Robbie was saying as he continued. Later I had to have him repeat it, go through the entire incident in detail. He didn't finish the story the first time. He stopped when I started bawling, sobbing noisily. I've seen more death than any man should ever have to. I had lost men before and it never hit me so hard. At first, I think it was Nuyi's death that hit me the hardest. I saw his face in my head, that melancholy hangdog look he had just about all the time, even when he was happy.

I buried my face in the thin pillow they had given me, trying to smother the sounds of my sobbing, maybe trying to bury the images I was seeing. At some point, Robbie quit talking and just waited for me to get it out of my system. When I finally opened my eyes, he was still there.

"Oyo's okay now, physically. So am I, and I asked one of the technicians here, and he said you'll be fit for duty in a couple of hours," Robbie said, but his voice was faltering through the whole recitation. But he didn't say anything about, the way I had carried on.

"How'd we get out of that mess?" I asked, and he told me about the artillery strike Souvana had called in almost on our own heads to wipe out what remained of those two enemy companies, and the shuttle that had pulled us out. How they had worked on me in the shuttle, how close it had been. Well, the surgeon had already told me about *that.*

"Souvana has the rest of the squad. We're bivouacked about two hundred yards from here, over to your left. Most of the company has been pulled out of action. We're regrouping for whatever comes next."

I closed my eyes. "In two days, I managed to get a third of my men killed, and damned near got myself killed as well," I said, not voicing the thought that raced behind it: *Maybe it would have been better if I had died too.* I guess Robbie caught the thought as well as the spoken words.

"What the hell are you getting at?" he asked, his voice a bit louder, more *solid.* "We're the freakin' stars of this show after blowing two power stations and taking out half a battalion of enemy soldiers. Captain Fusik has put both you and Souvana in for medals. And Nuyi for throwing himself in front of you, trying to knock you down when those grenades came in." I didn't learn until later that Robbie had also been put up for a medal, for keeping me alive until help got to us. "We even got a 'well done' from General Ransom."

That didn't make me feel any better. I recalled what Major Wellman had told me—a lifetime before, when he informed me that I had "volunteered" for the 1st Combined Regiment: "I don't see how a soldier deserves a medal for somehow surviving when damned near his entire platoon was killed around him." Well, this time I had only lost part of a squad, not most of a platoon, but. . . . Hell, with Wellman on the staff at regiment, I was sure to hear from him again, complete with sneers. He had a cushy staff job. He wasn't likely to do anyone a favor by getting himself killed, despite the nice little daydreams I had enjoyed when I learned that he was in 1st Combined.

I blinked, remembering something Robbie had said a little earlier. "You said Oyo was okay, *physically.* What the hell did you mean?"

Robbie shrugged. "He's taking Iyi's death . . . badly. I mean, they *were* identical twins. That's got to be bad for anyone, and those two were closer than any people I've ever come across. He just sits there, staring dead ahead, and he won't respond to anyone or anything. You know what the biraunta are like, with their tails coiling and uncoiling and swishing around all the time. Oyo's doesn't even twitch now. And the way they're so damned terrified of porracci? Well, Souvana tried to get Oyo off his butt to eat, or something, and Oyo just picked up his rifle and flicked the safety off. He didn't *point* it at Souvana or anything like that, but . . ." Robbie shook his head. "I got in the middle and took the rifle from Oyo, then convinced Souvana to back off, to let it slide until you got back. But something's gonna have to be done. I just don't know what."

I didn't know either, and I couldn't force myself to try to figure it out. I just couldn't find the energy to care.

A FEW MINUTES LATER A MEDIC CHASED ROBBIE off and brought me supper. There wasn't any real food, nothing to *chew* on—just broth, fruit-flavored gelatin, and coffee. None of it was satisfying, but it did stop the hunger pangs temporarily. "You can get something solid to eat later," the medic said. "The doc just wants to give your stomach a little more time to recover." There wasn't much I could do but accept the situation. The only way I was going to get any meat was to bite the medic's arm.

It was nearly sunset before the surgeon came back. He asked me how I felt and when I said I felt okay, he had me stand up quickly—just to see if I got dizzy, I guess. He looked in my eyes, flicked a light on and off, then peered into my ears.

"Believe it or not, you're ready to return to full duty," he said when he had finished probing my side and looking at all the data my monitor had recorded over the past hours. "You may feel a little tenderness in your side for the next couple of days, even a sensation like something is moving in there until your body finishes regenerating the lost tissue, but that shouldn't hold you back. Ask the sergeant at the desk where you're supposed to go." He pointed.

"Ah, what about clothes?" I asked. I wasn't wearing much except the loose shorts they give you in the hospital, sort of glorified underwear.

The surgeon grinned. "The sergeant will have new

clothes for you and as much of your gear as you had when you came in. I would guess that your unit has the rest of your things, whatever is left. Good luck, Sergeant."

THE SERGEANT PROVIDED A FRESH UNIFORM ISSUE. As for my gear, the only thing that had come to the hospital was my helmet, and it was no longer fully functional. There were several dings from shrapnel, and the electronic diagnostic routine uncovered three separate component failures before it announced that the diagnostics program itself was faulty and told me that I should have the helmet replaced or serviced by a technician.

I found my way back to where the squads and platoons from my company were, to the side of the clearing, under cover of trees. Everything was around the perimeter of the clearing, which was being used as a landing strip. I asked a corporal from third platoon where the company command post, CP, was, and he pointed to a tent. When I got there I found Captain Fusik and Tonio sitting on folding stools. Both looked as if they had been through nearly as much crap as I had. I reported for duty, officially, saluting and all the rest.

"Glad to see you're back on your feet, Sergeant," Captain Fusik said, getting up to return my salute. "Your squad has done one hell of a job. Sorry about the men you lost. I know it hurts. It still hurts when I lose people, and I've lost more than just your men since we came here."

"Yes, sir. I know. It's just . . . well, that doesn't make it any easier."

"Of course not. Look, we probably won't be going back into action before tomorrow. That's the latest I've had from battalion anyway. Get back to your squad and get yourself squared away. We're in the middle of reorganizing, probably three platoons to a company, to fill in the gaps. You'll be getting replacements but I don't know who they'll be yet."

"Yes, sir. Ah, my helmet's electronics are shot, sir, and my weapons are gone. We have someone to replace them?"

"Of course. Sergeant Xeres will see you get what you need."

Tonio had also stood when the captain did. Now, he took me by the arm and led me out of the tent. "I thought we lost you this time," he said once we were away from the captain.

"I thought I lost me too. Maybe I should have after losing a third of my men. Been a lot easier on everyone else."

"Stuff that shit, Dragon," Tonio said. "We've both lost men before. It wasn't your fault they got killed. We're fighting a war, and that means soldiers die. They ever find a way to fight wars without getting soldiers killed, they'll probably quit fighting them. Come on, we'll get your helmet fixed, then I'll take you to your squad and see what else you need to replace."

"Hold on a second." I stopped. "How come you were in the CP when I got there? Where's Greeley?" Greeley Halsey was the company lead sergeant.

Tonio shook his head. "Greeley bought it last night, along with Lieutenant Taivana." I whistled softly. The platoon sergeant and the company's executive officer. "For the time being, I'm acting platoon sergeant. For the time being," Tonio repeated. "I don't have the seniority to keep the job permanently."

"Crap, seniority doesn't count for everything, not in a war. You're the best man in the company for the job," I said. "The way we're losing people . . . and trying to build more regiments, you'll keep the job." If he did keep the job permanently, I would be in line for the job of platoon sergeant, a promotion—something that had always been hard for me to win. Maybe the brass wouldn't look so closely at my past record with a war on. As long as Major Wellman wasn't part of the promotion committee.

·   ·   ·

ROBBIE SAW US COMING AND CAME TO MEET US before we got to the rest of the squad. Tonio said he would talk to me later and turned to head back to the CP. I had a brand new helmet. The technician said that was easier than trying to work up fresh electronics in the old one since it was so damaged.

"I've got your rifle and the rest of your gear, Sarge," Robbie said. "They haven't given us any tents, but we've got sleeping rolls and tarps to put over our heads if it rains . . . and I hear it's supposed to."

"They haven't, by any chance, set up a field kitchen, have they?" I asked. "I'm starving."

Robbie shook his head. "No kitchen, no hot food, but we've got plenty of battle ration packs."

"Better than nothing. I'd better talk to Souvana first . . . then Oyo."

"I've got your stuff over there." Robbie pointed. "I'll pick out a couple of ration packs for you."

I nodded and he moved off. Souvana first. He was sitting at the edge of the squad area, looking away from the encampment, as if he didn't trust whatever guards were supposed to be keeping us safe. I don't know if he knew I had returned, but he heard me coming, turned his head to look, then got to his feet.

"You did good, Corporal," I said, before he could say anything. "Thank you for getting us out." First things first, and from what Robbie had told me, it was entirely due to Souvana that any of us got out.

Souvana made a low grumbling noise in his throat. "I did only my duty, Sergeant. I return the squad to you now."

I didn't feel like smiling so I didn't have to hide it, but returning the squad to me must have galled Souvana no end; if he had been a little slower that morning, or a little less successful, the squad might have been his to keep—if I had not survived. From the beginning of the 1st Combined Regiment Souvana had never hidden his belief that he was more qualified to run the squad than I was. After the past couple of days, I was almost inclined to agree.

"Though I do not relish the need to say this, I believe we might have to replace one more member of the squad, Sergeant."

"Oyo?" I asked, and he nodded. "I heard what happened. You do know *why* he acted the way he did, don't you?"

"Yes, Sergeant. He acted from overwhelming grief. I understand that, and I do not wish to press charges for what he did. But Oyo does not appear to be able to deal with that grief, and if he cannot, he poses an unacceptable danger to the squad when we go back into action. He should be remanded to the medical staff for treatment . . . or to be sent home as unfit for further duty, if that is their assessment of his condition."

"It may come to that," I said, and the sigh was in my mind if not in my voice. "But I would hate to lose another member of the squad if it can be avoided. I'm going to talk with him now. If I can't make any progress, we'll see if we can find someone who can help him. If not . . ." I let a shrug finish that sentence for me.

"Of course, Sergeant. We must make every effort to help him. He is part of our squad."

I nodded, slowly. *Our squad:* I didn't miss the way Souvana said that. Maybe the edge was gone from Souvana's natural competitiveness, at least for a while.

I WENT OVER TO WHERE OYO WAS LYING—AS FAR from the rest of the squad as he could get—and knelt next to him. At first, he gave no indication he even noticed me. After a couple of silent minutes, his eyes did move, turning toward me for just an instant before he went back to staring straight up into the night sky.

"I'm sorry about your brother," I said, little above a whisper. "I share some measure of your grief, though I can't possibly feel it as deeply you do." Oyo looked at me again, turned his head to meet my eyes. "There's no way I can make the hurt go away. I wish I could. I wish I could bring Iyi back. I can't. But we have to go on—the squad, and you."

"Half of me is dead," Oyo said. "How can a half go on as a whole? I cannot even think of what any future must hold without Iyi. It would have been much better if I had died with my brother. I *should* have died then, fast, all at once, instead of waiting to die slowly now."

"But you didn't die. I don't know anything about your religion, what you believe in, but there must be a purpose you can find, a reason to go on. It's bad enough that your brother died. Don't let his death destroy you as well."

"I can't think. I can't see anything but my brother's face. There is a mirror in my mind I cannot turn away from, cannot close my eyes to. Ever."

"We'll find people to help you. Maybe a biraunta doctor who can help you find a way through your grief."

Oyo stared vacantly at me, as if he was no longer aware that I was there. "Will you come with me?" I asked. After another long moment, he got to his feet. I took him to the field hospital and explained the situation to the sergeant at the desk.

"We'll get him help," the sergeant said. "There's a system in place." He looked at Oyo. "You're not the first to have this sort of problem, Private. I'm sure we can get you the help you need."

I went back to the squad then, after stopping by the CP to tell Tonio that we were another man short—at least temporarily. He nodded. And sighed.

CHAPTER 16

NIGHT. DARK. QUIET. THERE WERE NO LIGHTS visible around the encampment. I doubt that any were burning except in the tent where the surgeon did his operating, and the fabric of the tent was opaque enough that no light showed from it. Everyone else did what they had to do with the aid of helmet night-vision systems. I knew the only way I was going to sleep was with the aid of a medical patch, and I was reluctant to go that route after losing most of a day to unconsciousness. I had come too close to the permanent sleep. I wasn't all that eager to lose more conscious time voluntarily.

Although there had to be half a battalion of soldiers in and around the area—maybe five hundred men, rangers and line troops—there was rarely much activity close to me. Twice before midnight, shuttles came in with wounded or supplies, then left minutes later. That was the only real noise. The sounds of fighting were too distant to be more than a muffled rumble, like a summer thunderstorm miles away. The squads posted on sentry duty were as silent as possible, waiting for anyone to test our defenses. This might be a rest area, but it was on a hostile world, not far from real fighting.

I spent a couple of hours listening to the reports from CIC, trying to figure out what was going on, trying to catch up on everything I had missed, listening through endless repeats for the occasional insertion of something new. If the message rocket the local garrison sent off when we arrived had gotten through, the Ilion Federation might have a relief force already on its way; they might arrive in-system at any moment, giving us a few scant hours to prepare to meet them. If an enemy relief force arrived before we had the situation on the ground resolved in our favor, it might be all over for us. It might simply depend on how large a force the enemy had been able to assemble quickly.

There was no clear feeling that the situation on the ground *would* be resolved in our favor anytime soon—if ever. I didn't expect CIC to say, "We're getting our butts kicked royally," but none of the reports said that we weren't, or that we were "mopping up the last pockets of enemy resistance." Nobody was sounding the victory horn. We had hurt the defenders. They had hurt us. Fighting was going on in half a dozen isolated battles. Enemy casualties were being described as heavy. Our casualties were being described as moderate. I had been in the army long enough to know that the real meaning of that was that we were losing men as rapidly as the IFers were. Perhaps more rapidly. Adjectives never mean the same concerning your own force as the enemy.

Part of the capital city was burning, though CIC seemed uncertain how the fire had started. All towns within sixty miles of the capital were without electrical power, except in a few isolated areas—places that might have had auxiliary power sources—and even there power was apparently being reserved for emergency use. The intensity of the artillery duels had lessened. Both sides had lost artillery units, and ammunition was getting scarce on the ground. The enemy had no fighters in the air, but they had downed perhaps a quarter of our fighters.

Concentrating on the radio reports helped me not think about what had happened to my squad, but it was not a foolproof distraction. *I wouldn't have cried like that if my brother had been killed,* came to me during one repeated item on the feed from CIC. At first, I sloughed off that thought, but it came back to nag at me. My brother and parents. For all practical purposes, I didn't have any blood kin. If they were still alive—I didn't know, one way or the other—they had disowned me years before, and once I had gotten past the worst of my anger and hatred I had, for the most part, forgotten about them. As much as I could.

Nuyi had been more my brother than my brother ever had been. Dark purple skin, face like an overgrown iguana, and all, Nuyi had been more kin to me than anyone I shared DNA with. Nuyi. Iyi. Jaibie. Members of different species, alien in appearance, heritage, and background, but people I cared about, people who cared about me. Twice, Nuyi had risked his life for me—once during our first campaign together, on Dintsen, and then here on Olviat, where he paid the price. Offhand, the only human I could think of who I had ever felt closer to than I had to Nuyi was Tonio Xeres, and we had become close the same way—serving together, fighting together, suffering together. Our closeness came from blood spilled, not blood shared through birth, but blood thicker than blood, if you see my meaning.

MY SIDE STARTED TO BOTHER ME, THE WAY THE surgeon had warned me it might. It felt as if some tiny creature was doing jumping jacks and push-ups in the hole where I had lost all the meat. Robbie had told me how I had been wounded, speared by Nuyi's thigh bone. Nuyi's flesh had served as a brake, keeping the bone from going all the way through me. Thinking about that made the discomfort worse. My mind started to play around with images of some miniature version of the dead divotect inside that hollow space in my side. Or his spirit. Divotect believed in spirits, ghosts. I had learned that while we were trying to liberate Dintsen. One evening while we were talking, Nuyi had spoken of the spirits of divotect dead around us as if he could actually see them. It had made me a little jumpy.

My left hand and arm started to tremble as I fought the urge to touch my side. I took several slow breaths, trying to concentrate, but my breathing got out of control; I nearly hyperventilated. I squeezed my eyes shut and concentrated on breathing slowly inside my closed helmet to get some carbon dioxide recirculating. You tilt your head forward to close the gap under your chin; that was something they taught us in boot camp. Then I stood and stretched—at length, going through what was almost a set of warming-up exercises.

Keep a grip on or you'll get your head as messed up as Oyo's is, I told myself. There was a little anger—at myself—behind the thought. I knew better. I had been around.

Oyo. I didn't know if he would be coming back, or how long it might be before he got *his* head together enough to stay with the unit if he did. *If.* I hoped he would, and soon, not just for his own sake but for the sake of the squad. I wasn't optimistic. Sure, modern medicine can do wonders, and mental illness is almost unheard of, among any of the starfaring races. Any trouble caused by chemical imbalance, physical injury, or genetic aberration can be remedied as quickly as a scratched ass, but there are still some disorders medicine can't touch. The inner workings of the brain still hold some secrets.

Earlier, in the first hour or so after I got back from taking Oyo to the field hospital, the remaining members of the squad had each come over to talk with me—Fang and Claw together, Kiervauna and Robbie separately. Everyone wanted to see how I was managing. Kiervauna and the two ghuroh expressed regrets over our losses, and told me what they had seen during the incident—nobody's memories differed much from Robbie's. Maybe most of the others wanted some sort of reassurance, some hope that the rest of us wouldn't suffer the same fate Nuyi and Iyi had. And everyone wanted to know if I had learned anything about how long we would be where we were or what we might be asked to do next.

"All I know is what the captain and Sergeant Xeres told

me before," I told Kiervauna. "We're reorganizing the entire Ranger Battalion, one company at a time. They're moving people around to fill as many squads as possible. We'll probably be three platoons instead of four. It will probably be morning before we get our replacements." I said virtually the same thing to Fang and Claw. And to Robbie.

Souvana didn't come to see me. During one of my more restless periods, I went to him. He was still sitting up, looking outward, as if he had ordered himself to remain on watch all night, and I told him the same thing I had told the others, with almost an apology. "I should have told you before, but I didn't think to."

"Sergeant Xeres informed me, while you were still in hospital," Souvana said, whispering, glancing at me only for an instant. "He was not certain then that you would be returning, and informed me as acting squad leader."

"The squad would have been yours if I hadn't," I said.

"Yes," was his only reply, one flat word without any intonation I could notice.

"When the time comes for you to have a squad of your own, I'm sure you will command it with honor, Souvana," I said.

He stared at me for a moment then nodded. "Thank you."

It wasn't a peace treaty between us, but maybe it was a start at a truce. I grinned. "And someday, I'll figure out how to beat you in hand-to-hand combat." He didn't return my grin, but the snort he gave me was almost friendly—for Souvana.

IT WAS AN HOUR OR TWO PAST MIDNIGHT BEFORE I lay down to try to sleep. Daybreak was a long way off with the longer day, and night, on Olviat. I still didn't want to use a patch to sleep. We might be called on to help defend the area or to go out on patrol at any time and I didn't want to take a chance . . . in addition to my reluctance to retreat into oblivion. Regular sleep would have been welcome since I didn't know how long I might be on the go come morning. Replacements would be arriving from one of the other squads. I would need to take time getting to know them, fitting them into the squad. And—probably sooner rather than later—we would be sent back into the fight and it might be who-knew-how-long before another chance for relatively safe sleep might come my way.

A soldier learns to sleep when he can and, normally, I don't have any trouble sleeping in the field, even if the prospect is for no more than ten or fifteen minutes. Sometimes, that's all the time there is, and even a few minutes can keep you going for quite a time afterward. But the medtank had given me the equivalent of far more than eight hours of sleep. My thoughts did the rest. I had been as close to dead as anyone could be and still come back. I couldn't forget that, couldn't put it out of my mind for long. This wasn't the first time I had been wounded and spent time in a medtank, but it was the worst I had ever been hurt. I worried what it would do to me the next time I was in combat, the closest I had ever come to buying that infamous farm. Would the memory of how close I had come to death interfere with doing my job? Some people are never the same after a serious wound. Some just can't handle it in their heads, and there's no way to know in advance who can and who can't. You don't know until you've been put to the test again. And again.

Finally, though, I did doze. It must have been after three in the morning before I drifted off. Even then, it wasn't full sleep, but something just shy of the mark, not deep enough for dreams, too shallow to shut out the odd interrupting thought or image. That kind of half-sleep is a nasty trap when there's anything troubling you, and I had more than my share. Maybe I did get a little real sleep, for suddenly, it was dawn—well past seven in the morning—and Tonio was standing over me, calling my name, shocking me out of whatever measure of rest I had achieved. I grunted or something and blinked repeatedly, trying to clear my mind of sleep.

"What's up?" I asked as I sat up, then got to my feet.

"Three new men for you," Tonio said, gesturing to the right with his head, back over his shoulder. "Just three. The doctor said you might be getting Oyo back in a couple of hours, if things work out." That much was welcome news. I hoped it *would* work out, for Oyo's sake as well as my own peace of mind.

I turned to look at the replacements. They weren't *new* people, really, since they had been in the company since Fort Campbell, all privates in B Company's fourth platoon. Toniyi Ooyayni was a divotect. His skin wasn't quite as dark as Nuyi's had been, more a brownish purple; he was from what divotect called their First World, the world where they originated, Divo. Ilyi Nel Keffi was biraunta, his fur almost blond. At any rate, it would be impossible to confuse him with Oyo—if Oyo did return. The third new member was human, Neville St. John—he pronounced it Sinjin, after the English style. He was from the maritime provinces of Canada, but had been born in England.

"For the interim, Sergeant Desivauna will be first platoon sergeant," Tonio said after I had welcomed my three new men. Desivauna, a porracci, had been fourth platoon sergeant—the platoon that had been cannibalized to provide replacements for the other platoons. "He'll be around shortly."

I nodded. "If it's okay with you, I want to completely reorganize my fire teams."

"Your squad, go ahead," Tonio said. "How's the time to do it, if you're going to."

I TOOK THE NEW MEN TO THE CENTER OF THE squad area and called the others over. I made introductions, though it might not have been necessary. The whole company had trained together, and first platoon had squared off against fourth in several exercises. Then I gave everyone the news.

"We're going to move things around in the squad. I'll take Kiervauna as my assistant fire team leader and Robbie will go to second fire team as Souvana's assistant. Fang stays with second. Claw comes to first. Oyo will join second fire team when he gets back from the hospital, which could be in a couple of hours according to Sergeant Xeres." That part was an aside, mostly for Souvana's benefit. "Of you new men, Ilyi and Toniyi, you'll be in my fire team. Neville, you'll be in second."

We shuffled around until everyone was gathered in the right place. Then I told Souvana that we would take thirty minutes to make sure everyone knew how we wanted things to operate in our teams, then we'd all get together and I'd lay out things for the whole squad.

I was moderately surprised that Souvana did not voice any reservations about the new lineups. Maybe the changes were as logical as I thought—spreading the new men between the two fire teams rather than keeping them all in my team, and finally fully dispersing the species. I thought it should make the squad far more balanced than it had been. At least, I hoped it would.

WE SPENT A LITTLE TIME GOING THROUGH BASIC squad drills, covering the most common tactical situations, trying to make sure everyone knew what Souvana and I wanted. This was more talk than action. It wasn't as if we were trying to absorb raw replacements, but the new men had to know how we did it, and the veterans of the squad who were switching fire teams needed a little time to get used to working with new men at their sides. An hour of training wouldn't make the teams operate as smoothly as they had before we lost people, but I thought we would jell fairly quickly—if we had the opportunity.

Oyo returned while we were eating breakfast. The first thing I noticed was that he had shaved off the fringe of hair around his face. I didn't say anything about that; I figured it might be a biraunta mourning ritual. The second thing I noticed was that Oyo's tail was still, not bobbing and weaving, coiling and uncoiling. *That just means he's still depressed,* I told myself. Biraunta tails are as much an indicator of mood as dog tails on Earth. I had to expect that Oyo would still be upset over losing Iyi. It had happened less than thirty hours before.

"The doctor released me for duty, Sergeant," Oyo said when he reached me. "I believe I can function as I should—as far as possible. I will do my best."

"Sit down, Oyo." I patted the ground next to me and he squatted. "I'm sure you'll do fine, even if it's . . . difficult at first. Everyone understands. We'll help as much as we can." I told him about the replacements, and the way I had reorganized the squad. "We may have lost Jaibie because we didn't have a biraunta scouting for second fire team. This way, both teams will be covered." Of course, the reason both biraunta had been in my fire team was that porracci frightened biraunta, reminded them of some prehistoric predator from their home planet. That fear had been the biggest stumbling block in making the integration of Ranger Battalion work in the first place. It had taken a long time, and a couple of deaths in training, before we got to the point where we could function at all.

Oyo turned his head and glanced toward Souvana, maybe fifteen yards away. Then he looked back at me. "I have faced a worse nightmare than porracci since yesterday, Sergeant," he said. "They do not frighten me now. Perhaps what you say makes sense." There was little inflection in his voice, but he was far more functional than he had been the evening before.

"Maybe we both have something to prove to ourselves, Oyo," I said after a moment's silence. "You have to prove to yourself that you can function after the loss of your brother. I have to prove to myself that my wound won't haunt me so badly that I can't do my job. Maybe we'll both need help getting through the next days. But we've both got good people around us."

IT WAS A FEW MINUTES AFTER I SENT OYO OFF TO join the others in second fire team that I had a call from our acting platoon sergeant. Desivauna wanted a conference with all the squad leaders in the platoon. Immediately— that was the porracci way. We met near the company CP, out in the open.

Desivauna's fur was a muddy shade of brown, clipped to three-quarters of an inch. He must have weighed 360 pounds, maybe ten pounds more than Souvana. Among porracci in the military there is a fairly constant relationship between physical size and rank. Pure physical prowess is how they determine rank in their army. They take each other on in hand-to-hand combat, with the winner taking the higher ranking, and perhaps challenging the next porracci up until he finally loses. Real pecking order stuff. That isn't the way we do it in 1st Combined Regiment, or the command structure would be weighted more heavily toward porracci and ghuroh, the largest and strongest species in the regiment. Desivauna's arms showed several scars, reminders of dominance challenges; porracci normally don't have scars removed. They wear them as badges of honor.

"We will be going back into action this evening," was Desivauna's first statement. He didn't bother with greetings. He was brusque, all down-to-business, like most of the porracci I had come across. Porracci weren't much on diplomacy or trifles. "I don't have any details, but we will be operating primarily in one-squad teams, the way we have trained, but coordinating activities among teams. As I understand it, the entire company will be part of the same general operation. The purpose is, of course, to try to bring this campaign to a successful conclusion. We will be asked to harass an enemy unit to steer them toward a concentration of our line forces. General Ransom wishes to force a conclusive battle before attrition makes our position untenable, and before the enemy can reinforce their assets here."

I had to walk all the way over here to hear this? I thought. You haven't said anything we couldn't have assumed. Save the pep talk for when we need it.

"Make sure your squads have full loads of ammunition and that all weapons and electronics are serviceable. There is a resupply depot at the far side of the clearing, and each platoon will be scheduled for its turn. I will have more data for you when it becomes available. Dismissed."

CHAPTER 17

BESIDES THE NEW PLATOON SERGEANT, WE ALSO had a new platoon leader—Junior Lieutenant Eso Vel Hohi, a biraunta—since JL Taivana had been killed. Eso, who also became B Company's new executive officer because he was our most senior junior lieutenant, came around to visit each squad before noon. Although he was a member of the most diminutive species in the alliance, the biraunta JL had plenty of what they call "command presence" in leadership school. The way he acted and talked, the way he carried himself, demanded respect, and he got it, even from the porracci under his command. The lieutenant talked with me for a few minutes, privately, then talked to the entire squad There was nothing special in what he had to say, just the usual "we'll work together and do fine" noises any new commander makes. After he had made his spiel he took Oyo aside. They spent about ten minutes together before the lieutenant left and Oyo came back. I didn't ask what they had talked about—it was none of my business—but Oyo seemed a little less morose afterward.

A field kitchen had been set up during the morning, so we had a hot lunch. It was pretty much the same variety of food we got in our ration packs, but heating it and putting salt and pepper on made it seem to taste almost as good as a meal in garrison. And there was no shortage. We were able to stuff ourselves.

After lunch we went to the resupply depot and filled up on ammunition for our rifles, grenade launchers, and rocket launchers. We got one new rocket launcher; the one Nuyi had carried had been destroyed by the grenade that killed him. We also drew land mines and electronic snoops. A couple of men with problems in their electronics got them repaired, or had their helmets replaced.

I managed a few minutes alone with Tonio and he gave me a little information on how the overall campaign was going, more than I had been able to pick up listening to the feed from CIC.

"It could be worse," was the way he started. "We're managing to move all of the larger enemy units toward each other and consolidating our positions around them— all but one battalion of tonatin that is frustrating the hell out of General Ransom. They're evading our attempts to herd them toward the others, and they're hitting us efficiently enough to make it difficult to force the confrontation the general is looking for."

"I take it that's the job we're being given?"

Tonio nodded. "A series of coordinated strikes to distract them, fragment that battalion, and be enough of a nuisance to back them into the area where the general wants them, hopefully before first light tomorrow. We should be getting specific instructions within the next hour or so. How's that biraunta of yours doing?"

"Better. He's not half-catatonic any longer. I think he'll do okay." A shrug. "I guess we'll find out tonight."

"What about you?"

He didn't have to explain what he meant. It was something I had been wondering about as well. "I think I'm okay. We'll find out about that soon enough too."

I HEARD THE CALL GO OUT FOR PLATOON SER-geants to report to the company CP and made the easy guess that the meeting was to give out orders for the night's operation. It was forty minutes later before Sergeant Desivauna came back and called the squad leaders together. He had us get our electronic maps out and linked to his, and we spent half an hour going over squad assignments. As usual, our orders were result-oriented. They told us what our objectives were and the general area of operations, but the details were pretty much left to the immediate tactical commanders—the squad leaders, in this case. Only the where and when were taken out of our hands since we had so many squads working toward the same final objective in a restricted area of operations.

"Since we will need to stay in radio contact to coordinate assignments, it won't be possible to maintain total electronic silence during this operation, but I expect squad leaders to minimize their use of radio, and to restrict their men from making nonessential calls. Observe common-sense precautions, moving after each transmission," Desivauna said. Then he had each squad leader go back over his instructions, correcting anything that wasn't given back to him exactly as he had said it.

WE WEREN'T GOING TO GET A RIDE. WE HAD TO walk, and most of the squads were going to have to push themselves to get into position by the time our operations were scheduled to begin, ninety minutes after sunset. First platoon left the encampment four hours before sunset. That would give us close to five and a half hours to cover fifteen miles and get set. We might have farther to travel if the enemy battalion we were targeting moved faster than expected, or if they moved in the wrong direction. The way things had been going, I would have bet on one or the other, so I planned to push my men as hard as possible, especially during the first couple of hours, to give us more of a chance to adjust to any unexpected enemy moves.

Although the whole platoon was heading toward approximately the same destination, we were moving separately, by squads. The smaller the group, the faster it can travel, and it's that much harder for the enemy to detect. And, if one squad did run into trouble on the way, only that squad would be at risk. The rest would keep going. That was part of the orders. Go on to the objective. Leave any squad that's intercepted on their own.

If a squad got hit the way we had the morning before, there would be little chance of the sort of rescue operation that put down the tonatin who had us trapped. That brought a bit of a lump to my throat. *It won't happen to us again*, I told myself. *I won't let it happen.*

I knew it *shouldn't* happen on this operation, not going in, but there was no way to guess what the situation would be after we had all taken our turns hitting that enemy battalion a few times. CIC was moderately confident that they were tracking the position of every tonatin army unit of company size or larger, and they had a rough idea where most of the larger groups of armed civilians were. The civilians were almost all close to their towns, a last line of defense. We planned to stay well clear of those areas. Civilian militia units were the least of our concerns. They didn't have the equipment or training to be a serious threat. But if they got in the way, they were fair game.

I had briefed everyone on the route I planned to take, and exactly what our instructions were for anything we ran into. If I got killed, Souvana could take over and not lose time trying to get up to speed. Both our assistant fire team leaders also knew what we were to do. There always has to be someone ready to step into command.

I had my fire team in front, with Ilyi on point—up in the trees when possible. Oyo was ranging around on either flank and behind, doing what he could to make certain that no one snuck up on us from a direction we weren't expecting. Having so much territory to cover kept him busy, but I figured that was so much the better.

It started raining not long after we left the encampment—a series of light, intermittent showers. That sort of precipitation isn't a bother unless it goes on so long that the ground turns to thick mud. Our helmets and uniforms kept us from getting too wet—at least those of us without a lot of fur showing. And the hard, leathery skin of Toniyi, our new divotect, shed water as if it had been waxed.

We had been on the march for close to an hour, covering nearly four miles, before the sky got much darker and the rain got heavier, driven by a stiff wind and punctuated by lightning. The voice from CIC said that the storm system was growing and becoming fairly extensive, with one cell following another. It looked as if we were going to stay wet at least until sunset, when most of the storms were expected to dissipate.

Electrical storms would make it that much more difficult for the enemy to locate us. The shadows under the trees were almost night dark, and lightning can fool the detectors that might be looking for electronic emissions, and screw up night-vision systems momentarily. Apart from the slight chance of being hit by lightning—not necessarily catastrophic for a soldier wearing an insulated helmet, uniform, and boots—storms simply added to our security. I was willing to trade a little discomfort for additional safety. Any day.

WE DIDN'T STOP FOR OUR FIRST REST UNTIL WE had been on the move ninety minutes. We had started out fairly well rested—as much as any soldier can hope for in combat—so I wasn't worried about anyone's tail dragging too soon. Toniyi, the new divotect, was the one I watched. If he started to falter, I would know it was time for a rest, or a slower pace, but he showed no signs of tiring. In the storm, continuing to walk was hardly more uncomfortable than sitting or squatting to take a rest.

Ten minutes was all I allowed for that first break, and I timed it for one of the periods when the rain had let up a little. Rain is more of an annoyance if you're sitting in it than if you're on the move.

Twenty minutes after we started moving again, a new

storm cell passed overhead, bringing not only another burst of heavier rain but several lightning strikes within three or four hundred yards. We passed the scene of one strike where lightning felled a tree with a diameter of four feet. The wood where the trunk had been split was smoldering but was too wet to really burn.

That was when I decided that it was time to keep our biraunta out of the trees until the weather got less hazardous. It wasn't just that they might be more of a target up high, but I didn't want one of them falling because a tree got sliced underneath him.

BY SUNSET, WE HAD COVERED ALL BUT THE LAST half mile to the point where we were to set up. The enemy battalion had, surprisingly enough, moved in just the fashion that CIC had predicted—the first time it had lived up to expectations since it had started making a nuisance of itself. The paranoid part of my brain started to worry about that; who was tricking whom?

Because we had made such good time and didn't have to go farther to counter enemy moves, we had to take a longer break at sunset, to avoid getting too close to the action before the rest of the squads got into position. We also didn't want to get so close to the enemy battalion's line of march that one of their outriding patrols might stumble across us. Everything had been going so good that I wanted to minimize the chances of any last minute problems.

No one complained when I said that we would be staying put for half an hour or more unless the enemy did something unexpected. No one said much of anything. After four hours of a fairly rapid march across soggy forest terrain in full gear, the men simply sank to the ground in relief. So did I, once I was certain we had our perimeter covered and that everyone had a clear field of fire. I was tempted to put out a few electronic snoops, to give us enough warning of any approaching enemy to let us fade away or set up an ambush as the situation might demand.

No, I decided. *You don't need snoops. This is just a rest stop. You're too nervous. Save the snoops for when you really need them.* Maybe I thought my men might think it was because I was thinking about the way I had been wounded, and had men killed. Maybe they would think I had lost my nerve along with the chunk of my side. The wound did cross my mind; that tiny ghost seemed to turn a couple of somersaults in the hollow in my side. As for being nervous, of course I was—every time I got near the chance of battle. You have to have a little edge, knowing what *might* happen, but you can't let it consume you . . . or it will.

OTHER THAN THE BATTALION WE WERE GOING after, virtually all of the major tonatin army units had been backed up against the south bank of the river that bordered the capital. The area where the tonatin were was only lightly wooded. Part of it was in farm fields. And we had enough soldiers between the army and the capital to keep the tonatin from retreating into it where they might be hard to flush out.

There might well have been a number of small tonatin units—platoon size or less—outside the perimeter our people had forced most of the enemy into, but the lone battalion outside that area was to the south, doing everything it could to maneuver around past the troops we had facing their main force. Maybe they were looking for a place where they could squeeze our people hard enough to let the rest of their army break out of the trap they were in. That's what *I* would have been looking to do if I were their commander. If they couldn't break out, their fate was pretty well sealed—barring the arrival of massive reinforcements from off-world.

Which, of course, was entirely possible.

IN FOUR AND A HALF HOURS, THERE HADN'T BEEN fifty words spoken in the squad, and most of those had been me giving instructions during rest breaks. The new men were fitting in, and the men who had been with me all along were getting used to their spots in the new lineup. I hadn't expected foul-ups early, when there were no tonatin around to make mistakes expensive, but it was still reassuring. Somewhat. You judge what the others in the squad will do. You get comfortable—if that's the right word—with those around you.

I let our break stretch past thirty minutes. The last reports from CIC were still good. That tonatin battalion, now estimated at nine hundred men, was still moving toward the area where we planned to hit them. I worried a little about it being too easy, as if maybe *we* were the ones being suckered in instead of them—the way my squad had been suckered by the force we had been harassing two nights before. When that possibility started to take up more brain cycles than it should, I got my men on their feet and moving again.

THE OPERATIONS PLAN WAS FAIRLY SIMPLE. THE target battalion was moving from point A to point B and we wanted to divert them to point C—against that river that was helping keep the rest of the tonatin defenders of Olviat pinned, west of the capital. It was up to a dozen spec ops squads to sting them at the right times and places to herd them like cowboys taking steers to market in some Old West action vid.

Once we got them backed up against the river, close to the rest of their troops, our line units could simply extend the perimeter they had built, get the entire enemy force—less those few small units that were still roaming free—where General Ransom wanted to stage the climactic battle of the campaign. But if we hit that lone battalion at the wrong time or place, they might go in some other direction, where it might be harder to get at them again.

Up to a point, we would be able to handle minor changes in direction by the battalion with so many groups lurking along their line of march, changing the timing and location of later strikes to make up for mistakes or miscalculations, but we didn't want the need for improvisation to get out of hand. That was why we would be using the radios to coordinate our individual bites.

Captain Fusik and Tonio were going to be centrally located but far enough from the action to stay out of direct contact with the enemy, with one short squad from second platoon around them just in case. The captain and Tonio would watch the data feed from CIC and gather reports from the squads, and direct any changes. That was the theory. If they couldn't get through to us, for whatever reason, CIC could take over. If we also lost contact with CIC, we would still continue, but in that case it would be every squad for itself to some extent, with a bunch of buck sergeants like me doing a lot of guessing.

If the operation degenerated that far, we would take a lot more casualties than we would otherwise. I couldn't let myself dwell on that or I wouldn't have been fit to command my squad.

CHAPTER 18

IT WAS AS MUCH A MATTER OF TRUST AS NECESsity that squad leaders were not required to report when they reached their initial attack positions. A single click of a transmitter would have done it and been almost impossible for the enemy to pinpoint; two direction finders would have to be aimed perfectly at just the right split second. The transmission, even if only for a tenth of a second, would have been received by CIC and mapped to within inches, which would tell Captain Fusik and the whole chain of command which unit was reporting. But we wouldn't take the one-in-many-millions longshot of having even a single transmitter click intercepted. *No news is good news.* The only reason for a squad leader to break electronic silence before the attacks started would be that his men were in trouble.

That didn't happen. The activity was all on the CIC update channel, one-way coming from the flagship. The only significant news on the CIC channel concerning our mission was when the enemy battalion took a long rest break, starting ten minutes after I got my men up and going again.

I didn't waste much thought on the enemy taking *short* breaks. They had to do that periodically, just like we did. No species can keep going indefinitely without rest, and while tonatin might be a bit hardier than some of the races, they too had limits. Ten minutes, maybe fifteen, I figured the halt would last, what we would take in similar circumstances. When CIC hadn't reported the enemy formation moving again after twenty minutes, I still wasn't concerned. Maybe it was supper time.

After twenty-five minutes, I halted my squad again. We were in danger of getting close to the enemy too soon. *We should wait until they start moving again,* I told myself, *until CIC tells us they're on the go and still on course.* The catch was that CIC might not pick up on the resumption of movement immediately. The area *was* heavily forested. If the enemy battalion chose to go to total electronic silence and changed course when they started moving again, we might suddenly find ourselves either exposed or too far out of position to intercept them quickly.

We have to be watching them too closely for that. Nine hundred men have to leave some *trace even if they're being extraordinarily careful; they have to have a decent infrared fingerprint even if we can't see them under the trees.* I was trying to convince myself that this lengthy stop by the enemy wasn't necessarily the prelude to something sneaky, that it wasn't time for us to throw out the plan we had started with and start improvising.

You have to improvise when necessary, but I don't think I wasted more than a minute deciding that we would stick with the plan, move a little farther to make certain we weren't late. We would just have to be even more careful than we usually are about stealth. I started the squad moving again, using hand signals for that and to remind everyone to be careful.

There were twenty-seven minutes left until the first of our spec ops squads was due to take a nibble of the enemy battalion. That was if that battalion didn't just sit where it was instead of moving on to where we had expected it to be . . . and even that would only delay the start of our operation by a couple of minutes. Probably.

•   •   •

THE ENEMY BATTALION DID THE ONE THING I NEVER would have expected. It simply made no sense that I could see . . . which might be why the enemy commander did it. The tonatin battalion turned around and started hiking back over the route they had been following, after going in the other direction for more than three hours. They were on the move for several minutes before CIC noticed and passed the word to us on the ground.

Maybe that battalion commander was smarter than anyone has a right to be . . . or he was simply luckier. We had knocked out all of the tonatin satellites over Olviat, so they didn't have that source of intelligence to tell him we were closing in. While one or two squads might have come close enough to an enemy snoop without noticing it, it was highly unlikely that more squads had. There was no reason to suspect that the tonatin had scattered that many snoops in the first place. Before we arrived they hadn't had any need, and afterward they would have had difficulty doing it undetected.

However the move came about, our carefully scripted plan was dead. The first squads had been set to attack the front of the enemy formation, to slow them down and give them a couple of equally likely options for changing direction. The next few attacks were supposed to limit those options and start maneuvering the IFers in the direction we wanted them to go. But with the direct reversal of course, those first squads were going to be too far away to strike on schedule.

I had my map out and open, looking for plausible alternatives, when Captain Fusik came on the squad leaders' channel with new instructions. The two squads nearest what was now the van of the enemy battalion were to hit as quickly as they could to try to make the enemy commander think that we had a force that had been trailing him. Two other spec ops squads would hurry to get into position to hit the tonatin battalion if they didn't reverse course again.

For the time being, only those four squads would move to intercept the enemy column on its new course. The rest of us would make more minor adjustments until we knew whether we were going to be able to turn the enemy around again. My squad, along with our platoon's second squad, was to cross the old line of march to get into position east of the tonatin battalion, to try to turn them west if they did another flip-flop and resumed their original course . . . which is what we wanted them to do. If they didn't turn, we would be a bit closer and able to move to get in and take our licks sooner than we would have been able to had we stayed put. It *sounds* more complicated than it really was.

I brought my men together to whisper a report on what had happened and to pass along our new orders, then we started off as quickly as we could. I had my fire team in the lead, with Ilyi on point on the ground. Kiervauna was next. I followed him. Toniyi was behind me, then Claw. I didn't pay as close attention to the way that Souvana had his fire team lined up, except to note that Souvana was two spots behind me and Oyo was the rear guard, also on the ground.

We had to cover eight-tenths of a mile to get to the position Captain Fusik had marked for us, and I wanted to get there before the first squad hit the enemy. I estimated that would be in approximately seventeen minutes. It wasn't impossible, but with the need to watch for enemy patrols, snoops, and land mines, we weren't going to have time to spare.

Although the temperature was fifty degrees Fahrenheit after the storms, I was sweating within minutes from the combination of exertion and tension. My breathing was more labored than the hurried hike could account for, even with the seventy-odd pounds of gear I was carrying. I had carried heavier loads at a faster pace often enough in training. But this was the real thing, and the last time out, I had nearly not made it back in. Yes, I thought about that, but never to the point of distraction.

I watched the forest, scanning constantly. I had to remind myself to trust the men with me and not try to be the eyes for every position. At the same time I was listening to the feed from CIC, wondering when the next update would come in about the course and position of the enemy battalion. And I had to watch where I put my feet, of course, to make sure I didn't snag a boot on a vine or exposed root. Taking a tumble would have been inconvenient and slightly humiliating.

There was the weird sensation of time moving too fast and standing still at the same time. You focus too hard, or try to do too many things at once, and you lose track of time. That's the speed part of it. But at the same time your mind goes through so many things that you feel as if much more time ought to have passed. That's the standing still. The problem is that neither sensation is correct. You have to trust the time line on your display . . . *and* try to remain coherent and sane.

We crossed the path the enemy would have followed had they not reversed direction. I held the squad up for a few seconds while Ilyi and Oyo slid through the woods a hundred yards south to make sure that the tonatin commander hadn't left mines or booby traps, or part of his force. I didn't want us to walk into a trap blindly assuming there was no enemy close. We had to start thinking that the enemy battalion commander might be a lot smarter than we had been giving him credit for.

Once the biraunta came back and signaled that there were no enemy troops waiting to catch us, I moved the squad across the path quickly and we changed direction to aim directly at the point where the captain wanted us. When we got there, I was just settling into my position after seeing that my men were where I wanted them, when I heard the first shots. The first spec ops squad had snapped their first mosquito bite on the enemy column.

Those first shots were a long way off—more than a mile. If I hadn't had my external audio pickups set at maximum gain, and had one pointed in precisely the right direction, purely by chance, I might not have heard anything.

Damp, heavy air and all the intervening trees worked to deaden the transmission of sound. But the noises weren't my imagination. The attacking squad leader radioed, "Good hit," on the tactical frequency. Then his squad would have withdrawn, pulling back before the enemy could respond. The next squad was to strike thirty seconds later, from the other side.

I didn't hear any shots from the second attack, but I heard the squad leader's report. There was a gap of four minutes before another squad took a nibble, this time adding a couple of grenades to the mix, and that attack was close enough to hear. After that, most of our squads were in position and the bites came with some regularity, spaced out along the length of the enemy column and coming from both sides, concentrating on the southern half. The only angle left *completely* untouched was the north end of the column. We wanted them to turn around again, to do another about-face and head back the way they originally were.

If that happened, my squad and three others would be in position to start turning the enemy west. That would give other squads time to move to their next positions. The plan could go wrong at almost any point. All the enemy commander had to do was make the right—for him—choice at every turn, either because he was so damned smart or because he was luckier than anyone has a right to be. But when the choices have to be made instantly and frequently, under fire, there is every chance that any commander will make an occasional mistake, no matter how damned brilliant he is, and we planned to be in position to take advantage of any mistakes.

It was fifteen minutes after the first ambush before we received word that the tonatin battalion had reversed course again, coming in our direction. I warned my men to get ready. When our turn came we were going to hit harder than the others had, using RPGs as well as bullets freely, maybe even a rocket if the opportunity arose. We were on the east side of the track the enemy was following. We wanted the IFers to turn away from us.

Ten minutes passed. The IFers were moving slowly, taking cover every time one of our squads hit them, and fighting back, sizing up the opposition before the bulk of the force started moving again while leaving enough strength in place to handle our attacks. That strung the column out over more distance than before, making them more vulnerable to our hit-and-run tactics. I started to hear reports that the enemy commander had detached a couple of platoon-sized patrols to attempt to engage the ambushers up close. There wasn't much chance of that happening, and the enemy commander must have realized that. He recalled his patrols, set them to covering the flanks of the battalion, and did what he could to draw his force together.

Claw was the first man in my squad to spot the enemy's point squad. The enemy squad was a hundred yards south and eighty yards to the west. I gestured for my people to get lower and remain motionless. We were going to let the point squad move past us without challenge and, we hoped, without them spotting us. After we opened up on the van of the main force, the other squad that had crossed the line of march with us would do what they could to take out the point squad.

That point squad, twelve men, moved past us, rifles covering both sides of the trail as well as the route ahead. Heads were turning methodically, scanning. Those men obviously knew their jobs, and the series of ambushes had made them particularly nervous. I wished them a merry trip to hell, then turned my attention to the trace behind them, waiting for the first company of the enemy's main column to come into sight.

Another four minutes. I focused so completely that I didn't have room in my head for any thoughts about the last mission I had been on. It wasn't until much later, after things calmed down, that I thought back to this moment and decided that I had passed the first test. I hadn't lost my nerve.

Finally, the tonatin battalion came into sight. The soldiers at the head of the column were well spaced out, minimizing the damage a single grenade or burst of rifle fire would do. They were obviously expecting trouble, pushing the pace a little more than was wise. Speed and vigilance take their toll on each other. The faster those soldiers moved the less able they were to spot the minimal signs an ambushing force might give. The tonatin were obviously anxious to get wherever they were going, and however much they might worry about trouble along the way, their commander was only willing to compromise so far.

I could understand that. But I was sure as hell going to do everything I could to take advantage of the situation.

Wait! The lead element drew even with our positions, eighty yards to the west. At that range, a blind man could scarcely miss hitting soldiers who were on their feet. I could see the tonatin quite well—camouflage uniforms, helmets, weapons, and the gear hung from backs and shoulders. I could see the strange hands gripping rifles. Tonatin hands had four fingers, all about the same size, thick and long, set two opposite two, making the hands function something like the mechanical claws in those arcade scams where you put your coin in with the mostly futile hope of grabbing a prize. Tonatin were adapted to use those claws as efficiently as humans use the arrangement we have; there was no awkwardness about it.

I counted silently as pairs of tonatin passed me, one on the near side of the enemy formation, the other on the far side. I had decided that once forty tonatin—about a platoon—had crossed my field of fire, I would start the attack. That would leave the patrol covering the flank still some distance south of us, too far away to close and interfere before we could do our damage and withdraw.

Thirty-eight. Forty. I simply opened fire, moving my aim across my field of fire and holding the trigger of my rifle long enough to spray twenty or thirty rounds. We wanted to make it harder for the enemy to decide that there were just a few of us, make it that much more difficult for their commander to decide whether to put all his men down to meet what might be a major attack or try to keep us occupied with a platoon or two while the rest of his people kept going.

Keep them guessing as long as possible is almost always tactically sound. I reported our attack while I was firing, the minimal number of words. Altogether, the attack lasted well under a minute. We popped off a few RPGs, expended close to a magazine of ammunition for each rifle, then started pulling back, east, under cover of hot-smoke hand grenades that would blur both visible light and infrared detection. We used standard fire-and-maneuver tactics with one fire team covering the other, leapfrogging each other ten or fifteen yards at a time. We stayed low and worked to keep as many tree trunks as possible between us and the enemy close enough to target us.

Breaking contact took longer than the ambush had, and no surprise—some of the enemy soldiers were still firing toward where we had been a minute or more after we had vacated those positions. Once we were out of immediate danger and I had ordered an end to any shooting by us, we stopped long enough to make certain that I had all my men, and that no one had any incapacitating wounds. Then we moved. We had to get farther from the enemy before they put out a force to neutralize us, and we had our next ambush spot to reach before the IFers did.

HIT AND RUN, THEN HIT AGAIN. COMPANY B KEPT at it without any major problems for several hours. It was nearly midnight before one of our squads got caught between two tonatin platoons and paid the full price. No one from that squad survived. There were a few casualties in other squads—killed and wounded—but there was no precise count given while the operation was under way. The wounded were treated as best they could, though there was no chance to evacuate anyone, or get them to more sophisticated treatment . . . which probably cost a couple more men their lives.

At least my squad had its luck running again. In four ambushes, we had two inconsequential injuries. Souvana had a thin strip of fur burned on the back of one hand from a bullet that had grazed without penetrating. Fang got a two-inch-long splinter of wood—chipped off when a bullet hit a tree next to him—in the shoulder. St. John pulled the splinter out. Neither Souvana nor Fang was inconvenienced enough to mention it.

Somewhere along the line, the tonatin battalion commander must have deduced what we were trying to do, and he did everything in his power to thwart our design. He started turning his people into the attacking spec ops squads instead of away from them. That's how we lost the one squad. But we had Captain Fusik—and the full staff of CIC, with their computers—working to counter every counter the tonatin leader came up with.

I can't answer for any of the other squads, but my men and I must have covered eight miles in five hours, even allowing for the time we waited for the enemy to get to us at each ambush. After our third strike I told my men to start being careful with ammunition expenditure. I couldn't see an end to the operation, how long it might be before we could get more ammunition, and if we ran dry, we would be useless.

In those five hours, we moved that tonatin battalion a quarter of the way to where we wanted them, but in the last two hours I think we lost more ground than we gained. I was getting tired, and I figured that most of my men had to be as well. We weren't to the point of collapse, but we were no longer at our peak efficiency. Even lying in wait at a time like that is a rather intense experience, not restful. You're waiting for danger, waiting for an exchange of fire that could bring a bullet—or grenade—carrying your obituary. The ebb and flow of adrenaline from anticipation and fear has to take its course, even though the medical nano-agents in our bodies are programmed to counter that to some degree. Offset our ... deterioration in capability with the knowledge that the enemy couldn't be anywhere near peak efficiency either. They had been on the move considerably longer without more than twenty or twenty-five minutes rest at a time.

No, that didn't make me feel any better. It never does. Even now, thinking back, the simple memory of what it was like starts to knot my stomach up a little.

IT WAS AROUND MIDNIGHT WHEN CAPTAIN FUSIK started doing what he could to give each squad a little time to rest, but the more time he gave us, the more time he gave the enemy, so there were limits. I could sympathize with his dilemma, but that didn't give me a real chance to climb down from the extended adrenaline high. I was so tense that the muscles in my forearms were as tight as vacuum-welded steel. I remember thinking that if they tightened up much more, no bullet would be able to penetrate—a ridiculous notion.

Another three hours passed. We—my squad—had staged seven ambushes altogether. I was down to two full magazines for my rifle and maybe half a magazine in the weapon, about 250 rounds altogether. Most of my people had to be as low, which had me more than a little concerned. If we got into a firefight that we couldn't withdraw from quickly, we might be in serious trouble. *Mention it the next time you report a hit,* I reminded myself. I had to consciously remind myself of everything by then, almost as if I were still in boot training trying to keep my drill instructor happy. There's a reason why *that* is virtually impossible.

I caught myself yawning while we were lying in wait for our eighth ambush. I couldn't stop; the more I tried, the wider I yawned. My body wanted sleep, no matter what the price. I had to lift my faceplate to rub at my eyes and face, trying to massage myself back to full alertness. From the latest report I had, the enemy column was at least ten minutes away. I worried that I might fall asleep waiting for the enemy, and that would have been . . . unacceptable.

The tonatin battalion was still five minutes from us when I heard a call from Captain Fusik to all squad leaders. Our Company A was being moved into position to help us. Company A had been hurt as badly as B Company, so they had also reorganized into three platoons. The plan was for them to hit as one unit rather than break into squads. B Company's squads would move together and form into larger teams as well. It would be at least an hour before Alpha would be in position.

"The estimate is that we've inflicted between 10 and 15 percent casualties on the IFer battalion," Captain Fusik said. "Since we haven't been able to herd them where we want them, CIC has decided to attempt to increase the attrition."

He didn't say anything about ammunition getting too short for us to pin eight hundred enemy soldiers very long, and we were too close to the van of the tonatin battalion for me to break electronic silence to remind him. I barely had time to whisper the essentials of the news to the rest of the squad.

CHAPTER 19

FIVE MINUTES CAN BE AN ETERNITY, BUT NOT THIS time. Instead of sniping for a minute or less and then running, we were to hit the van of the enemy column with everything we had and keep at it until the situation became untenable. We wanted to hold up the tonatin battalion as long as possible to give the rest of our units time to get into position to lock them in place. Once we got that battalion stopped, CIC would have our artillery drop a few heavier surprises on them. But we would not get a *lot* of help from the heavy stuff. Most of what we had available had to be saved for the main enemy force and for counter-battery fire against whatever artillery the tonatin defenders still had.

Kiervauna would fire the first shot—one of our rockets—this time. Both men with rocket launchers would get in a couple of strikes. Then it would be rocket-propelled grenades. Then rifles. One, two, three. We would let the current point squad get close, as near as I dared. The rockets would go after the van of the main force. The RPGs would go against both the point and the main force. If the point squad was close enough, we might toss a few hand grenades their way. When it came time for the rifles, our first priority would be to finish the point squad, the nearest threat. Then we would turn our full attention to the lead company of the main force.

Before we got too deep into the fight—before the enemy commander had a chance to detach any of his people to flank us—I hoped that a couple more of our squads would start attacking. If we didn't get help within two or three minutes we would be in deep trouble. We would have to try to withdraw, and there wasn't time to place land mines between us and the tonatin to slow them down. They were too close.

Three minutes. I wiped sweat from my hands and settled so I was looking over the sights of my rifle. Kiervauna was a few feet to my left, watching me as much as out where we expected the enemy to appear. I would give him the signal to launch his first rocket. He would show the rocket the target—one of the enemy soldiers—then launch it. The rocket was smart enough to detonate when it got close to a target, even a moving, living target. If it went off a few feet over the heads of the enemy, as intended, it could do considerable damage.

Two minutes. I looked around to make sure I knew exactly where my people were. Then I had to wipe sweat from the palms of my hands again. I knew it was nerves, fear, but fear is normal, natural, something to use, not something to cringe away from. I looked at the side of my rifle's receiver to make sure that the safety was off and the selector switch was on full automatic.

One minute. Unless the enemy stopped moving or the estimate from CIC was wrong, the point squad would come into view any second. This time I only wiped the sweat from my right hand. I didn't want my trigger finger to slip. I worked at getting my breathing even and shallow, worked at calming my mind. Waiting.

The combat uniforms of the tonatin were as effective as ours in minimizing thermal signature, but our night-vision systems do not rely exclusively on detecting infrared. Our targets were sure to be moving, which also helps. I saw movement—a helmet between low-hung branches. I scanned around that spot and in a few seconds counted six men along the side of the path, so close to the trees that they had to duck under the lowest branches. They were 120 yards away.

I raised my left hand a few inches above my head and made a signal for my men, a pointing finger indicating where the enemy was. But I didn't look to see if the others had noticed my gesture. I kept my gaze toward the enemy. It would only be necessary for Kiervauna to see my next hand signal, the order to fire. That would be the signal for the rest of the squad.

That gesture wouldn't come until the main force of the enemy battalion was within range, and the point squad was too close for comfort. That would take another minute or two. Until then, we needed to remain as nearly motionless as possible. The point squad might be within forty yards when we opened up. Too damned close.

The enemy's point squad was smaller than before—and probably wasn't the same squad as the last time we had hit. That duty gets shifted around to move fresh eyes to the front, and to make sure that the same men aren't always feeling the most pressure. There were eight tonatin I could see in the point squad. They were within sixty yards. There was fifty yards between the last man in that squad and the van of the column behind it.

I gave Kiervauna the signal.

We opened up with two men firing rockets. They were joined by two men firing rocket-propelled grenades. Then the rest of us opened up with rifles, joined quickly by those who had started with rockets and RPGs. The enemy point squad had been slightly out of range of hand grenades. Maybe the porracci could toss a three-pound grenade fifty yards, but none of the rest of us could, certainly not with the kind of accuracy we needed.

The standard rifle that all of us but the biraunta used had a cyclic firing rate of nine hundred rounds per minute. That meant we could empty a 100-round magazine in under seven seconds if we held the trigger down. The biraunta rifle had a slightly lower cyclic rate, and the magazines their rifles used didn't hold as many rounds. But none of us emptied magazines as quickly as we could have. We didn't want to run out of ammunition this close to the enemy.

Still, we put out a fairly heavy amount of fire over about a minute and a half—easily over a thousand rounds. We laid a lot of hell on top of the IFers who were within range. Then I told my men to start being more conservative. We went back to short bursts, three or four rounds at a time. I reported to Captain Fusik and asked how long it would be before we had help.

"Listen for it," he said, and almost before the last word was out, I heard new gunfire enter the fray from our left, closer to the van of the enemy column. The IFer point squad had ceased to exist by that time. Souvana moved his fire team closer to them and reported that there were no survivors.

A third spec ops squad joined the firefight after another forty-five seconds, and after that the fighting became more general, with the rest of our squads pitching in as soon as they arrived. The enemy battalion was trying to establish defensive positions, not an easy job with the column of two's spread out over a mile of curving forest trail. All they could do was kiss dirt on either side of the trail and get what cover they could.

Captain Fusik ordered me to start moving my squad left, to join the next squad. Alpha Company was three-quarters of an hour away, pushing toward the fight as quickly as they could. We were also given a "heads up" warning because our artillery was beginning to target the enemy column. Fifteen seconds later, the first rounds exploded. From the sound of the blasts, I guessed that they were the heavy rockets. They carry a larger explosive charge than the shells the big guns fire.

"Captain, we're going to run out of ammunition before much longer," I reported when there was a moment of silence following the detonation of the first rockets. "I doubt that any of my men have much more than a single magazine." Personally, I had one full magazine plus a nearly empty partial in my weapon. My guess was that all of the squads had to be in the same shape, but it wasn't up to me to tell the captain that. The other squad leaders would be quick to point out their own shortages.

"We're working on it," Fusik said. "I'll get back to you when we can get more ammo in. You'll just have to stretch your supplies the best you can."

I couldn't stop my mouth. "You mean like fire half a bullet at a time? Or maybe we should toss IOUs for bullets at them?"

"Do what you can," Fusik said, and the words seemed to drip ice. Well, it wasn't the first time I'd put my foot in my mouth with an officer, but if we didn't get more ammunition in fairly soon, it sure might prove to be the last.

I CARRIED A PISTOL IN ADDITION TO MY RIFLE, AND I still had a full complement of ammunition for that, four magazines of needle rounds. It might keep me going for a minute or two after the rifle ran dry. Apart from that, we might be reduced to bayonets—if the enemy didn't just sit off where they were and drop RPGs on top of us. If I kept us close enough to let that happen.

"Cease firing," I told my men. "Pull back by fire teams. Souvana, take your men back first." We had been told to move to the next squad. They were a couple hundred yards away, a little closer to the enemy than we had been. Still, I didn't see any need to take a straight line. We could make a wide curve that would take us out of range of enemy RPGs for a few minutes, and put enough tree trunks between us and the enemy that a bullet would have a hard time finding one of us.

We moved slowly, as if we were still easy targets, not using fire-and-maneuver after the first couple of moves. Until we were ready to hit again, I'd just as soon let the enemy forget us. When we were near the apex of our arc, three hundred yards from the enemy, I stopped the squad and had everyone check on remaining ammunition, and told them to be as conservative as possible once we got back into the fight. "I don't have any idea how long it's going to be before we get fresh supplies, but figure it won't be until after A Company gets into the act," I told them.

"We will need to limit ourselves to single, aimed shots to have any hope of holding out that long," Souvana observed.

"There's not a man in the squad who can't be effective firing single shots," I said, and Souvana nodded.

I was just about to give the signal to start moving again when there was a sudden, dramatic increase in the amount of gunfire. Everyone in the squad turned toward the noise. It wasn't simple curiosity. We had to know if it posed any threat to us. We were too far away to see what was happening. The trees that kept us fairly safe from enemy gunfire also kept us from seeing much. I got us moving along the route I had picked, and got into my place in the line, listening for something on the radio to tell me just what the hell was going on.

It wasn't long. There were suddenly a lot of reports flying on the company channels. The tonatin battalion commander wasn't doing what we expected. Again. He was withdrawing his troops under heavy fire—as many as he could. The first estimate I heard was that he was leaving perhaps a short company to hold us off while he pulled the rest out, due west, away from the bulk of us . . . and directly toward our A Company.

I stopped my squad again, anticipating orders to change course and head west as well, maybe to try to get in front of the enemy force to slow it down. We would have had to damned near run to do *that*. But two minutes passed without any orders for us. Captain Fusik was busy dealing with other squads, trying to figure out what we needed to do— I guess. He probably also had conversations going on with Colonel Hansen and CIC. I've seen officers trying to balance four or five conversations at once.

The firefight—our squads against that lone tonatin company left to guard the retreat of the rest—seemed to get extremely intense suddenly. The IFers were burning ammunition as if they had endless supplies. I knew that couldn't be the case. After all of the small firefights, those tonatin had to be getting short of ammo as well, even if their standard load was considerably more than ours was.

"Dragon." At first there was just the one word. I acknowledged the captain's call and then he continued. "We hold here, do what we can to finish off the troops the IFers left. Continue moving to join with your platoon's second squad."

"Yes, sir," I said, careful not to say anything more. I liked Captain Fusik. He was okay, for an officer, and I had been trying not to mouth off to him . . . the way I already had that night. I figured he'd understand, once we were out from under the pressure. "We're on the way." I signaled for the squad to start moving.

THIS WASN'T A "MOPPING-UP" OPERATION SINCE the IFers had left almost as many men as we had to fight them. They managed to get into a halfway-decent perimeter, and the tonatin were good soldiers. They must have known that they were being sacrificed to give the rest of their battalion a chance, but they held fast, and gave us every ounce of grief they could. When they got low on ammunition, those who were still able to fixed bayonets, got up, and charged. It was insane, like something from some ancient poem extolling war. It was also more than a little terrifying to be on the end of that charge, even though the IFers had virtually no chance.

We had been engaged in this firefight for nearly half an hour, our positions a hundred yards from the enemy. My men were still being stingy with bullets, firing single rounds. Even so, I think every man in my squad was well into the last magazine for his rifle. It was almost a relief to see the remaining tonatin get up and run toward us. There weren't near as many of them left—not much more than the equivalent of two platoons. Call it ninety men. Their numbers dwindled quickly once they were on their feet.

Fully half fell before they closed the gap to fifty yards, and only a handful made it all the way to our line.

Even they didn't get the chance to use their bayonets. I killed one with my pistol at a range of five yards. Down the line a short distance, I saw one tonatin get all the way in before a porracci from second squad grabbed his rifle while the ghuroh next to him slit the tonatin's throat.

This fight was over. There wasn't any gunfire. There wasn't a single tonatin left on his feet or able to fight. Still, it was nearly three minutes after the end of the abortive charge before Captain Fusik came on the radio—using the squad leaders' channel—to give us new instructions.

"We take care of our wounded, then check the enemy and tag their wounded for pickup later. Then we head northwest, to rendezvous with the people bringing in ammunition. We'll carry our wounded who can't walk. There are medics with the supply detachment." He sounded tired, but I didn't expect that we would be given a rest. The fact that we were going to meet our ammunition resupply was a pretty good indication of that, so I wasn't surprised by what the captain said next. "Once we have fresh ammo and turn our wounded over to the medics, CIC will give us a vector to get back into the fight. We have to support Alpha Company as quickly as possible. The IFers still aren't moving in the right direction."

CHAPTER 20

THE SUN ROSE AS IF IT HAD NOTHING BETTER TO do but still couldn't muster any real enthusiasm for the ritual, and it was only visible for a few minutes above the eastern horizon. The sky directly overhead was heavily overcast, gloomy. According to the weather report from CIC, the clouds were stacked through several thousand feet, and the bottoms were only two hundred feet up. It had been hours since any rain had fallen, but there was a heavy dew, and the air felt heavy, hard to breathe. That morning would have been a serious inducement to depression even without a war.

We rendezvoused with the men carrying the extra ammunition, and took everything they would give us. Since they had to resupply the entire company—what was left of it—they were a bit on the stingy side. Four magazines per rifle was the limit, along with two clips of RPGs for each grenadier. We were promised more later, assured that the regimental quartermaster had plenty of supplies on the ground and was making preparations to make certain everyone got ammo before they needed it.

I didn't call the sergeant who told me that a liar to his face, but I was thinking it, and I'm sure the sergeant knew it because he went on trying to reassure me. I walked away. I'd heard promises like that before, and the harder they try to sell them, the less faith you can have in their redemption.

That rendezvous also served as a rest stop. All of the spec ops squads had rejoined. In trying to herd that IFer battalion, our company had two dozen men killed and close to thirty wounded who had to be turned over to the medics. There weren't enough people in the resupply detachment to handle all the wounded, so Captain Fusik had to detail a squad from third platoon to help. That left the company at less than half-strength, about seventy-five effectives.

After fifteen minutes, barely time to wolf down a ration pack, Tonio passed the word to get ready to move. My squad drew the point, so we started off while the rest of the company was getting organized. I split the squad by fire team, but we moved parallel to each other. That let me put both biraunta out in front and, since we were in a heavily wooded stretch, I let them get up in the trees.

Even more than usual, I was conscious of the responsibility, and the danger, of the point. In the past twelve hours we had helped wipe out two enemy point squads. There were wild thoughts of irony and payback trying to distract me from the job at hand, "do unto others" stuff, as my head tried to accept some guilt for the way we had done our job—and likely saved the lives of some of our own people.

Somewhere ahead of us the rest of that maverick enemy battalion was still maneuvering to stay free of the static fighting we had forced on most of the defending army. That battalion commander had proven himself extremely capable under extremely adverse conditions. He was unpredictable, a major contributing factor to his success. The staff and computers of CIC hadn't been able to do a decent job of forecasting how he would react to the various pressures we had applied.

They have to be running short of ammunition, I told myself, *and they almost certainly don't have any way to get new supplies unless they move into the perimeter we've forced the rest of their army into.* That was supposed to be a comforting thought, but I didn't find much comfort in it. For all I knew, they might have headed to a previously prepared cache of ammunition, a hidden supply dump. It's something *we* might do if we had been the garrison on a world that might be attacked. *They might already have that ammo, all they can carry,* the worrying part of my brain told me.

Our intelligence might not be able to find a small ammo dump in the forest if we searched for it from above for a year. The tonatin defenders knew this territory better than we did. On and on. I fought to maintain concentration, but it became increasingly difficult. It had been a long time since I had come out of that medtank, with little chance to close my eyes and rest—let alone *sleep*—and we had spent much of that time on the move. I was tired. We all were.

It didn't help in the least to remind myself that the tonatin we were moving to intercept had to be as tired as we were. Tonatin were more . . . durable than most species in the Alliance of Light, according to everything I had seen. Porracci might match their stamina, and maybe the ghuroh could come close, but none of the rest of us could. I had read reports that a company of tonatin soldiers could march fifty miles in a day without having a single man fall out, then do it all again the next day . . . and the next. If a human army company tried that, it would be incredible if they finished the first day with a third of the men who started the hike.

Our A Company engaged the enemy an hour after dawn, maybe forty minutes after we left the supply rendezvous. The tonatin column went right through A Company, fighting on the move, holding to the course their commander had chosen, leaving their dead and wounded where they fell. A Company suffered 10 percent casualties in a fight that lasted six minutes, and it was the captain of A Company who broke off the firefight, withdrawing on either side of the enemy column.

When I heard that, I thought that A Company's commander would probably lose his job after the campaign. It wasn't until later that I heard that he had been seriously wounded in the fight. He didn't live long enough to get to a medtank. His lead sergeant was also dead, and there was only one officer left in the company, a divotect junior lieutenant.

The major battle, the one involving the bulk of our forces and all of the IFer units except the one battalion, had been continuing for more than a full day, with no one on either side getting much sleep. According to CIC, we had a slight numerical advantage, partially offset by sniping attacks by small groups of enemy civilians. Those had become an almost constant annoyance. Civilians, mostly armed with hunting weapons, were making things dangerous for support units and patrols, and they didn't seem to give much weight to the fact that their attacks were generally suicidal. Maybe they thought defending their world was worth the price. One of those attacks managed to kill the regimental operations officer, a lieutenant colonel, and half of his staff. I couldn't work up much enthusiasm for the thought that maybe Major Wellman was one of the dead. I knew I wouldn't get rid of him that easily.

THREE HOURS. WE COVERED ONLY SIX MILES, changing course twice in response to the latest moves by the enemy battalion, and once to rendezvous with what was left of A Company, with Captain Fusik assuming command of the combined unit. Combined, we didn't equal a fully manned ranger company, but we would be more potent together than separately, especially since A Company was desperately short of officers and sergeants.

The enemy battalion was moving directly west during the last hour we were tracking them, farther from the main battle north of us. I had given up trying to guess what the tonatin battalion commander thought he was doing. Maybe he was just guessing, making lucky choices. Or maybe he was being a damned good commander, trying to draw as many enemy units away from their main force as he could, weaken the line holding the bulk of the defenders against the river; to give them a chance to break out and maybe turn the tide of battle. My own guess is that the tonatin battalion commander was both smart *and* lucky. There's always an element of luck in combat.

Three hours. Oyo dropped out of a tree and scurried over to me. "I spotted an electronic snoop seventy yards from here," he said after I stopped the squad. "I don't know if it spotted me. I was only fifteen feet up." He pointed into the trees. "It might have registered my presence." That would depend on how it had been set. The only reason to tilt a snoop so it looked up would have been if the tonatin suspected that we had people to use up in the trees.

I couldn't call Tonio or the captain for instructions, but I was too tired to fully trust my own choices. I had to stop and think this through—carefully. A mistake could be disastrous. There was a small chance that an enemy would leave a single snoop, or occasional snoops, to give them some indication of where the opposing force was, and to give us reason to hesitate. But without working satellites to relay the information, they would still have to have someone close to gather whatever intelligence a snoop might pick up. The greater chance was that the snoop was one of many scattered at a predetermined distance from a defensive perimeter, to let the soldiers inside that perimeter know when trouble was approaching.

I went back and forth over the possibilities. Ilyi, our other biraunta, had also come back after he saw that Oyo had. He hadn't seen any snoops, or any evidence of enemy positions. "I want both of you to go back out," I told the biraunta. "Go out to each side. See if there are more snoops planted. Look for enemy positions. Try to get out three hundred yards—unless you run into trouble sooner."

As soon as they were moving, I called Claw over. "Go back the way we came. Find Captain Fusik or Sergeant Xeres and tell them we've come across an enemy snoop and we're checking it out. Then get right back here." I had to let the captain know we had stopped or the entire company—both companies—would be tripping over us in a few minutes. If the enemy had planted that snoop to get us bunched together in one particular spot. . . .

I TOOK THIRTY SECONDS TO SPLASH WATER ON my face, then put a medical patch with a stimulant on my neck, where it would get into my bloodstream quickly. I had a hunch something was going to happen soon and I wanted to be as ready as I could be. Until Oyo and Ilyi got back, I wouldn't know much, but I got the squad as well-situated as I could in case the sky fell on us.

It was fifteen minutes before the biraunta returned, within twenty seconds of each other. Oyo had spotted nothing new. He was the first back, and was just finishing his negative report when Ilyi dropped out of a tree thirty yards away and ran to me.

"I spotted two more snoops," Ilyi reported. "One sixty yards from the first, and the third another fifty yards on. They make an arc, the three of them." He used his hands to illustrate the layout. "But I saw no trace of enemy soldiers, and I went nearly two hundred yards in from the arc of the snoops." He paused. "I think I was detected by the middle snoop."

I turned back to Oyo. "You're certain there were no more snoops on your side?"

He shrugged, a gesture as natural to biraunta as it is to humans—with the same range of meanings. "Relatively, Sergeant. I did not want to get close enough to be spotted. There is a chance I might have missed one, but I do not think it is a *great* chance."

"Ilyi, run back to pass the news to Captain Fusik. You should pass Fang along the way." But Ilyi hadn't even had time to acknowledge the order before Oyo pointed south and we turned to see Fang coming. "Hold up a second, Ilyi," I said. "Let's see what he has to say before you go."

Fang didn't seem the least bit winded after running

nearly a mile. "I reported to Sergeant Xeres," he started. "Captain Fusik joined us. The captain said that we should investigate and send him word, but if there are enemy soldiers waiting, we are to find a route around them and start moving as quickly as possible. CIC reports that the enemy battalion is still on the move, and changing course a little to the south of west."

I nodded. That would take the enemy battalion farther from the main battle. "Ilyi, tell the captain that we're moving in an arc to the left. We'll keep a watch on the area of the snoops as we go past. Get back as quickly as you can."

He nodded and ran to the first suitable tree, then climbed it. He could move faster there than he could on the ground. As soon as he was out of sight, I got the squad up and moving. I put Oyo on our right flank—the side nearest the snoops—and just slightly ahead. We moved by fire team again, with Souvana's team on the right.

No one needed to be told to move smartly, or to keep their eyes and ears open. The farther we got from those snoops, the safer we would all feel, even if it was only the safety of ignorance. My hands were sweating again and my throat was dry. My body, at least, still thought combat might come at any second.

We couldn't ignore the snoops. We were supposed to investigate. Once we got past the arc of the three snoops we knew about, I sent Oyo into the area behind them. Moving high in the trees, he might get in and out safely even if there were enemy troops waiting. He was gone nearly twenty minutes. He was visibly excited when he dropped out of the trees near me.

"There are no troops," he reported, struggling to catch his breath, "but I saw something on the ground and went down to investigate. They left something half-buried. I did not touch anything, in case it was booby-trapped, but I think it was a supply cache—ammunition and food, perhaps."

I nodded. "If they have one dump like that out here, they might well have others. And there might be enemy troops just about anywhere. Get back on point and we'll start moving again." This time I used Claw to carry the message to Captain Fusik.

In the next twenty minutes, we traveled a mile without any hint of the enemy. I was starting to breathe easier by then. Ilyi got back from his trip with simply an acknowledgment from the captain and word that the rest of them would follow us and close the gap. If trouble came, help might only be five minutes away. Not that the remnants of two badly battered companies would be much help if we ran into that enemy battalion. Yes, the latest intelligence report had them more than five miles away from us, but intelligence isn't always right.

ANOTHER FIFTEEN MINUTES AND TWO-THIRDS OF a mile passed before Claw returned. "We're to stop for a time, Sergeant," he said. "The captain plans to blow up that enemy cache, whatever it is. When we hear the blast, we are to continue." He gave us a new heading as well, more directly toward that enemy battalion. Two platoons from C Company, Ranger Battalion were being diverted from other assignments to try to intercept the rogue tonatin battalion and slow them down, to give us a better chance of catching them. And CIC was going to "try" to work in a couple of artillery fire missions.

We settled in an oval perimeter to wait for the explosion. It wasn't a long wait, hardly enough to let us catch our breath and take a quick sip of water. We heard one loud explosion, followed by the stutter of several minor secondary explosions—perhaps grenades cooked off by the initial blast.

"Okay, that's it," I said as I got to my feet. I had my faceplate tilted up just far enough to call out to the men without having my voice muffled. "Up and on 'em." I rubbed at my eyes, then pulled my faceplate back down. We moved back into our two columns and the biraunta headed out in front. There was no slacking off. We were all wound tight, wondering if we might be running into an ambush, or maybe a few nastier surprises left to guard the approaches to that cache that had just been blown.

AFTER ANOTHER THREE HOURS OF THE CHASE, MY nerves were stretched almost to the breaking point. It might have been better in a way if we had run into trouble. That would at least have given some release to the tension. It was the absence of any trouble and the feeling that our luck could not continue indefinitely that made it so miserable. That sounds crazy, but that was how I felt. Waiting for the sword to try to chop my head off had me ready to scream, even though I was getting so tired I felt as if I might fall asleep on my feet.

In those three hours, the battalion we were chasing changed course twice, and CIC provided us with new headings to try to cut down the distance between us. The lag between the time the enemy changed direction and when CIC notified us meant that we gained on them *very* slowly. We were—maybe—within a mile and a half now. The two platoons from C Company were, I was told, marginally closer. The artillery fire missions against the IFers had not materialized, and the latest word was that they would not. What ammunition we had on the ground for the remote-controlled rocket launchers and howitzers was being hoarded for use against the main enemy force. To our north, the main battle continued, though with less ferocity than before. Those three hours might have seen the deaths of two or three hundred soldiers, ours and theirs, without bringing the battle visibly nearer resolution.

The only good news, as far as I was concerned, was that there was no sign of an enemy fleet bringing reinforcements. As long as no more IFers arrived to join the fight, we still had a decent chance of winning.

• • •

THAT TONATIN BATTALION KEPT MOVING, SO WE had to keep moving as well. Through the rest of the afternoon, the longest break we got was ten minutes, time to let exhaustion roll over you and nearly knock you out. Getting up after a stop like that is rough. By sunset, most of our butts were dragging badly. It's a mental numbness soldiers have suffered through probably since the first armies formed up with spears and swords. You keep going because you have to, because there is no realistic alternative. You can't just sit down and say, "That's enough. I can't take any more." That's mutiny. In my squad, maybe only Souvana and Kiervauna showed no outward signs of exhaustion. Even the ghuroh were moving more slowly, and the rest of us—human, biraunta, and divotect— had reached the point of needing to fight to get one foot in front of the other. I had to keep Oyo and Ilyi on the ground. They were so tired that a misstep and a fall from the trees was possible.

The body gets tired, the muscles flaccid and uncoordinated. The mind goes numb. Vision and hearing become less acute. Reaction time stretches. Men turn into zombies. When you reach that point even stimulant patches no longer provide a sufficient boost. And men—of any species—make too many mistakes when they get that tired. If I had been anywhere near Tonio or the captain, I would have started bitching my head off. We weren't closing with the enemy in any great hurry and, if we did, we would be in no shape to handle a firefight. But I was so tired that even the thought that we might be walking into a slaughter wasn't enough to get my brain functioning at full speed.

Finally, half an hour after sunset, Captain Fusik sent a runner up to tell us that we were stopping for "an extended rest." My squad was to pull back and help form a perimeter with the rest of the unit. I was too tired to feel relieved. I got the squad turned around and we headed back with the runner. I hoped that the captain realized that we needed a *long* rest, time for everyone to get a little real sleep, but I wouldn't count on it until I heard it directly from the captain or Tonio.

We got back to where the rest of companies A and B were setting up a perimeter and found our slot in the line. The order was passed for each squad to go on half-and-half watch, thirty-minute shifts. "Tell your men to sleep fast," I was told. There was no word on how long this stop would be, how soon we would be off in pursuit of the enemy again.

I had my team take the first sleep shift. Souvana ought to be good for an extra thirty minutes. I sure as hell wasn't, and if I were to lead my squad I had to be as rested as possible. My last conscious thought before my mind shut down was something along the line of, *This is probably when the IFers will attack.*

CHAPTER 21

IT WASN'T. WE MANAGED THREE COMPLETE ROTA-tions, giving everyone the chance for ninety minutes of sleep—in three segments. That doesn't sound like much, but even the periods between official turns at sleep could provide some rest, without counting the likelihood that some of the men dozed while they were supposed to be on watch. I caught myself on the edge of nodding off more than once. As long as there were *some* eyes watching, I wasn't about to make a fuss about men nodding off, though I did wake them when it became apparent.

Then *the Word* was passed that we were going to move out. Everyone was to eat a ration pack and be ready to go in fifteen minutes. I made sure my men were stirring, and got through my own routine of stretching—trying to jack my mind back up to full alertness—then pulled out a ration pack and ate, hardly tasting the food or paying attention to the mechanics of eating.

I was still tired—most of us had to be, even our porracci with their vaunted endurance—but the little sleep I had managed would keep me going for quite some time, if necessary. I could think halfway straight again, and that's the important thing. As long as the brain is functioning at some semblance of normalcy, you've got a chance to respond to whatever happens.

Before the order came through to move out, I walked over to Tonio, hoping to get a few seconds to ask what the situation was. I guess every squad leader and platoon sergeant had the same idea, so all I got was the same canned response: "We continue after that IFer battalion. They stopped moving half an hour after we did, and just started up again fifteen minutes ago. The latest intel says we're a mile and three-quarters behind them. C Company is within a mile of them, on an intercept course. They should be able to slow them down and give us a chance to catch up. We're going to make it before dawn."

That would be some achievement, on no more sleep than we had managed. When they want to, tonatin can hike us into the ground, going faster for a longer period than most other species. They hadn't taken as much time to rest as we had, but they didn't *need* as long, and probably wouldn't admit it if they did.

WE STARTED MOVING ON SCHEDULE, AND WITH NO more than the expected amount of grumbling. Captain Fusik didn't try to push the pace right away. He let us ease into the routine, gave us time to get accustomed to moving on sore feet, with muscles that didn't want to cooperate. He gave us time to get our minds clear of the remnants of sleep. We had been on the move for thirty minutes, with my squad on the point again, before the captain sent word forward to pick up the pace.

I had anticipated that, so I didn't even groan inwardly. I passed the word on to the biraunta who were scouting ahead of us again. If we were determined to catch that IFer battalion and engage them, I would prefer to do it before dawn, while we still had the minimal advantage night might give us.

After an hour on the march, the captain gave us a five-minute halt. Twenty minutes after we started moving again, we heard distant rifle fire. It was ten minutes later before a messenger brought news forward that the two platoons from C Company had made contact with the enemy battalion and would try to hold the IFers until we could join in. The firefight was only a mile from our position.

"Heads up, now," I told my men after the messenger headed back toward the column behind us. "We might run into trouble any time now." I'm not a prophet, just a professional pessimist. That's a survival trait for a soldier. The trouble came less than a minute after I spoke those words.

DAWN WAS STILL MORE THAN AN HOUR AWAY. Either Oyo or Ilyi got off the first shots. It was simple to tell the difference between the light biraunta rifles and the heavier tonatin weapons or the rifles used by the rest of the species in the Alliance of Light. The sound was unmistakably different, the biraunta shots an octave higher in pitch than the tonatin rifles, and about half that compared to the rifles the rest of us in the Alliance used. The few seconds warning gave me a chance to disperse the squad, and let us get to cover before the IFers took us under fire. It probably saved lives in the squad. I didn't have time to wonder if either of the biraunta would survive. Up in the trees, they would have become vulnerable the instant they started shooting.

Oyo reported, "At least two platoons of IFers, maybe three," over the radio, and I relayed that to Captain Fusik.

"We're moving up on your left," Fusik said. "Two minutes."

I acknowledged that with a single click of my transmitter. There wasn't time for words. I had spotted several enemy soldiers moving toward our position—two men charging forward while a dozen or more laid down covering fire. That's meant more to make you keep your head down and disrupt your aim than to kill you. With inexperienced or poorly trained troops it can work all too well. The effect isn't quite as dependable when you're up against well-trained veterans.

I'm fairly sure I dropped one of the rushing enemy soldiers, and several others went down and didn't get back up. But until Captain Fusik and the rest of our people reached us, the numbers were on the side of the IFers, and they showed no inclination to give up and pull back. If the enemy battalion got all of its force concentrated, the numbers would still be on their side. All we had were three very truncated companies, two on this side and one on the other side, under three hundred men. Despite the losses we had inflicted on that tonatin battalion, it still had to have twice as many soldiers capable of firing a rifle as we had.

Neither side could count on reinforcements from the main engagement. The IFers were unlikely to be able to break out of the perimeter, but General Ransom wasn't about to weaken our effort there. That was where the battle for Olviat would be settled. We were a sideshow, and definitely on our own. CIC wasn't even going to allow us artillery or air cover.

The terrain was neutral, not likely to favor one side over the other. We were in virgin forest, old growth, varieties of trees and bushes native to Olviat. There wasn't a lot of undergrowth at ground level, but there was some, and every little bit helps when you're trying to hide from enemy eyes and bullets. The ground was mostly level, with a very slight slope toward the river a dozen miles north of us. I do mean *slight,* maybe one foot in fifty, too little to be noticeable.

The leading element of the enemy force was within eighty yards of us when the rest of the men Captain Fusik was leading joined in on our left flank, suddenly contributing overwhelming gunfire and a dozen or more RPGs to the firefight. That did rather more than break the back of the attack. If there had been two platoons coming toward us at the start, maybe half of one platoon was able to pull back.

They didn't go far, just out of range of our RPGs while they waited for the rest of that short battalion to join them, and then the entire force started to press toward us again, along a broader front now. I switched radio channels to my direct link to Tonio.

"Now what?" I demanded. "They can run right over us if they've got the balls to finish the job."

"Take your squad and try to slide to your right," Tonio said, tactfully ignoring my comment. "Make them think about defense instead of offense."

"We'll do our best," I said.

"If you get a chance, maybe you can shoot some of those balls out from under them," Tonio said before I switched to my squad frequency.

BOTH OYO AND ILYI HAD MADE IT BACK SAFELY, though Oyo had a slight wound—a tonatin bullet had sliced across his backside, an inch above his tail. The bullet had scraped fur away and scored the skin beneath, leaving a black line, but the wound was not bleeding seriously. Oyo was ready to move out ahead of the rest of us as usual. He seemed more animated than I had seen him since his brother had died. I didn't ask, but I thought that he was eager for a little payback.

The rest of companies A and B put out a heavier volume of fire to cover our move. At first, we crabbed along on our bellies, doing our best to get intimate with the ground. Only after we had put thirty or forty more yards of ground—and a couple of dozen thick tree trunks—between us and the enemy did we get up and start running. We still stayed hunched over as far as we could get without falling flat on our faces. At times like that, I feel as if I have a fluorescent bullseye on my butt.

We moved directly away from the firefight until we were three hundred yards from the nearest IFers. Then we went another eighty yards to be on the safe side. The purpose wasn't just to get away from the bullets. If we were going to have maximum impact when we rejoined the fight, we didn't want the enemy to see us moving. Our effect would be significantly greater if we came as a big, nasty surprise, if they had to worry that perhaps we were a new—perhaps much larger—force brought in to finish them off.

I had the squad strung out in a single column, with five to eight yards between men. This was a game of follow-the-leader, with Ilyi darting from one tree to the next, choosing the ones with the thickest trunks along our route—anything for a little extra measure of safety. Toniyi was second in line. I followed him. Claw was behind me, and Kiervauna was at the tail end of my fire team. Robbie McGraw was the lead man in the second team. Souvana was all the way at the rear—not exactly where he should have been, but I wasn't going to raise a fuss just then. Souvana might often be a royal pain in the ass, but he was as good a spec ops soldier as there is, though I'd probably never admit that to his face.

We spent ten minutes moving west, covering three-tenths of a mile. I wanted to hit the IFer battalion near where I expected its middle would be—not quite halfway between the men with Captain Fusik and the men of C Company. If the captain was also sending a squad around on the south flank, we could really give the enemy commander something to worry about—the possibility that his men would be totally surrounded. It would take him time to learn how few we were on the flanks, and maybe he would make a rash decision to try to break out of the "trap" before he had a complete picture. He hadn't made many rash decisions so far, but . . . a man can always hope.

Ilyi glanced back at me after pausing. I signaled for him to stop moving west. As soon as I had the attention of the rest of my men—those who were close enough to see me directly—I went through a series of hand signs, knowing the information would be repeated for those who were farther away. It was time to turn south again, and to narrow the gaps between us. Skirmish line. We moved quickly to the new formation—eight men across the front, two to four yards apart, with Souvana and me slightly in back of the line, centered behind our respective fire teams. This was *not* leading from the rear. Souvana and I were never more than three yards back—just far enough to keep an eye on the entire formation. A bullet would hardly have noticed the extra time it would need to get past the line to one of us.

I set my head-up display to show me the blips of active enemy electronics in the area as I scanned it. There weren't many, and none seemed to be directly in front of us. When you only have commanders passing orders, and maybe a subordinate acknowledging them, you don't get a lot of blips. The IFers were at least as disciplined about active electronics as we were.

We moved slowly now. We kept the line as "dressed" as practical, stopping at trees, searching the terrain in front of us carefully before moving to the next hesitation point. You do everything possible to minimize your exposure. When we turned, I thought we must be 380 yards from the enemy—but I allowed myself a *wide* margin of error in my mind, fifty yards plus or minus . . . and reminded myself that even that might not be sufficient. The IFers could have been moving as much as we had. There could be half that battalion moving toward us and a lot closer than I thought.

You can't count on living long in this business if you don't take every possible enemy response into account— what they *can* do, not what you think they might. The enemy commander had shown himself to be pretty damned smart. Men like that don't suddenly turn stupid and fall completely apart. Even if they make mistakes—no one I've ever met was totally immune from the occasional screwup—they're generally small and quickly corrected.

The farther south we went, the slower we moved, and the lower we crouched, each man instinctively doing everything possible to minimize the target he would present to an enemy. Our pauses became longer. The question wasn't *whether* we would encounter the enemy, but *when*. Every step we took south brought that *when* closer.

When we reached a point 180 yards from where I had estimated the enemy was, I stopped the squad for a couple of minutes and did a very painstaking survey of the area ahead with my faceplate cranked up to its maximum 2X magnification and the gain on my audio pickups at maximum. Maybe the audio wasn't sensitive enough to hear a worm crawling through the ground, but it would pick up the slightest metal-on-metal noise at a hundred yards under ideal conditions, and it could pick up labored breathing at thirty yards. I looked for movement that didn't fit. I listened for anything that might not sound natural. I'm certain every man in my squad was doing his own survey. When I had scanned our front twice, working back and forth across, I turned the magnification on my faceplate back down and looked along the line of my men. Had any of them spotted anything I missed, he would be waiting to signal me.

No one was. I whistled softly—a poor imitation of some bird from Earth, I think—just enough to get the nearest men to glance my way. I signaled to start forward again, and the rest of the squad keyed on them. We repeated the entire sequence after another thirty yards—stop, survey, then continue—with the same negative result. We went another twenty yards then stopped again, still without any of us seeing or hearing anything out of the ordinary.

We weren't looking far enough to the side. The attack came from our right, about forty-five degrees out.

SOMEONE ON THE OTHER SIDE GOT TOO EAGER for their own good. He opened fire from more than 150 yards and was joined by several of his comrades after less than a second. That's the only thing that saved us. Most of us. Ilyi took a burst across his shoulders and upper chest. The heavy tonatin ammunition tossed him backwards and he hit the ground hard and skidded into a tree trunk ten feet behind where he had been standing. There wasn't time to go see if he was alive or to attempt first aid if he was. At least a platoon of IFer troops were moving toward us, and they had at least another platoon giving covering fire.

I dove for the cover of the nearest tree and started shooting back before Ilyi skidded to a stop. The rest of the squad went for cover and started shooting back as well. Kiervauna had the presence of mind to get his grenade launcher into action and loosed an entire clip of four RPGs as fast as he could pull the trigger. In Souvana's fire team, Fang was slower getting his grenade launcher around, but he spread a clip out starting just after Kiervauna had gone back to his rifle.

Eight rocket-propelled grenades dropped in an area sixty yards wide and twenty deep—all within six seconds—can put the hurt on one hell of a lot of people . . . and slow the survivors down considerably. As the last grenades exploded, I was calling Captain Fusik to let him know what we had encountered—and to suggest that we could use a considerable amount of help anytime within the next twenty seconds.

"We're fully engaged," Fusik replied. "You're on your own until we can shake something loose. Try to stay mobile. Pull back and continue moving west once you break contact."

Yeah, right, I thought. "I've got one man down. I don't know if he's dead or alive, but if he's alive, he's in pretty damned bad shape. He's one of our biraunta, so we might be able to carry him and not lose much time, but that will mean two fewer men firing back at the IFers."

"Do what you can. Better to lose one man than ten though."

That was logical, but it's a hard logic to swallow when you know the people. Ilyi was new to the squad; I didn't know him as well as I knew the men who had been with us since the beginning, or even Robbie, who had joined us on Earth before this campaign; but he was still one of *my* men. I wouldn't abandon him unless there was absolutely no alternative. I switched to my squad frequency and gave the men our new orders. "Kiervauna, see if Ilyi's alive. If he is, pick him up and bring him along. The rest of us will give you all the covering fire we can."

We were just starting to move when several enemy

RPGs exploded. Luckily, none of them came within thirty yards and no one was hurt by the shrapnel . . . or by the slivers of wood a couple of them splattered around when they impacted against tree trunks. I felt a couple of tiny bits of wood impact against my helmet, but nothing reached my hide.

I knew that Ilyi was still alive when Kiervauna picked him up. The rest of us started spraying long bursts of rifle fire against the enemy positions, suppressive fire to give Kiervauna and Ilyi more of a chance to get away. Fang had taken time to reload his grenade launcher and he spread another clip of RPGs where we could see the enemy concentrated.

We ran like hell, with one or two men holding back for a few seconds to continue firing at the IFers, then moving forward while a couple of others stopped to fire for a few seconds.

EXCEPT FOR THE FIRE COVERING OUR WITHDRAWAL, the firefight had lasted less than a minute. Between us and the IFers, maybe a thousand rounds of rifle ammunition were expended, and between fifteen and twenty RPGs. We had made a complete shambles of an acre and a half of prime forest. Several trees had been felled or damaged so badly they wouldn't stand much longer. Limbs had been torn loose. Twigs and leaves ripped apart. Several small fires were smoldering, but there had been too much rain in the past couple of days for there to be much danger of them surviving very long, let alone spreading.

After we got back a hundred yards, we stopped firing. Our hope was to make the break complete by doing everything we could to make sure the IFers lost track of where we were. There was still gunfire behind us, but none of it was coming near us, and that was the important thing. We pushed on for another thirty yards before we stopped to catch our breath. I went to Kiervauna, who was still holding Ilyi. He hardly seemed to notice the biraunta's weight.

"He is in very bad shape," Kiervauna said, whispering as if to keep Ilyi from hearing him.

The brief look I had seemed to confirm that estimate. The light biraunta body armor had not stopped the two enemy slugs that hit it. I doubted that it had even slowed them down appreciably. Even human body armor isn't always enough to stop the heavy tonatin bullets. And two slugs had missed the armor, catching him in either shoulder. In addition to blood loss and shock, he had to have broken bones in both shoulders.

"We can't stop to treat him yet," I said, having difficulty getting the words out because I was out of breath. "Let's go on a little farther. We'll stop as soon as I think it's safe."

IT WASN'T SOON ENOUGH. WE HADN'T TRAVELED another forty yards before Kiervauna stopped, looked at Ilyi's face for a moment, then leaned forward, putting the side of his helmet against Ilyi's chest. After a few seconds, Kiervauna set the biraunta's body on the ground, then glanced my way and shook his head. Ilyi was dead.

Before I had a chance to react, we were under enemy fire again.

CHAPTER 22

I SUPPOSE WE HAD ALL BEEN DISTRACTED BY ILYI'S death, even if only for a few seconds. The distraction was deadly. The first burst of enemy gunfire nearly took Fang's head off. The rest of us dropped to the ground safely, but we weren't well situated. After we got flat, we scrambled for what cover we could find and started to return fire.

The IFers had opened up from 150 yards away. Maybe someone on that side got a little overeager. If the IFers had waited until they were closer, they might have wiped out the entire squad. As it was, Fang was the only one killed in the initial salvo. No one else was hit.

I radioed Captain Fusik as soon as I could, to let him know we were under attack again, but I didn't know how many of the enemy we had stumbled into, or how much difficulty we might have breaking loose. My guess was that we had run into more than a platoon of IFers, but I wasn't sure how much more. The rest of Captain Fusik's command was still engaged with the enemy, so there was no promise of quick help. Once more it was, "Do what you can."

Yeah, right. I saved my snort of disgust for after I had turned off my transmitter.

My men had responded as well to the ambush as any could while I was on the radio. This was not the time to worry about conserving ammunition. We were putting out enough fire to make it difficult for the IFers to get close without taking heavy losses, but they *were* moving, trying to get around on our right. Souvana had his fire team concentrating on the soldiers who were trying to flank us, even getting off two rockets, before discarding the launcher because there were no more rounds for it.

Robbie had gathered what we could use from Fang—grenade launcher, his last clip of RPGs, and rifle ammunition—and started firing grenades at the enemy, pumping grenades through the launcher tube until he had none left. Kiervauna was more selective, stingier with his few remaining RPGs.

"I'm certain we're facing at least two full platoons, perhaps an entire company," Souvana told me over our private link. "There might be more flanking us out of sight. They could be coming on both sides to slip the horns of the bull around us."

"I know, so it's time we boogie out of here," I said. I don't know how Souvana's translator button interpreted *that,* but he got the message. He agreed. "We'll pull back straight north, then start east toward where the rest of the company is," I said. "Right now we can't do much by ourselves but lose more men without doing a hell of a lot of good."

Souvana didn't argue the point. I guess even porracci macho doesn't necessarily extend to the absurdity of demanding a "last stand" against insane odds. Between us, we took ten seconds to decide on the method of withdrawal. We had to leave our dead—for later retrieval, if we had a later. My fire team made the first move, then took new positions and put down covering fire to let Souvana's team pull back past us. The tonatin put up more fire than we did, so our moves had to be slow. This time, we weren't able to make a couple of moves like that, then get up and run. The IFers were moving as quickly as we were so we weren't able to break contact so handily. We had to stay down a lot longer, and that slows you considerably.

I was satisfied that we moved quickly and erratically

enough to keep the enemy from accurately targeting us with RPGs. They didn't try with many, so maybe they were extremely short.

We worked through four rotations of fire-and-maneuver, with the moving fire team staying almost belly-flat. I thought that we had gained maybe twenty yards on the IFers. That wasn't enough to take us out of danger, and we were having difficulty maintaining that gain, let alone increasing it. We started bending east, which took us farther from some of the enemy but kept the rest at about the same distance.

The first time I got up and tried to do my moving running in a crouched-over position, a bullet hit the right side of my helmet, a glancing blow that set my ears ringing and twisted the helmet around—and also twisted my neck a little. I dropped flat and turned the helmet back the way it should be . . . then moved my head tentatively to make sure it still worked and wouldn't fall off. I closed my eyes for an instant and tried to calm my heartrate.

My hearing took longer to return to something approaching normal, for the ringing noise to subside. Apparently Souvana had called my name several times before I responded, surprised that my radio was still working. "I'm okay," I told him. "The bullet glanced off my helmet. Let's get moving again."

I took more care about staying low after that. If some cosmic bookkeeper was keeping a ledger on lucky breaks, I had to be close to overdrawing my account.

IT WAS A LONG FIFTEEN MINUTES LATER BEFORE we were finally able to break contact with the enemy. My guess was that they were still uncomfortably close, but we had lost sight of each other and stopped firing. It was time for us to do a little spirited jogging, to put more distance between us and those IFers.

There was a squad from A Company in contact with the enemy to the south. C Company was engaged on the west. The remainder of A and B companies were engaged on the east. At the moment, my squad was the only one in the area not in direct contact with the IFers we had been harassing. We had done our share and would undoubtedly be called upon to do more before long. I just wanted to get us a few minutes' respite before going back in, time to get our heads back together and catch our breath.

Catching my breath also left time for my thoughts to catch up with me. I had lost two more men, Ilyi and Fang. Only half the original members of the squad remained. Who would be the next to die? Would *any* of us make it off Olviat?

I pulled out my map and folded it, trying to get a better idea of where everyone was—and trying to get my mind away from our losses. We were still a quarter mile from the bulk of A and B companies, and only about twice that distance from C Company; they were pushing east, driving against the enemy battalion. The squad on the south had moved toward C Company.

Indecision in combat has always been rare for me. You see what needs to be done and you do it, or you do what you're ordered to do. This time . . . what I really wanted to do was to call Captain Fusik and ask for instructions, make him take the responsibility, but we were out of contact with the enemy and using the radio might do nothing more than give them a chance to get a fix on our position. So I had to take my thumb out and make the decision myself, and quickly, before the enemy tripped over us again. *So decide,* I told myself, trying to ignore the way my head ached from the glancing hit my helmet had taken, and the way my ears were still ringing softly. Then I sucked in a deep breath and made my decision.

"WE'VE GOT TO GO BACK IN," I SAID AFTER GATH-ering the squad close enough to talk to them without using the radio. "Try to hit those people who surprised us, turn the tables. If we head in going just west of south, we might catch them on the flank. We can't let them think they've got a hole they can escape through on this side."

That was the important thing. The three companies of rangers—what was left of us—had been assigned the task of handling the short enemy battalion. We hadn't been able to steer them close enough to the main battle to force them into the perimeter with the rest of the IFers, so we had to make sure they couldn't attack our people from behind. It was clear that we were considered expendable, as long as we got the job done. And if we couldn't get the job done in fairly short order, the general was going to have to find another way to do it. We wouldn't last forever.

"We don't have all that much ammo left," Robbie pointed out. "We've all used quite a bit here. Me, I've got one full clip and maybe twenty rounds in my weapon."

"I know," I said. "We still go in." He stared at me for a few seconds, then nodded.

I only needed a minute to get the essentials of my plan across and make sure everyone knew what we were going to do. Then I took a drink of water and suggested that the others do the same. We all put fresh magazines in our rifles. For most of us, that meant our *last* full magazine. "Spend them wisely. Let's get moving," I said, then I took my fire team out first.

Each fire team was a man short. We moved in parallel columns, with enough spacing between men to make it difficult for a single enemy marksman to take out more than one with a single burst, and to give us a chance even if they started lobbing grenades. We moved slowly, cautiously, going from tree to tree, doing our best to blend in with the scenery. We had used up just about all of the night. The shadows were already a bit lighter, turning from black to gray as dawn approached. Sunrise was no more than twenty minutes away, and as soon as the sun cleared the horizon, visibility would increase dramatically, costing us what little advantage darkness gave.

Oyo was on point for Souvana's team. I had Toniyi, our divotect, on point. His dark, leathery skin was well-suited for this forest, and he would offer virtually no infrared signature that enemy gear would be able to pick out from the background. I hadn't had a chance yet to get to know him as well as I had known Nuyi, but he seemed competent, and maybe just a little stronger. He was less talkative as well—not that we had had much chance for idle chat since he joined the squad.

I didn't expect that we would need long to reach the IFers again, and I was right. It was only six minutes after we started south again when Oyo halted Souvana's team and my team stopped as well, waiting for some signal from Oyo to tell us why he had gone to cover. He got low, with a tree trunk behind him, and turned to make a complicated series of gestures. He had seen a squad of IFers a hundred yards off, at an angle of about thirty degrees to our line of march, on the right; southwest.

This was what we were waiting for. I moved my team a bit forward, then to the right, until both teams were facing the direction of the enemy. Oyo had spotted the IFer point squad. There were more troops behind them, moving with their weapons at the ready, anticipating trouble.

Trouble was what we intended to give them.

I wasn't at all nervous. I felt almost unnaturally calm. Looking through my rifle sights I got my breathing slow and even. I waited, wanting some idea of just how many of the enemy we were about to engage—and wanting to get them spread out to give us as many targets in the first critical seconds of the firefight as possible. The opening volley is often the only chance you get to make a significant impact on the enemy in an ambush.

We were facing at least a company of the tonatin troops—a short company, with maybe only a hundred men, but that still gave them a minimum of a twelve-to-one advantage, and I had no way to know how close the rest of the enemy battalion might be. Kiervauna was the only one left in the squad with RPGs—the great equalizer—and his final clip was in the weapon. We were going to have to hit hard with what we had, then move before the IFers could mount a counterattack. This time we would move toward them instead of away . . . obliquely; we weren't going to get up and charge directly at the enemy. I've never been *that* insane.

I took a breath and held it while I squeezed off a short burst from my rifle, spraying three enemy soldiers who were closer together than they should have been. I'm sure I caught all three. By the time they heard the sound of my rifle, the bullets were too close to give them a chance to duck. The rest of the squad was firing by then as well.

We were in position to spray an eighty-yard swath of the enemy, and we did a good job. Then, while the IFers were ducking and trying to spot where we had fired from, we were moving, southeast, at an angle to the tonatin line of march, a little farther from the positions of the enemy we had seen but closer to the bulk of what was left of the battalion that had been hung around our neck.

It was comforting to have the enemy's return fire aimed toward where we had been instead of where we were. After we had moved eighty yards, we stopped and took another cut at the enemy from the new angle, then moved before they could adjust. The problem was we stayed on the same heading instead of changing direction.

We were on the move when two RPGs ripped through the forest canopy, from in front of us. We dropped to the ground, heading for the best cover within diving range, and waited for the grenades to explode. Thankfully, neither detonated near enough to cause casualties, and we were up and moving again as soon as the shrapnel had spent itself, heading in the direction the RPGs had come from, only a slight change.

I radioed what we were doing to Captain Fusik. He had us located on his map, and we were no longer so far apart that we couldn't directly assist each other. The rest of our company was four hundred yards to the east, pressing west. Company C was within two hundred yards of the portion of the enemy we had just ambushed, and now had them under fire—so *they* couldn't come after us. Comforting.

"Grab the best positions you can, Dragon," Fusik told

me. "Try to hold where you are. Keep the IFers from getting away from us. We're moving in your direction."

Well, the best positions available weren't all that great, but there were enough trees with thick trunks to limit the directions from which we would be vulnerable. I got my men down in about a semicircle so we could cover the most likely avenues of assault. "Don't get too spendthrift with your ammo," I told my people as they found their lines of fire. "We don't know how long this is gonna last."

THERE WASN'T TIME TO IMPROVE OUR POSITIONS by scraping away dirt or moving deadwood to give us additional protection. We had enemy troops coming at us from the south, spread in two skirmish lines twenty yards apart, and they acted as if they knew almost exactly where we were—the direction if not the distance. We spotted the enemy 220 yards out, but I had my men stay down and hold their fire. Unless the IFers started using RPGs again, I wanted them close enough for our rifles to do maximum damage when we opened up. I used the rangefinder in my helmet optics to find a line 140 yards out. If possible, I would hold off until the first IFer skirmish line reached that mark before firing—the signal for the rest of the squad. If the tonatin didn't spot us before that point—if they *did* only know the direction and not the distance—we might really cripple the unit coming toward us before they had a chance to do anything about it.

Of course, I wasn't leaving us any wiggle room. Once we engaged, we wouldn't have much chance of disengaging unless the IFers simply turned and ran away, and, with the way they outnumbered us, that didn't seem much more likely than me getting a battlefield promotion to colonel. We were going to have to hold out until Captain Fusik got people close enough to force the IFers to turn their attention away from us.

The enemy skirmish lines were moving slowly, pausing often. Heads were turning from side to side, scanning.

Rifle muzzles were tracking back and forth like the noses of bloodhounds on the scent. They were 175 yards out. A minute or so later they were 160 yards out. I still couldn't see any hint that they had spotted us. At that distance, they would hardly have continued walking slowly toward us if they knew where we were. They would have either gone to cover or started running.

Come on, another twenty yards, I thought. *Get where we can wipe you all out at once.* I was conscious of blinking once. The twenty or so tonatin we could see in the first skirmish line were the only ones who counted—immediately. Those farther to either side and those in the second skirmish line were a problem for a very short-term "later," assuming we took care of the nearer ones. Spray the nearest enemies, then lift your fire a little and hope to get some of the men in the second line even though they would have time to drop to the ground before you targeted them.

The first skirmish line reached the mark I had noted—140 yards out. I started firing. It took only a small fraction of a second for the rest of my people to open up. Noise. Fury. Tonatin soldiers fell, hit. Others dove for cover, some wounded, some not. We continued to spray short bursts toward where we thought the enemy soldiers were, first in that nearer line, then toward where the soldiers of the second skirmish line had gone to cover. Kiervauna got off his last RPGs.

For nearly twenty seconds—longer than we deserved— it was all one way, with us on the right end of the gunfire, raining doom on the enemy. I don't know why the IFers needed that long to start returning fire, and I didn't have time to be properly grateful. We simply took every ounce of advantage we could from it, putting down as heavy a layer of fire as we dared while none of it was coming toward us. I emptied the magazine in my rifle and got the partial magazine that was all I had left loaded before any enemy fire started coming toward our positions.

Even then the enemy fire was sporadic, scattered, some of it obviously misdirected. It wasn't coordinated . . . and it wasn't nearly as heavy as what we were putting down. I was too busy to sort through the possibilities, but I had an instinctive feel. The first possibility was that we had hurt them far more badly than I thought, or at least crippled the command structure of the enemy right in front of us. The second was that there were fewer of the enemy than we had feared. The third was that they were as short on ammunition as we were.

Those were the good possibilities. There was one other, perhaps more likely—that they were intentionally limiting their fire in front of us because they were busy sending troops around to encircle us and finish us off properly. When I could, I scanned the area behind us. The chance of the IFers coming at us from behind was an itch I couldn't scratch. We were committed, with no way out until more of our troops reached us.

My guess was that it would take at least fifteen minutes, and probably much longer, for anyone from the rest of B company or A Company to take the heat off. And I wouldn't have bet that we had that much time left, no matter what odds I was offered.

Out beyond the right end of our short line, where one of the grenades had exploded, a small fire had started and was managing to grow rather than dying the way most of the other incidental fires had over the past couple of days. Maybe the rocket had hit dead wood or dry brush. It didn't look as if it had much chance of becoming major, but it might rob the IFers of a little cover, force some of them to move. Or, if the fire got smoky, it might give them more cover.

There was movement in front of us again. The IFers were edging along on the ground under what covering fire their comrades managed to put down. I saw one tonatin 120 yards out. He got behind cover before I could shoot him. I had noticed one thing: He had a bayonet fixed to the business end of his rifle.

"Fix bayonets," I ordered. "They mean to come right into our laps." I got my bayonet in place while I kept an eye on the tree that one tonatin had moved behind. He couldn't move at all without showing something. I wasn't particular. If I could shoot a foot off, that would certainly slow him down.

The way it worked out, a foot *was* what he showed, and I put a single shot into it. The IFer jerked around a little, reflexive movement, and for just a second his left shoulder was exposed and I put another round into that. I didn't think he was going to have much more to do with the fire-fight.

THE IFERS WERE GRADUALLY BROADENING THEIR advance against us. We had to spread our fire over a wider area as they came at us from either side, taking single, aimed shots when we could, trying to hold the time when we ran dry back as long as possible. There were several dozen IFers in the skirmish lines, but they weren't putting out much more gunfire than we were. Farther off, we could see more moving in, but we couldn't waste ammunition on distant targets when there were closer ones. I warned my men—again—to be careful with their ammunition.

Time had become almost meaningless. The timeline on my helmet display seemed to have slowed to almost nothing, but there was a lot going on outside my helmet. None of my men had been hit since the start of this latest fire-fight. We stayed flat, with only our weapons and the minimal amount of heads and arms showing. The trees that sheltered us were taking a beating. I had noticed wood splintering off the trunk next to me a couple of different times. The rattle of wood chipped away by the impact of a high-velocity bullet against a helmet will get your attention.

I took my pistol out of its holster and set it on the ground by my left hand where I could get to it quickly if I had to . . . without letting go of my rifle. If it got down to that, I could fire the pistol with my left hand and use the bayonet on my rifle with my right hand—the stereotypical two-fisted hero.

I hoped it wouldn't come down to that. If it did, we would likely all be dead within seconds. The hero business has never been what they make it out to be in adventure vids.

When I could spare a fraction of my attention, I kept up a running commentary for Captain Fusik on the command frequency. A couple of times he gave me what were supposed to be encouraging remarks about how close help was and how we just had to hold out a little longer. My mind filtered out the bull . . . and most of it was bull. I could hear increasing gunfire to the left, which meant that the major part of this fight *was* getting closer, but at the moment it seemed that the pressure the platoons on that side were exerting was just forcing more IFers toward my squad. I couldn't see that it would make much difference if we were overrun by retreating instead of advancing IFers. Dead is dead.

Fifty yards out, a half-dozen tonatin got up and started running toward us. They didn't get far, but by the time the last of them had fallen, another group of the enemy was charging, thirty degrees around the arc. They got a little closer, and the fire team that got up and charged after them got even closer, to within forty yards. It might be costly for the enemy, but if they kept coming like that, it was only a matter of time—and not much time—before they would get to us.

The third and fourth enemy skirmish lines were both within 160 yards, firing at us from cover now, trying to keep us pinned down while the unlucky suckers up front ran forward until they were killed. I glanced at the gauge on the side of my magazine and saw that I was down to only a dozen rounds of ammunition. I was just settling back into a firing position when I felt a quick burning pain in the heel of my right foot. I glanced back and saw blood. A bullet had taken off part of the boot and creased my heel. I guess I hadn't been careful enough.

Even if we could get up and run, I wouldn't make it far

like that, but the blood wasn't gushing, so I wasn't going to pass out from that, and the pain . . . well, there was too much else going on for me to give much thought to the pain. If the IFers kept coming, a sore foot would be the least of my worries . . . before all worrying ended for me.

"Get ready," I said on my squad channel. "The way they're going, they'll be in our laps soon. Let's take as many of them with us as we can." Yeah, that sounds hokey as hell, but there weren't any critics lying there in the forest.

Fairly soon, we would have to get to our feet to meet the enemy. They were so close that lying on the ground wasn't doing much to minimize our exposure. Once they could see us they could hit us. I guess I wasn't the only one in the squad who had taken a minor hit, but no one was complaining or screaming.

The enemy was thirty yards out—the unlucky few whose turn to rush forward had come. Again, it was half a dozen men. This time, those men dropped to the ground before we could drop them, and I needed a second to realize *why*. The rest of companies A and B had arrived, and the leading squads were almost as close to the rushing IFers as we were.

The fight didn't end instantly. In fact, it got considerably hotter for maybe ten minutes, a general firefight with most of what remained of the battalion of tonatin against three very shorthanded companies of Alliance rangers. C Company came in from the west thirty seconds after the other companies. The IFer battalion had been pushed in from three sides and hadn't been able to escape over our dead bodies.

There was even, at the end, hand-to-hand combat—bayonets and fists, knees and heads. By then, my rifle was out of ammunition and I had used the clip in my pistol and had no chance to reload it.

Then the fight was over—suddenly. After the tonatin battalion commander was killed, his successor gave up. He had been seriously wounded as well and died minutes later, but not until after he had given his men the order to surrender.

CHAPTER 23

OUR ESTIMATE HAD BEEN THAT THERE WERE ABOUT nine hundred men in the tonatin battalion when we were first set on them. When they surrendered, there were fewer than one hundred alive and without serious wounds. After my foot had been patched—the medic decided that the wound didn't need a medtank—I hobbled around in front of the area where we had made what I had feared would be our last stand. In twenty minutes I counted eighty tonatin bodies, the soldiers who had died trying to get to us, and I hadn't covered a third of the battleground.

The three companies from Ranger Battalion who had been involved in chasing down and destroying that tonatin battalion had suffered almost as much. Altogether, those three companies could muster fewer men than one fully manned company. That counts all of the losses we had suffered on Olviat. The three companies had been chopped up so badly that General Ransom didn't even attempt to put us into the lines of the main battle—the fight that was still going on to the north.

The way it turned out, we weren't needed. After the destruction of the one battalion, and the losses the rest of the tonatin defense force had suffered, the fight only went on for another three hours after our little piece of the campaign ended. We did take part in some of the mopping-up operations that went on for the next several days, in the retrieval of bodies, and so forth.

Someone established communications with the civilian authorities and started the business of occupation going. Weapons in civilian hands were confiscated. The weapons and electronics of the military were collected. All of that material was transferred up to our ships. Nothing of obvious military value would be left for the tonatin. We would feed it all into nanotech replicators back home to make new gear for us.

Confiscating all of the military hardware meant searching for additional caches of weapons and ammunition. There is a very good chance that we missed more than we found, but we did find nine camouflaged ammo dumps like the one we had spotted earlier.

Three weeks after the end of the fighting on Olviat, the 1st Combined Regiment headed back for Earth. The rest of the invasion force was left as an army of occupation—at least until the politicians running the Alliance decided what to do with the world. As far as I was concerned, they could deflect a large asteroid into a collision course with the planet and wipe it out. I wouldn't shed a tear.

WE WERE SENT BACK TO FORT CAMPBELL FOR another period of gathering replacements and training. It wasn't until our third evening back there that I worked up the nerve to go to Gen'ral Jimmy's to see Chrissie Orlmund. I still didn't know what I was going to do about her—us—but I couldn't put off the reunion any longer. Chrissie wasn't in the bar. I asked the bartender if it was her night off, or what.

"She don't work here no more," the bartender said. "Sorry to be the one to tell you this, Sergeant, but she took up with some junior lieutenant boot camp instructor and quit. I think she moved too."

I blinked several times while my brain processed that information. At first, I wasn't sure whether to be relieved that the problem had disappeared or hurt that she had thrown me over for some JL the minute I was gone. I might have stared blankly at the bartender for fifteen seconds. Then I laughed, which caught me as much by surprise as it did the man behind the bar. He knew how involved I had been with Chrissie.

"Give me a beer, Jack," I said, "and have one yourself."